This is a follow-on to Jason's first book titled *Vorclaw*. Jason was born in Pittsburgh Pennsylvania in 1974. Since he was eight years old, he delved into science fiction and fantasy, following the works of J.R.R. Tolkien and Gary Gygax. His favorite book, however, is *Great Expectations* by Charles Dickens. Jason began writing during his many deployments and travels as a member of the United States Air Force. After travelling all over Europe and the Middle East for nearly 24 years in the military, he is ready to put writing at the forefront of his life. Jason's true motivations are his daughters Eve and Ella who have read more books by the time they became teenagers than he had in his entire life!

To my brother Dan who had one of the best characters during game nights but always fell asleep during the game!

Jason Kalinowski

SOJOURNS IN VANA

AUSTIN MACAULEY PUBLISHERS™

LONDON · CAMBRIDGE · NEW YORK · SHARJAH

A CIP catalogue record for this title is available from the British Library.

ISBN 9781398431171 (Paperback)
ISBN 9781398431188 (Hardback)
ISBN 9781398431195 (Epub e-book)

www.austinmacauley.com

First Published 2022
Austin Macauley Publishers Ltd®
1 Canada Square
Canary Wharf
London
E14 5AA

Table of Contents

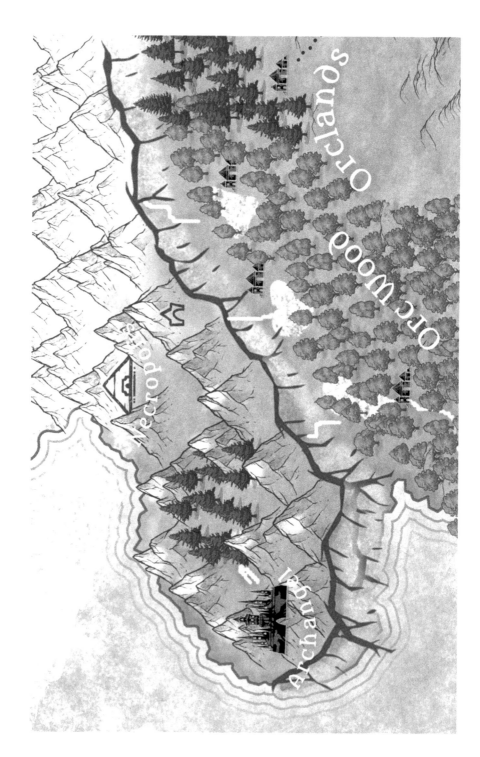

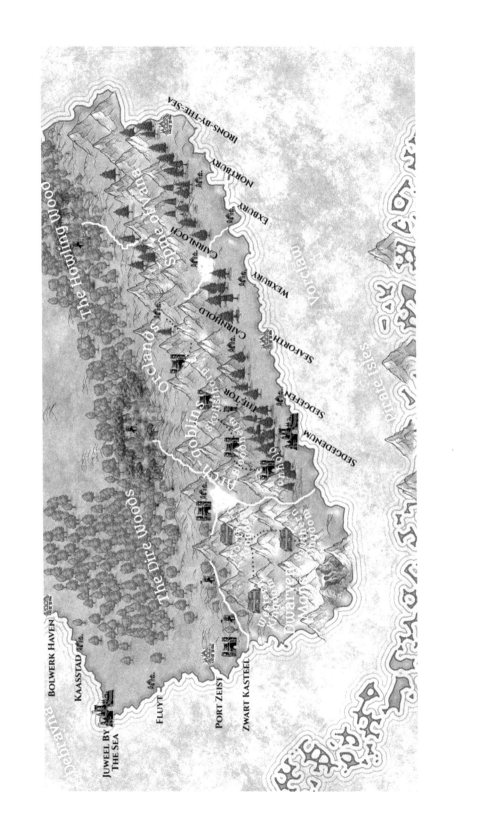

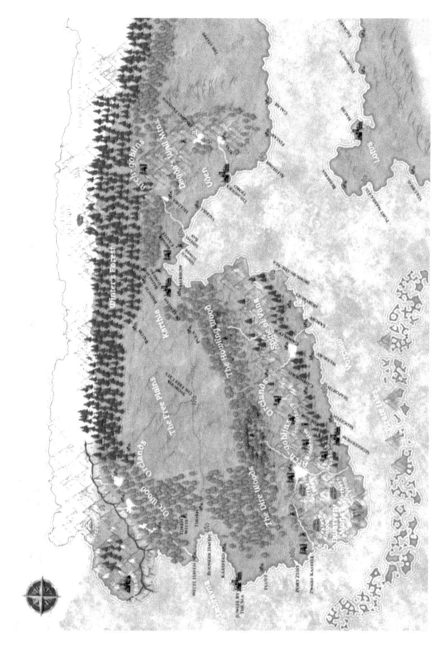

Introduction

The arch-goblin-warrior known as Lorez sat comfortably at the cave opening above a necropolis where his companions had entered. Although his homeland was in the arch-goblin stronghold of Blood-helm, located in the mountains outside the country of Vorclaw, the armored arch-goblin was nowhere near it. As he ate his apple and dead squirrel rations, the arch-goblin-warrior marveled at how he had come to be up in these mountains just south of the Land of the Great Glaciers.

He inherited, so to speak, a large warrior elf named Leif Foehammer who was raised by humans. Lorez's complicated story was set in the task to escort this elf and a party of humans to this necropolis. He was to ensure they went in and hopefully return with the soul of an ancient revenant known as Rom-Seti. It was the same revenant who attacked his vampire-queen—Queen Ooktha. It was more convoluted though. He was given a device called a soul sucker by his queen and instructed to hand it over to Leif once they departed Vorclaw; through the magical means of course, this item had the power to capture the soul of the undead.

The team's instructions were to weaken the revenant's life force so the soul sucker, a small Jade Tower that could fit into a man's fist, could capture the soul of this powerful undead being. Once the command word was spoken by the wielder, the item would pull on the soul and store it within. How the party was to weaken their target, Lorez didn't really know. If they were to return with the soul of the revenant, then there was to be peace between both the arch-goblins and Vorclaw, or so it was led to believe.

A Vorclawean general however, had secretly bargained with Lorez's own arch-goblin chieftain, Chieftain Merka, behind the back of their leader, Queen Ooktha. General Baltus Blackpool would hand over the fortress, known as the Tor or Fort Adamant, to Chieftain Merka's tribe. During their negotiations, Chieftain Merka revealed that Queen Ooktha herself also planned to betray Vorclaw. While General Blackpool and Queen Ooktha hatched their devious plan to attack the Vorclaw capital, Queen Ooktha intended to do more than raid the city; she was going to stay much longer than agreed. With this new information, General Blackpool readied his own soldiers for her betrayal.

Meanwhile, poor Leif and much of the party was led to believe that this task would result in a supreme peace. However, this task was only just a way for Ooktha to get revenge on Rom-Seti for his attack, nothing more. It also kept her involvement secret from Rom-Seti should the mission fail and she

11

could also remain in the good graces of the Union of Undead. Leif was also led to believe this mission would allow him to go freely from his arch-goblin captures but still travel between his home in Vorclaw and the land of his lover who also happened to be, Queen Ooktha.

Lorez laughed out loud at how devious and twisted it all was and how the only ones that truly knew it all was himself, General Blackpool and Chieftain Merka. Oddly enough, Lorez hoped they succeeded. He enjoyed Leif's company and respected the young elf soldier that his chieftain captured those many months ago. Lorez watched Leif battle in the arch-goblin arena, warned his people of the kelpie-folk attack aboard ship, championed the arch-goblins against the orcs and won; the two black smithed together and even battled lycaons just a few days prior. Leif wanted to let the lycaons off with a warning but the rest of the party, Lorez included, thought it best to dispatch the lot. What was odd, he thought, was he could smell the beastly lycaon's at this moment. It must be his imagination?

However, after hearing a noise from within the cave, he now realized that lycaon's were in fact, advancing on his position. The lycaons they dispatched days ago, must have had friends and now tracked them through the mountains!

Part I: Into the Fray

Chapter 1
The Unexpected

The skeletons and the revenant known as Rom-Seti had vanished. It was difficult to discern at first because of the green burst of light and wind that exploded from the small Jade Tower device known as a soul sucker. The whole occurrence made everyone disoriented. But the undead that were present either vanished or were sucked into the tower. Their entire bodies, even the severed arm of Rom-Seti, were gone. All that remained were the skeletons previously vanquished by Dru and Damon prior to Sker invoking of the soul sucker. Rom-Seti's spells were also gone, even most of the fires were extinguished.

As soon as Leif gained his senses, he was upon Bjorn who lay on the floor. Damon made his way to Erik who lay on the floor as well.

Dru made his way to join Leif and Bjorn.

Sker shivered with fright just before the doorway. Both Erik and Bjorn were helped to their feet.

"Talk to me Bjorn," implored a concerned Leif.

"I am alright, I think," he responded whispering and grasping his neck.

"Your neck," interjected Dru, "Its flesh is burnt red."

"Aye, and it hurts," responded Bjorn regaining his voice and sitting up. Rom-Seti grasped the large priest of Matronae by the neck shortly beforehand causing apparent damage to Bjorn's skin.

Dru made his way over to Erik and his eyes widened at the sight of him. "You look like you been to the underworld and back," said Dru. Erik's face was swollen and bleeding from the barrage he sustained from Rom-Seti's *armed defense* spell. Erik spat out a tooth at Dru in response while trying to ascertain what just happened and recalling the bludgeoning, he took from the multicolored arms that materialized from the floor to beat him senseless.

"Well done mage," said Damon. Erik beamed a bloody smile with a new gap between his remaining teeth. However, Damon was not complimenting the mage but being sarcastic. "Oh, you think I was praising you? You almost got us killed thanks to your ineptitude."

"How do you mean?" demanded Erik.

"You assured me you could defeat the revenant with all your enhancements. But you were defeated by a bunch of monster arms!"

"The *armed defense* spell is a powerful incantation that I did not foresee, Sorry," said Erik.

Leif made his way to Sker.

"You done well my friend," said Leif, kneeling to his lizard-goblin friend. "I guess the real praise goes to the runt," said Damon referring to Sker. "Are they all in there? Is he in there?" asked Damon of Sker still holding the Jade Tower. Sker did not know and handed the item to Leif.

Leif stood up and peered into the Jade Tower with some of the remaining fire light in the background. "I can't quite tell," stated Leif. "But given there isn't any of the undead left in the room, saved the ones you already vanquished, I would bet they're all in there."

"Bjorn," queried Erik, "Can you heal me?" he asked standing upright now.

Dru still supported Bjorn, keeping him on his feet. It was clear to all that Bjorn was not well. His neck was red, and his appearance seemed drained. Bjorn summoned a *divine cure* for the wizard's wounds. Erik's seemed better somewhat but Bjorn seemed even worse after his efforts. The large man fell to one knee. "Anyone else need aid?" asked Bjorn of the party but no one dared, not even Damon who could see Bjorn was unwell.

"We need to get you out of here and to a healer," said Leif. "Can you summon your master to extract us?"

Before Erik could answer, a large creature was trying to come through one of the normal sized doorways.

"By the gods," shouted Dru, "What is that?"

"It's a flesh-golem!" replied Erik. "It's made from a giant of some kind. We must be gone from here!"

Dru and Leif helped Bjorn to his feet and the party escaped down the corridor from which they entered. The flesh-golem broke through the stone worked door frame as soon as they had exited, using a great mace.

The creature's flesh also tore from its shoulders, but it did not notice pain. It only knew what its master, Rom-Seti shouted moments earlier in his native-otherworld tongue. *"Come to the throne room, kill the intruders, and do not rest until they're all dead!"* The creation did as his master commanded. Now it tried to wriggle its oversized bulk of flesh, muscle and bone down the narrow corridor from where the intruders escaped.

Once Bjorn got moving, his adrenaline took over and he started to make his way more easily down the passage. Once they got back into the grand library, Bjorn was able to move under his own strength although his throat and neck ached.

They all made it outside, escaping down the great ramp of the red stone pyramid. Leading the way was Damon Crag followed by Erik, Sker, Dru, Leif and Bjorn.

"Look!" shouted Damon. "The dead are awake!"

The undead that were at the bottom of the ramp were indeed moving around looking for something to attack. Damon's warning also served as an accidental announcement to their presence.

The assassin obliged the undead and went for one with his swords. He dispatched it with a block from upon high with right sword and took out the undead skeleton warrior by slicing at the knees of the creature with his left. Once it was squirming on the ground from lack of legs, Damon snuffed it out by crushing its skull with his boot.

Erik cast a minor spell, a *mage's dart*, at the skull of the next skeleton warrior, shattering its head causing it to go limp. He did so with the next undead and the next. All the party was now out and down the ramp. They were about to take off the way they came and back up to the mountainside where Lorez should be waiting. However, they saw Lorez in the distance, running at full speed, a mass of undead creatures in slow but hot pursuit.

"He is leading them right to us!" announced Erik.

"Thank you for stating the obvious," said Dru.

Directly in front of them was a great chasm filling slowly with water that came from a small stream to their right from around the pyramid. Beyond the chasm was the necropolis. To the south and on their left, Lorez was unintentionally leading the undead horde to them. To the south and to their right, beyond the stream, was a wall of natural rock but still a path that lead them into the necropolis. Going around the chasm and then into the necropolis seemed the best choice. Otherwise, they would return into the pyramid, face the flesh-golem and become trapped inside by the undead hordes.

The decision was made for them once the flesh-golem emerged from the red stone pyramid.

"This is so unexpected," said Damon. "How much time do you need to create the *mage's gate* to get us out of here?" asked Damon of Erik.

"More than we have with that looming," replied Erik.

The flesh-golem moved with longer than normal strides down the ramp.

"Let's get to the other side of the stream and make our defence there," shouted Leif.

"Move then!" shouted Damon.

They made their way across the slippery rocks of the small stream. It was not deep at all, knee high at best in places. They slipped in several spots, slowing their escape. Bjorn fell and in his weakened state went down stream a few feet with the minor current coming close to the edge of the chasm. The flesh-golem was down the ramp by the time the first of them, Damon, made it across. He was followed by Leif, Dru, then Bjorn and Sker. Erik, battered from battle and sickness over the last few days, also slipped. He struggled to get across the stream from lack of strength. "Help me!" shouted Erik, his robes waterlogged and weighing him down.

The flesh-golem was already making its way for the party, ignoring Lorez and the undead horde slowly following the arch-goblin.

Damon shouted at the creature to gain its attention further upstream. Dru joined him shouting as well. After Leif helped Bjorn to his feet, he turned in horror to see the flesh-golem was already upon them. The creature had sought easy prey, the closest, Erik.

He had his back turned as he was still fumbling to his feet trying to get clear of the stream. Leif went for Erik shouting a warning with his sword and shield leading the way, but it was too late. The flesh-golem swiped at Erik knocking him unconscious and sending him down the stream, over the small waterfall and down into the chasm below.

Leif easily dodged the backhand swipe of the creature's mace. Leif drove his *dao* sword into the gut of the monster. It did not even flinch and responded with another swipe of that great mace that landed hard but also deflected upward off Leif's shield. Leif then retracted his sword and backed away to avoid the backhand return swipe. Leif's attacked landed a gnarly gash on the creature's forearm and again, it did not even flinch.

Both Dru and Damon now flanked Leif, all three taking turns slicing at the flesh-golem as the creature emerged from the stream. All the while everyone was careful to avoid that great mace. Had the three swordsmen had more time they surely would have been able to eventually cut an arm off with all their cuts and slices. However, time was not on their side as some more undead skeleton warriors began to emerge from the pyramid.

Then Bjorn, when the flesh-golem was turned facing up stream at Dru, launched a body assault into the shoulder of the monster. Bjorn's head only reached the shoulder of the creature, but he had enough mass and strength to send the creature off balance and back into the stream where it slipped to one knee. Bjorn then took a swipe with his own mace at the side of the flesh-golem's exposed knee cap. The monster fell into the stream and began a slow decent downstream. It wasn't enough to send it over and the monster regained control and stopped. It stood up erect but was now hobbling on the damaged knee. Again, it showed no fear or pain.

"How do we kill it?" begged Leif.

"I don't know that we can," said Dru.

"Hack it to pieces when it comes out of the stream," said Damon.

As soon as it was close enough again, they all took swipes at the flesh-golem who in turn began its own wild swings of its great mace. However, the sudden appearance of Lorez, whose heavy boots seemed unaffected by the slippery rocks, resulted in the unthinkable. The arch-goblin came in diving at the knees of the flesh-golem from behind. Then the strong arch-goblin lifted his own body up and sent the creature over backwards and back into the stream, headfirst. Then Lorez grabbed the feet of the creature and pushed it right over the falls.

"Well, that was unexpected," said Bjorn.

"And none too soon, the undead horde is advancing on us," said Damon. Dru looked over the falls and saw a withering flesh-golem that was still alive if that's what it was called. However, he also saw a bloodstain on the rocks and the corpse of Erik the mage.

"Come on," shouted Lorez. "We have to go."

Around the chasm they went only this time they travelled on the opposite side from which they had come. Into the necropolis they went, leaving the undead horde to cross the slippery stream.

* * * * *

General Baltus Blackpool's soldiers arrived by ship just outside Sedgedunum. The ships were provided by Admiral Kahee prior to his departure from Fort Adamant. The rally point for General Blackpool to link up with Admiral Kahee was preset months in advance in expectation of the capital going under siege by the arch-goblin horde. It was General Blackpool who conspired with the arch-goblin ruler, Queen Ooktha to make the onslaught happen.

Many working pieces, reasoning and conspiracies played a part in making the seemingly surprise attack of Sedgedunum happen. General Blackpool had his reasoning; his wife was an accidental casualty during a wizard's duel between two aspiring mages from the Sedgedunum Wizard's College. She was killed many years ago in the capital while he himself was protecting the country. He was never notified officially and found out about her demise through the wife of his sergeant major who cared for the general's son, Dru Blackpool, until Baltus returned. The general never forgave the ruling council nor the Sedgedunum Wizard's College for that matter.

Admiral Kahee's reasoning on the other hand was different. The admiral was a childhood friend and he had turned a blind eye to the admiral's son's piracy exploits. Whether out of guilt or friendship, Admiral Kahee, for some reason, was compelled to aid the general's desire for revenge.

The shape-changer named Mimdrid had once tried to replace Baltus Blackpool by unsuccessfully attempting to kill the man. However, the shape-changer was spared and instead, recruited by the general to further benefit the man. Unfortunately, evil begets evil it seems as several other players stood to gain in the conspiracy but also developed their own agendas and profiteering behind one another's backs.

The general's own brother Anthon, from The Shadow Company, was more than happy to aid his older brother. Once considered a disgrace for being expelled from the Sedgedunum Wizard's College, Anthon had his own agenda, as determined by The Shadow Company.

Queen Ooktha herself agreed to the union for a different reason. She needed a means to maintain her hold over the three arch-goblin chieftains. Therefore, when Baltus came asking for her to invade, it was at a perfect time concept that would unite the three tribes in a common goal. However, she planned on staying much longer than the agreed week before retreating. She intended to ransack the city of all the wealth she could and for as long as she could. She was well aware of General Blackpool's plan to ride in with a force from Fort Adamant in seven days and take only a few losses on her part. However, she hatched a plan with her horde near Fort Adamant to lay siege to the fort instead.

While Baltus agreed to give the arch-goblins a week to plunder, he too had his own hidden agenda. He had no intention in sticking with that plan of arriving after a week. Instead, he planned to arrive a few days into the assault, trap most of the arch-goblins in the city and wipe out as many as he could. He would use the invasion as his catalyst for regime change and revenge for his wife's untimely death by appearing the hero by arriving with a force of his own. He also ensured the arch-goblins near Fort Adamant did not actually lay siege but instead brokered a deal too good for the chieftain to refuse. The general promised to surrender the fort and offer that chieftain a chest of gold and silver. That agreement was hammered out through Mimdrid and his own brother Anthon. And it went perfectly!

General Blackpool landed his force at Sedgefen, a small village just outside the capital. The general knew it well as it served as the home to his old friend Sergeant Major Magnus Foehammer and his wife Disa. They were the parents of Bjorn and their adopted elf son, Leif. The flotilla surrounded the small town's harbor. They began to offload horses, weapons and troops just before dawn. The general had wagon carts for troop transport already staged. As daybreak approached, they could see smoke rising from the distant capital. By emptying Fort Adamant and coordinating with Admiral Kahee to pick up troops from other parts of the nation, General Blackpool was able to muster two battalions of Vorclawean soldiers, over two thousand strong. The logistics of it all might seem too perfect to the ruling council but he was on that council as the commander of the military. Besides, after this was all over, the council may have a diminished role in the welfare of Vorclaw, if any at all.

* * * * *

Magnus Foehammer continued through the night building defensive fortifications along the roads and ground they had gained back into the northwest of the city. He returned to the docks after a while to see the makeshift infirmary that his wife Disa and the other clergy had created. He also looked for Ruko the sea captain and his men who joined Magnus on his initial assault into the eastern section of the city.

Magnus was surely defeated by a vampiress that appeared on behalf of the invading arch-goblins. However, a sea captain named Ruko announced to the vampiress that he was Magnus Foehammer. Why his name meant anything to the creature or Ruko was a mystery. Further still she then asked Magnus if he was Leif's father. Magnus mourned Leif as he had been considered missing or dead. The vampiress knew of his adopted elven son, but before he could dare question them, Disa arrived with a new band of volunteers to aid Magnus and turned the undead creature before he could gain any more insight regarding Leif.

Both Disa and himself now believed Leif was alive or at least had contact with the vampire. However, those sailors and that sea captain were nowhere to be found. The whole evening was so unexpected.

* * * * *

It took Anthon Blackpool years to construct the iron-golem. Using spells from the Shadow Company and resources quarried by the arch-goblins of Ironhold the creature was lost in one night. After painstakingly toppling the Wizard's College, the tower came down upon the creation, ending the iron-golem. Although disappointed, the wizard was in fact satisfied. He had taken his revenge on the wizards who excommunicated him. What was unexpected, the sun was coming up and Chieftain Merka's warning of Queen Ooktha's plot to kill him never materialized. Perhaps his unexpected wizard entourage, the two mages on loan from the Shadow Company, dissuaded her?

* * * * *

Queen Ooktha was back in the western arch-goblin city deep in the Mistful Forest called Ironhold. The city was nestled in the far back reaches of the forest budding up and into the mountainside. It was predominantly empty to because of the assault taking place.

She had a private chamber within a well-guarded sanctum. There, she rested and drank the blood of an arch-goblin victim who got too near her this night. She was badly wounded but not beyond repair. Disa Foehammer, using her priestess powers of Matronae, burned Queen Ooktha using that *divine light*.

Oh, how her skin burned but the blood soothed her. She rubbed it on her skin as well hoping it might expedite her healing. What she needed really was rest. She locked herself in her chamber to recoup from the unexpected attack from the mother of her elven-lover, Leif Foehammer.

Chapter 2
The Break In

Chieftain Blist, whose arch-goblins controlled the northwest part of Sedgedunum, stood with his foot atop a dead human while eating a leg of a dog he carved up. A soldier, a servant or a citizen, Chieftain Blist did not care whose corpse he stood on. What mattered was that he was successful in capturing this part of the city. Depending how much his tribe pillaged would make him a legend.

He intended to plunder it for as much he could. Prior to the assault, he inquired with Anthon Blackpool which part of the city held the wealthiest treasures and made certain his arch-goblins were heading straight for it. Blist had to go through Ironhold to get to his city of Skulls-thorpe, but passage should not be a problem given Queen Ooktha made her home in his underground city of Skulls-thorpe and not Ironhold.

Ironhold was the home to his fellow warlord, Chieftain Gutter, the rotund arch-goblin who governed the city closest to Sedgedunum. Blist did not consider Gutter his equal in strategy and found it unsurprising that he had to send his arch-goblins to help secure fronts in the northeastern blocks of Sedgedunum, without question.

In the northeast section where Magnus just left, the fighting settled into fronts. Where arrows, spells and cross bow bolts exchanged volleys, the arch-goblins were slowly being pushed back. However, in the northwest section of the city, where the Wizards' College tower fell, there was a standstill of fronts. The longer the standstill in the west, the more the arch-goblins could pillage for precious items, slaves and weapons. Slaves were hard to come by as many city-folk were at the docks prior to the assault, celebrating the Festival of the Seas. Much of that part of the city, the wealthiest part, was already emptied from homes into the streets. Items were loaded on to carts for transport or already making their way back to the arch-goblin stronghold of Ironhold. Drove by arch-goblin elders and young children, the convoy of carts and pack animals were pulled by horse, donkey and cattle. They were slowly following the path made from the original assault, through the Mistful Forest. Some newly acquired slaves, servants mostly from the wealth of Vorclaw, made a run for it by overpowering their young and elderly arch-goblin oppressors. However, most of those escaping were run down either by the arch-goblin youth or lizard-goblins that accompanied them.

It was an arch-goblin youth that spotted the oncoming trouble. The arch-goblin youth retracted his spear from an old human who tried to escape from the slave convoy. It was the sound of hooves thundering that drew his attention. It was an impressive sight of cavalry with several hundred horses strong. He then noticed many soldiers double-timing behind the horses. After a few moments of admiring the military precision in which they moved, it finally occurred for the arch-goblin to turn and run back into the forest to notify the slave convoy that Vorclaw had mustered its forces.

* * * * *

General Blackpool smiled a little when the city came into view. He could see that his brother's plan to fell the wizards tower using an iron-golem mined by the arch-goblins of Ironhold had worked. It took his brother and a team of Shadow Company wizards' years to create the beast and a day to undoubtedly expire.

The smoke still rose from within the city in the morning light. A muddy trail now existed leaving the north gate and into the Mistful Forest where the arch-goblins were moving their loot from the city. With the morning sun present he had nothing to fear from the vampiress, Queen Ooktha. With a bit of luck his brother had already vanquished her.

"Isaac," said General Blackpool addressing Major Isaac Goldwater, formerly the Fort Adamant Garrison Commander. "Run them down and into the forest for half a mile or until they have scattered away like roaches," directed General Blackpool. "The infantry will turn into the city at the north and east gates and guard your rear."

"Draw your weapons!" shouted Major Goldwater to his cavalry commanders who echoed his command. Major Goldwater, although cavalier in his personality, was extremely loyal to General Blackpool and relished at the thought of impressing his general. "Let none of these creatures see another day," he said to General Blackpool, who smiled in return. "Advance to the forest!" he shouted. Off the horse regiments went. They started as a trot but eventually, it became a stampede.

Most of the old arch-goblins stood and faced the onslaught while the younger arch-goblins either ran or hid behind carts of stolen goods. None survived long. Onward the horses turned and into the Mistful Forest pursuing and slaughtering.

While the horsemen were attacking anything moving outside the city and into the forest, General Blackpool led his soldiers on foot sending two thirds of his forces to the eastern gates and the remainder to the northern gate.

"Captain Ty," began General Blackpool. "Take the men to cover the rear of our dragoons by attacking at the north gate. Nothing gets out! Nothing attacks the rear of our cavalry until their job is done. Is that understood?"

Captain Ty was surprised at the responsibility given to him. He did not trust General Blackpool and like his own mentor, Major Titus, who was killed in battle with the arch-goblins on a convoluted mission earlier that year, did not believe he put the good of the nation at the forefront of his decision making. Therefore, Captain Ty was now questioning what his old mentor, Major Titus, was concerned with. However, it made sense as his current battalion commander, Major Ickingham who commanded the White Eagles, was not among them as the general sent him to another assignment. No matter, the task was at hand to attack from the north and trap the invaders and protect the cavalry.

"I understand, sir," responded the captain.

"I will flood the east gate and push them your way. It should be easy kills for you and the returning cavalry. Anyone that goes out the west gate however, let them. Many will be cut off from the north by our horsemen if they do so. We will pick them off in the west once we've swept the city clean."

"And captain," said the general.

"Sir!"

"Give no quarter and take no prisoners, man!" said the general so all of Captain Ty's other officers and senior enlisted soldiers heard.

Major Goldwater smiled at Captain Ty, "Good luck Lucius," he said referring to Captain Ty by his first name.

* * * * *

Captain Ty's men encountered escaping captives of the arch-goblins in their advance. Their intelligence provided insight into what was happening within i the city as well. Captain Ty learned much of the northern city was overrun but, in the east, people were fighting back. However much of the north was being looted, especially in the west were the wealthiest lived. The stories infuriated the captain.

"No prisoners!" shouted Captain Ty. That comment surprised him. He considered himself professional, insightful and calm. But in this case, either the stories or maybe General Blackpool's comments about *no prisoners* invigorated him somehow. He charged, leading his men to the gate. He sent some north to aid the cavalry to pick off anyone escaping the horsemen. The rest he led to the north gates. Surprisingly, the gates were wide open. In fact, they were no longer even gates but smashed piles of wood by some powerful force.

In he led them attacking whatever arch-goblin and lizard-goblin he could find. Many of the arch-goblins were already forming a barrier to hold back the approaching soldiers in the small square within north gate. Captain Ty stabbed one arch-goblin and shoved another back with his shield. He kicked a lizard-goblin who was brandishing a spiked club and sent the thing tumbling. The square erupted into a great battle.

"Arrows up in the windows," shouted one of his soldiers.

Several Vorclaw soldiers felt the sting of crossbow bolts and arrows. Not all those soldiers died but some had.

It was then Captain Ty noticed his folly. Many of the felled arch-goblins and lizard-goblins were sacrificial. All avenues out of the square were now blocked and archers were now firing from all windows and roof tops. "Attack the west!" shouted Captain Ty. He hoped to break through the barriers of carts, boxes, rubble and in some cases, corpses piled up. Some of his men made it over but were eventually slaughtered. They pushed on and made it down one road only to confront another barrier. The arch-goblins were ready there too with more arrows and even rocks from upon roof tops. Captain Ty's first command at an assault was a failure and he swiftly ordered a retreat. He lost dozens of soldiers at a one-to-one loss excluding the downed lizard-goblins.

* * * * *

Chieftain Blist was still not happy with that victory at the north gate. Although his quick preparation and guidance forced a retreat, he knew his forces were trapped in the city. Furthermore, reports were filtering into him that a larger force was moving on the eastern gates while a large cavalry force went north into the Mistful Forest after his loot convoys. With Chieftain Gutter engaged in skirmishes with the City Watch and volunteers, he had to decide on his best course of action before Gutter's arch-goblins benefitted over his own clan. decide.

He could pull his troops out of the western gate and flank out of the city into the forest. Maybe then he could come back on himself and pinch the Vorclaw troops between Gutter's forces and his own. However, would Queen Ooktha be angry that his troops fled at the first sign of trouble? Another variable that he did know about was the location of the wizard, Anthon.

Chieftain Blist was aware of the plan to eventually kill Anthon but was certain it would not happen now. Queen Ooktha was wounded by a priestess. And now, the wizard if alive, would be a great asset in escaping. Also, where did these soldiers come from? Surely, they were not with General Blackpool; he should be under siege by Chieftain Merka in the mountains around Fort Adamant, ensuring a longer campaign for him in Sedgedunum?

As the thoughts swirled in his head, he had to maintain order. Arch-goblins and especially lizard-goblins were starting to worry. They were making their way up the stairs to the city walls. Blist too made his way up to get a look.

"We're trapped my lord," shouted one of his warriors.

Chieftain Blist, much larger than most arch-goblins, grabbed that arch-goblin warrior and threw him off the wall on the side of the Vorclaw soldiers looking on.

"Ha!" shouted Chieftain Blist. "Look at those fools trapped outside their own city!" he shouted with a toothy grin. "We beat them in their city and just pushed these new fools back out!" he shouted laughing. It became infectious as some of his warriors eased up seeing their chieftain was less than concerned. Then he let out a war cry towards the several hundred disorganized

25

soldiers outside the northern walls. His warriors did the same shouting at the Vorclaw soldiers.

Chieftain grabbed one of his captains and told him to muster some archers for the wall but do it by keeping out of sight of the soldiers over the wall. After about five minutes of taunting the arch-goblin archers were in position. There weren't many, barely twenty in all. Chieftain Blist had them notch, target centre mass and loose arrows, then fire at will after the first organized volley. The whole arch-goblin force on the wall hooted and shouted with joy when several Vorclaw soldiers took arrows until they moved out of range. Only a few were hit and fewer still killed but it was a morale builder for arch-goblins for sure.

"I want regular reports on their troop movements!" shouted Chieftain Blist. He was pleased with instilling confidence in his troops, but he knew he had precious little time to plan his next move. He sent a runner to the eastern gates which were still intact and to Chieftain Gutter to find out what was happening in his section of the city.

* * * * *

Carts turned on their sides and used as a barrier exploded by a *fireball* blast! Flames engulfed the cart and several flailing lizard-goblins. The arch-goblins took some damage, but none were killed. Although the magical attack was far from him and was barely able to see it happen, Chieftain Gutter, the rotund arch-goblin of Ironhold, hadn't realized yet the predicament he was in. He hadn't yet received information that the western gate was overrun that morning by a host of fresh Vorclaw soldiers. They were accompanied by several wizards, seemingly from out of nowhere, who volunteered to join the military forces. The wizards destroyed barriers created by the arch-goblins that allowed their looting. Chieftain Gutter had not taken nearly one quarter of what he intended and therefore stubbornly pushed more of his forces forward to the front so his youth and elder arch-goblins could build more loot carts.

"Why are these carts not moving out of the city?" shouted Gutter to a young arch-goblin, grabbing him by the shirt.

"Master," he replied. "I know not."

Several arch-goblins ran past the chieftain and drew his attention away from the boy. However, they were towards the front of the wagon train of stolen goods and not the battle.

"Run up to the front and find out what's stopping them," said Gutter pushing the youth.

Several more arch-goblins, wounded arch-goblins, were quickstepping past him.

"What happened to you?" demanded Chieftain Gutter.

"My lord," began one arch-goblin who was panting from running and covered in blood. "We are being overrun by the eastern gates."

"Vorclaw Army pours through the gate," shouted another running towards the chieftain.

The chieftain and his bodyguards advanced on the front to see what was going on. The sound of another explosion quickened their pace. They all drew their weapons seeing the fray developing before them. A mass of Vorclawean soldiers were fighting in the streets against his own soldiers. The impromptu barriers he staged were being blown apart by wand-wielding wizards. Some of the wizards, the chieftain thought looked familiar; he believed they frequented his mines helping Anthon forge the iron-golem.

"We've been betrayed!" he realized. The force coming driving towards his wagon train of stolen goods would be upon him before night fall. He knew his arch-goblins were going to be overrun. "Retreat!" he shouted. "Back to the forests and Ironhold!" It was then the arch-goblin youth returned.

"My lord!" the arch-goblin boy shouted over the clang of metal and screaming. "Wagons blocked by fighting at the north gate!"

Chieftain Gutter now understood the gravity of his situation. He was being overrun in the south, blocked in the north and a wall in the east.

"Start organizing a retreat to the west," Gutter shouted to his commanders. "To the west!" he bellowed, "escape out of the west gates!"

He then turned to his bodyguards. Leave this place in flames, burn everything you can to cover our escape."

"We've been betrayed," he said again to himself. He was sure of it.

* * * * *

Magnus Foehammer was back at it. The retired soldier was leading another band of volunteers into the western parts of the city. This time he made good headway but unfortunately had to reclaim some of the ground he lost the night he was almost killed by that vampire. Were it not for his wife Disa turning the foul creature, he was not certain he would be alive, or worse, a vampire himself. Disa armed him this time with holy water, a symbol of Matronae and some garlic, just to be certain.

Magnus punched one arch-goblin in the neck as the arch-goblin's mighty jaw or tusked teeth might break his own hand. Then he stabbed at another striking true in the gut. The large man then retracted his sword with a mighty swipe back the other way, sending a lizard-goblin flying in the air in two pieces. It was indeed a bloody battle. Several residents had fallen in this push north, but Magnus heard reinforcements coming from behind. From where, he did not care or have time to think about it. His mind was presently on the battle at hand. He took a small spear to the thigh when he wasn't looking but it wasn't that bad, and he wiped the spear aside. It was another lizard-goblin who cut the large man. He hated these little creatures and kicked that one in the face. It flipped end over end, teeth pouring out of its mouth. The creature turned to look back for his spear but ran away when the idea seemed better than to fight on; so, did several arch-goblins. Bizarre as it was, Magnus did not complain as that spear wound to his thigh needed tending quickly. Magnus then heard a familiar voice and realized why the arch-goblins had run away.

"Sergeant Major Magnus Foehammer," said General Blackpool from upon horseback referring to Magnus' rank he held when he retired from the army. Many other soldiers where now filtering onward and around them. "You are a sight for sore eyes my old friend. I thought I might find you in this fight."

"What in the nine hells is going on?" asked Magnus. "Where did they come from and why? And who in the hell knocked down the Wizard's College?"

"This has the Wizard's College stink all over it I believe," lied Baltus dismounting. He then went over to hug his old sergeant major.

"Disa," asked the general, "Is she?"

"She is fine," replied Magnus. "She and some other clergy of different faiths set up a wounded rally point and tend those harmed by all this…whatever this is?"

"Of course, she is. She is a good woman."

"I see you have the White Eagles again?" said Magnus noticing the tunics of their old battalion in which they served together.

"Yes, but it is a combination of soldiers from Fort Adamant and other troops."

"How did you amass them so quickly?" asked Magnus, only half curious but now tending his leg.

"Oh, we got a magical hail for aid from the capital. We used magic to speed horses, coordinate shipping and amass troops as soon as we heard at Fort Adamant. Unfortunately, we had to empty the entire garrison and so that's probably now taken by the arch-goblins," said Baltus, knowing it so.

"Amazing!" said Magnus. "Although I don't see how it is possible in my mind's eye just yet but then again, that's why you're the general," he said with a wink but then winced in a bit of pain uncovering the wrap to his wound.

"You should return to Disa, get yourself healed."

"And miss the chance to fight by your side once again?" asked Baltus, hinting that he wasn't going back.

"Magnus, I am glad you decided to disobey me again," said the general with a smile and a pat on Magnus's shoulder and the pair started walking together.

"Besides, I need to find this vampiress," said Magnus.

"Vampiress?" asked Baltus.

"Yes, there is a female vampire. There is also a pirate and they both involve my son, Leif."

"Interesting," said the general. "Tell me what you know."

Chapter 3
City of The Undead

They made their way into the necropolis, hacking many undead along the way. It got to the point of exhaustion from the overwhelming numbers of skeletons and zombies. They hunkered down in a building and bolted the door with old furniture. Bjorn plopped on to the ground in pain again from around his neck. He was also finding it difficult to breathe.

"Use the *lavender wands* and be silent," Bjorn said. "Rub the wands along the door creases. It will repel them, making them forget we're in here. It turns these lesser undead creatures away."

Dru did as directed while Leif, Damon, Lorez and even Sker, the lizard-goblin held the door shut at the clawing undead. Eventually, once they remained quiet, the undead moved on.

Dru gave Bjorn a vial. "Drink this," he said. "It is a potion to heal wounds, even grave one like yours I believe."

"Thank you," Bjorn said and drank. The potion was indeed helping. "Where did you get it?" Bjorn asked.

"I know people," said Dru with a smirk.

"Did you get this potion thinking I was going to fall in battle?" he said with a half-hearted laugh.

Dru shared in that laugh but only until Damon Crag told them to be silent.

"Save your strength, brother," Dru whispered to Bjorn.

Lorez finally eased his body from the door once there was quiet from the other side. There was not an upstairs but there was a hole in the roof. "Sker," whispered Lorez. "I want you to go up on the roof and tell me what you see. Keep low and quiet."

Sker was shivering with fear and looked to Leif for support.

"Sker," said Leif, "You have saved us once my friend. Now we need you to do it again. Tell us what you see outside our building and how many undead."

"Sker, do it for Master Leif," said the lizard-goblin.

"You're a brave soul Sker," said Leif and he helped the lizard-goblin through the hole in the roof.

At first Sker would not move forward but after a few encouraging words from Leif, the trapped team learned there were only five remaining undead. After several more instructions, Sker explained the road from which they came, many undead wandered the streets but much fewer were heading away from the Great Pyramid.

"The sun will set soon, and I think its best we be gone from this place by then," said Damon.

Dru's eyes went to look at Bjorn who was sitting on the floor resting his head in his hands. "You going to be able to move soon?" asked Dru

"In a minute," he responded, not lifting his head to look.

"Arch-goblin," asked Damon sternly. "What happened? You were supposed to wait for our return but instead we find you being chased by the undead. Why did you come out of the mountain you clumsy fool and wake them? Searching for treasure were ya?"

"Tread carefully human. Do not accuse me of something I know nothing about."

"Then explain why you were being chased from a place you were not meant to be," replied Damon Crag. "Why were you in the city?"

"I was forced out of the cave by a band of lycaon's," Lorez said forcefully. "They were led by something like a lycaon but not really a Lycaon. It was golden and not dark skinned," said the arch-goblin. " I had no choice," he said after several moments of wondering what was leading the Lycaon's. "By the time I got into the city the dead were already aroused."

"I told you all not to kill them," said Leif bringing down Sker from the ceiling and letting him rest on his shoulder. "Now you all have brought the wrath of the lycaon's."

Damon narrowed his eyes at Leif but then looked at Lorez and rolled his eyes realizing it was now irrelevant.

"These *lavender wands* really do keep us hidden," said Dru quietly focusing on the current situation. "Perhaps we can go from building to building and use them to hide our tracks and make our way back into the cave."

"We cannot," said Lorez quickly. "The passage is blocked by lycaon's."

"We fight out way through the lycaon's," said Damon. "How many of them?"

"Twenty, at least," replied Lorez.

"No," said Leif standing up from his adopted brother. "Bjorn will not last a confrontation with a force that size with the undead on our tail."

"We cannot stay here Leif," said Dru. "We don't know what else is here and how many more undead are roaming around. And what if the flesh-golem climbs out?"

"The small human is right," said Lorez referring to Dru. "The undead will find us eventually."

"Thank you for both agreeing and somewhat insulting me," responded Dru.

"I am not suggesting we stay here," said Leif. "We should make for the other end of the city, opposite the pyramid. I looked at the city from above and I thought I saw what looked like a gatehouse at the other side. We make for there and if any follow we'll either shut them in or lose them in the mountains."

"No!" said Bjorn, loudly. Everyone hushed him to keep quiet, but he made almost as much noise in the act. "Leave me here, I will be fine. I will only slow you down."

"Nonsense, you idiot. We're not leaving you," said Dru.

"I have done my duty," said Bjorn. "I have found my brother and he is alive. I am content."

"Well, I'm not content, you horse's ass," said Leif. "You are coming with me, or we all die together."

"Speak for yourself," said Damon Crag.

Leif ignored the vile man and continued speaking. "Besides, if you fall now, I cannot tell mother or father you fell at the hands of a bunch of slow and weak skeletons and zombies. They would call me a liar."

"You forget, I think I helped capture a revenant," Bjorn replied trying to make a joke.

"I see you've still got your sense of humor," said Dru. "Now get your lazy arse up, you big oaf. Here, take my last elixir. It should help cure you some more, but I am told too much will make you sleepy."

Bjorn drank down Dru's last potion of healing. "By Matronae's blessings this stuff is horrid. Who made it?" asked Bjorn standing.

"You don't want to know," said Damon knowing the maker and that priestess's faith.

Bjorn said a prayer to himself. He mouthed the words to find strength. Suddenly he seemed better, well enough to stand without aid. He had a determined look on his face. That prayer however must have alerted the undead for they heard a familiar low-pitched hiss of the undead as if something alerted them to the presence of the living. After several more moments, Bjorn grabbed his mace and readied himself.

"Are you ready then?" asked Leif and Bjorn nodded from behind his shield and mace in hand.

"You lead then, elf since, it is your plan," said Damon.

"Sker, hang on to me," said Leif. "It is Dru's plan to take shelter in a house and use the lavender to hide our scent." He nodded to his brother Bjorn with a smile who nodded in response. "Lorez, open the door," said Leif.

Out they went, Leif and Born hacking the undead outside the building into pieces. The brothers led the way with Damon in the middle followed by Dru and Lorez. To the western reaches of the necropolis they went, hacking any undead that stood in their way.

Leif and Bjorn did the same. There were a lot of them. The adopted brothers would pass back any undead that did not go down with their one or two swipes for Damon to finish them off. Not much was left for Lorez or Dru but to cover their flanks and rear. Damon also stepped forward anytime either Leif or Bjorn was caught up with an undead that would not go down with a few hits or refused to be passed back. After about ten minutes of battling, they drew a crowd of undead and so again they sought shelter to rest and outlined the doors and windows to their sanctuary with the *lavender wands*.

* * * * *

The necropolis held many dark creatures and entities within its walls. Mummies, ghouls, skeletons, zombies and possibly other creatures lurked. In addition, Dru Blackpool's comment about the flesh-golem climbing out of the rift was more accurate than anyone realized.

The creature, albeit slowly, was indeed trying to make its way out of the rift. The creature's original guidance from Rom-Seti was to kill the invaders. The guidance was vague, but the creature would complete its task.

Rom-Seti was indeed captured within the Jade Tower along with his skeleton warriors. While Rom-Seti tried repeatedly to escape he learned that he could call to his flesh-golem from within his Jade Tower prison. He tried the same with the undead minions milling about but they would lose focus due the *lavender wands*.

While he still could, Rom-Seti directed the creature through a passageway that led back up within the pyramid structure. He could only hope the creature would get through the maze up and out the pyramid before he lost contact. Rom-Seti worried and suspected there was great damage to his creation after a fall into the rift. The creature's left hand and arm were useless, broken in several places. The creature also had a limp from cracks to the pelvis. It may take some time, but Rom-Seti hoped to get it to follow his captures and slaughter them in their sleep. He would then use the flesh-golem to return the Jade Tower to the Red-Pyramid with the hopes of physically breaking it and hopefully releasing Rom-Seti's captured evil soul. Rom-Seti also called out to a multitude of undead minions however they were led astray despite the *lavender wands* his captures possessed. Rom-Seti wanted them all dead to make them his undead slaves.

* * * * *

Revenant Niss could no longer see the battle in Rom-Seti's chamber. It worried her that Rom-Seti might survive the attack she aided in. She wasn't worried about the spell she cast during the battle to help the invaders; Rom-Seti could not prove her involvement and her casting would be his word against hers. No, she was more worried about the invaders being captured and revealing how they came to be there in the first place. It would not take much for Rom-Seti to extract that information and start connecting the dots to her, Queen Ooktha and even to her silent partner in all this; there was also another revenant who hated Rom-Seti with a passion.

Therefore, she went to her silent partner who stirred within his abandoned elven city, many miles south of Rom-Seti's necropolis. This revenant was a friend and mentor to Revenant Niss. The two knew each other in life. While Niss was human, her silent partner was elven. She was his former student and lover.

In undead life as it was sometimes known, her goals were to gain knowledge. The elven revenant, on the other hand, had a very different goal. He performed as guardian until a time came where his people might return to his city and reclaim it. Then his duty would be fulfilled and would request of them to vanquish him.

It was Niss herself, when she was alive, that presented him the capability to become a revenant. Her mentor did so to expel the attackers from his city those many years ago. That attack was orchestrated by none other than Rom-Seti himself. Rom-Seti's presence in the Union of Undead was why the elven revenant refused to join the union. In fact, save for Rom-Seti and Niss, no other members of the Union of Undead knew of his existence or whereabouts.

Speaking only in elven, the revenant known as Pallentine, sat in a broken gold and glass throne room. It wasn't his throne however it was his chair from one of his studies. It was a marvelous chair indeed but he refused to sit in a throne that was not his. The revenant was never a king but a battle mage and lord protector of this elven city, who nearly lost all. Yet he did save this city called Archangel from being destroyed by Rom-Seti and his evil allies.

Revenant Niss who wore no mask or veil to hide her withered undead face was a contrast to her mentor who was ashamed of his own looks. Perhaps elven vanity demanded he wear a mask. It was made of hardened wood in the guise of a saddened elven male.

"The attack happened as planned," said Niss. "It was a spectacular battle from what I saw. I disarmed Rom-Seti's magic shielding through the mirror."

"Is he captured in our Jade Tower creation?" asked Pallentine in the elvish language. He rarely spoke common and again his own vanity, what was left of it, demanded he speak it.

"I do not know," she replied in common although she understood his words clearly. "The battle damaged my mirror ceasing all contact. And I've not yet confirmed with any of the Union of Undead to see if they too have lost contact with him."

"Then we shall wait," he responded. "I cannot scry into the Red-Pyramid, it's too well warded. You shall know the answer at the next full moon, the day of your next meeting with your Union."

"That is not for another fortnight," she responded.

"What would you have me do?" he asked irritated.

"Scry for them, or I will. I must know."

Another voice from the side of the room spoke providing an alternative solution. "Do not forget," said a male elf, a living one, and ally to them both, known as Teodor. "They are to return to Sanctuary once complete," the living elf said referring to the meeting place where Leif was given instructions on how to reach Rom-Seti's necropolis. "If they are successful, they will return there in several days: well before your next meeting with the Union of Undead. The Mistress of Sanctuary will contact me upon their return," finished Teodor.

"Yes!" said Pallentine in elvish pointing a bony finger into the shadows.

"Were you not able to track their progress through the cave complex?" she asked, unsatisfied.

"I was of course but I stopped once they neared the necropolis fearing detection," responded Pallentine.

After several moments of silence, Pallentine spoke up again. "To put your mind at ease, I will check the cave complex and the path back to Sanctuary starting tomorrow."

"Why wait?" she asked.

"It is nightfall and if they are alive, they are not likely to be running through the city facing Rom-Seti's minions after sunset. But if I cannot find them in the caves or on the path to Sanctuary, then we wait to see if they reach Sanctuary."

* * * * *

"We must leave!" shouted Dru. "They are upon us!" he shouted pointing behind the advancing party.

Leif and Bjorn Foehammer had waded through the undead creatures leaving damaged and withering monsters in their wake. Lorez and Damon dispatched any still posing a threat. Dru kept an eye out calling out anything coming in from the sides. They only stopped once since Bjorn gained his renewed strength. That was only to get their bearings on which way to go and to catch their breath. Now night had fallen and many more creatures came forth. Fast moving ghouls were now appearing.

Bjorn's confidence rose fighting next to his lost brother Leif. The two complemented each other in cutting them down, one two, three undead at a time. However, now they were being pursued by a large number of undead from behind. The team all broke into a sprint heading for the gate house. Their glowing magical weapons were leading the way as no natural light existed other than the stars. Leif was the first to the gate house. Great wooden doors stood closed, but a small building attached to the gate house held the promise of escape.

"It's locked!" said Leif. "Sker, get up there and see if there is some way to open this door!" The runty lizard-goblin leaped from Leif's shoulders up into a window to look for something. Otherwise, the party was going to be surrounded.

Bjorn stood in the middle and walked forward to greet the oncoming undead horde, his mace outstretched. "The power of Matronae commands your souls to the eternal rest!"

A brilliant white light blazed from that holy symbol. Skeletons withered and fell. Zombies either caught fire, turned away or fell apart. The few mummies and now ghouls burned and hollered in pain. There were five mummies in all and as many ghouls. The smell of the ghouls was horrid and the ones burning made them smell better. All the undead stopped and backed off, hissing at the party. They remained outside the light of the magical glow

34

of their weapons. The undead semicircle was looking for a way to get at the living flesh.

"Why couldn't you have done that earlier?" asked Damon.

"Why don't they attack?" asked Dru.

"They're weary of the power of Matronae," said Bjorn with renewed vigour. "Be gone from my sight or face the power of Matronae!" shouted Bjorn and again another radiance of power emanated from the man.

The mummy closest burned and fell in pain until his body was consumed by the holy light and exploded. The rest scattered into the darkness. That took a lot of energy from Bjorn who was surviving off two healing potions, prayers to his goddess, and pure adrenaline. He was physically, and now becoming mentally, exhausted. But he would not let his friends know it.

"Get ready, they will return," said Bjorn.

As predicted more zombies and skeletons returned. The skeletons armed with swords, axes and spears came on first and Bjorn again called upon his power of *divine light* granted by Matronae. The skeletons fell with their next strides in a heap, bones bouncing on the ground and heads rolling forward.

A ghoul made it through and leaped at Damon Crag. One undead creature was not a problem for the assassin. He quickly put his two short swords into the chest of the creature. Knowing it would not die and offended by the powerful stench, he used the momentum of the assault to pass the ghoul over to Lorez. The assassin's swords came out with a shove and the creature landed at the feet of Lorez. The arch-goblin, who was a seasoned warrior, crushed the creature's skull with his mace.

"The next time you do something like that, let me know," said an irritated Lorez.

It was then that Dru was hit in the back with a pair of keys.

"Try them!" said Sker from the window. "Only keys in room."

Dru tried the first key, and it unlocked the room to the gate house.

"Come quickly!" said Sker. "Steps leading up to wall. Way out me thinks"

In the gate house they went with Dru locking the door behind them. Indeed, the steps led up to the top of the wall. Dru pulled forth a rope from his back, tied it off and down they went, escaping the necropolis of Rom-Seti. At the same time, the flesh-golem emerged once again from the Red-Pyramid, following Rom-Seti's call and the undead massed at the gate waiting for the golem to provide their release in pursuit of their master.

Chapter 4
Queen Ooktha's Children

The elven vampiress burst through the door, breaking it into dozens of pieces. Her arch-goblin guards went scrambling. She was still angered by her defeat in the city and was anxious to hear what had come of the day's battles and blunders.

In a chair before Queen Ooktha was a young woman, no more than twenty years of age, tied to it. The girl, very beautiful, had her hair tied back for easy access to her neck. "What is your name my dear?" asked the Queen. The poor woman only screamed in response. So, Queen Ooktha, with a look of disgust upon her face at the lack of dignity by this maiden, delved into her neck to drain her of life-giving blood. The girl's scream became gurgles of blood. Death came quickly to the young woman as her neck was ripped open, killing her before she could possibly become a vampire.

"Guards!" she announced. "You may use her for feasting," she said. Queen Ooktha then jumped into the air and transformed into a bat. She overlooked the scene in Ironhold. She expected more carts of goods and more slaves but pleased that the spoils were coming in. Therefore, she made haste for Sedgedunum. She was angry and wanted vengeance on that priestess.

* * * * *

The two chieftains made their base of operations well with in the north-western section. They had a direct line to the western gate but not too far from the wall and not too far from the skirmishes. All concepts of looting were now gone, what they had already taken was what they got.

Food wasn't an issue for the arch-goblins or lizard-goblins. They could eat almost anything found in their path. Water wasn't a problem either, there were plenty of wells within the north-western section of the city. Chieftains Blist and Gutter both knew they could withstand a siege for an extended period of time. However, with Anthon and his wizards switching sides, as Chieftain Gutter conveyed to him, it would be a matter of time until enough wizards massed to decimate their ranks.

They had lost most of the north-eastern parts of the city and left them ablaze in their wake. The fires and fighting kept Vorclaw's army and citizens occupied, halting any more real advances and both chieftains thought it best to retreat. They decided on heading out of the western gates but dared not leave without Queen Ooktha's approval first. They had sent warriors to secure the area around the western gate. In fact, only a handful of scouts probed their defenses and retreated from there.

"They haven't attacked the western gate because the bulk of their forces are advancing from the eastern parts of the city," said Chieftain Blist looking over a map drawn out on parchment. "The rest are outside the northern gates."

"Then we should retreat out the north gate and kill as many as we can while we escape," said Gutter.

"No, the west gate is the obvious choice, we can get the most out through there and then flee deep into the woods and turn north to Ironhold," said Blist.

"You do that, I am taking my arch-goblins home out the north gate!" responded Gutter.

"No, we must not divide our forces now," responded Blist. "And besides you don't have enough to survive a departure directly through the northern gates. They are digging in. No, we wait for Queen Ooktha to see what she knows before we do anything, "added Blist.

"And in the meantime?" asked Gutter.

"As if you have to ask, you fool. We wreak havoc on the city! If Anthon did betray us just to level that wizards' tower, then we need to show him and that general the cost of betrayal. We are going to burn this city to ash!"

"Gentlemen!" came an angry female voice. "What else goes on in my absence aside from Anthon's betrayal?" demanded Queen Ooktha who appeared from out of nowhere.

"Most of the east is gone due to a surprise assault from unknown forces," stated Chieftain Gutter. "We have secured a line that gives us control of the northern and western gates. We have been burning buildings in our wake."

"Vorclaw has troops dug in at the north," added Chieftain Blist. "We repelled their assaults on that gate and they won't be coming there anytime soon."

"And what of the western gate?" she asked.

"I have secured it on both sides of the wall," replied Blist. "We can do an orderly retreat out that gate, into the western wood. Then turn north and eventually head for Ironhold."

"Or we could punch through the northern gate and kill many Vorclaweans as we leave. They cannot stop us all from leaving," said Chieftain Gutter.

"Why are we trying to leave so soon?" asked Queen Ooktha. "We have this section secure do we not?

"For now, yes," replied Chieftain Blist, "until they put out the fires, rally their forces and their wizards or priests recharge their spells."

"How long then?" she asked.

"By tomorrow night, they will get through our barriers," Blist responded.

Queen Ooktha was not pleased with that assessment. She wanted revenge upon the priestess who turned her from the fight. Furthermore, if what Gutter said was true, Anthon's wizards had defected, and she wanted to extract revenge on him. Suddenly, a revelation hit her like a lead weight. After several moments she blurted out, "How clever, Baltus!"

"My queen?" asked Chieftain Gutter.

"Don't you see?" she asked. "Our ally, who we planned to betray, has been one step ahead of us the whole time. He used us," she said smiling at the simplicity of it all. "General Blackpool planned to betray us from the very beginning," she said. "He pinned us in this corner of the city by design. And by arriving with these soldiers and wizards, he planned to become the savior of the very war he created."

"If this is true," began Chieftain Blist, "What might the status be of the hordes of Blood-helm attacking Fort Adamant?"

"That is a good question, I don't know," she said, contemplating her next move, as she stared at the map on the table.

She wondered if now was the time to break her vow, something she swore never to do. She never wanted to be a vampire and never wanted anyone else to endure what she had; to endure the hunger, the exile from light. Yet, to give her arch-goblins time to organize a retreat and still loot, creating some vampire minions and raising some dead might provide more time for her arch-goblins to organize a better retreat. No, she decided, not yet. The situation was not as dire when she still had most of her army intact and had other children she could summon.

"Continue to hold fast, my chieftains. Continue to loot and prepare to take what you can carry out of the west gates while we purge other forces out the north gates. Work together and I will give you some much needed time. By sunrise, be ready to depart!"

The two arch-goblins were surprised by her decision and confused by what she meant by giving them "some much needed time. But they did as she instructed.

* * * * *

Captain Ty had a sizeable force at his command. He could easily swing his force around to the west gate and attack the arch-goblins there, but he received strict orders not to do so. Major Goldwater went south to the east gate and met up with General Blackpool in the city. Therefore, the young captain had established a perimeter that would trap the arch-goblins if they dared to exit through the north gate. He even established patrols running near the west gate and into the forest to ensure they weren't flanked or attacked from the rear. The east was wide open to him if he needed it.

"Nothing will get through there, sir," said the sergeant major.

"Well done to you and the boys," replied Captain Ty.

It was then that the howl of wolves rang out in the night.

"Bring fire!" screamed a soldier on the outskirts of the perimeter. His voice trailed off with the sound of gurgling and growling.

"Wolves!" shouted another soldier from another part of the camp. "Wolves, everywhere!"

"To arms!" shouted Captain Ty. "Rally back to the perimeter!"

Just then Captain Ty and sergeant major saw two wolves attacking a soldier. The two ran to him scattering the wolves with yelling taunts and swipes of their swords. They were able to rescue him although he was visibly shaken by the ordeal.

"Turn around, sir!" shouted the sergeant major. "Dire wolf," he whispered in disbelief.

Behind Captain Ty appeared the largest wolf either of them had ever seen. It was as tall as them at the shoulder and its fur was as black as the night. The beast seemed to target Captain Ty and lunged at him, burying him under fangs and fur. Captain Ty was too close to make effective use of his sword and tried instead to reach for his dagger but couldn't. The dire wolf's powerful neck whipped him around though like a dog's chew toy. Were it not for the captain's armor, fangs would surely have torn into his flesh. Losing his sword, the captain racked and punched at the beast with his fists which only angered it.

The sergeant major attacked trying to save his captain from being mauled but was unable to get to the side of the dire wolf for a clean hit. So too did the young soldier they had just saved. The creature seemed to understand the sergeant major's intentions and kept the captain between itself and the sergeant major, all the while shaking the captain in its jaws. The sergeant major only did what he could and that was to shout for aid. Aid did come.

Men came running with spears, swords and torches poking and prodding the beast while trying to surround it. But it was clearly intelligent to some degree and backed away while keeping hold of the captain like a prized piece of meat from a hunt. The men found it difficult to surround the dire wolf. Their attacks seemed to do little to no damage with what hits landed or appeared to land. It wasn't until a sneaky dwarven soldier got a cross bow bolt into the left hind quarter of the creature. The dire wolf let out a yelp on reflex, tossing Captain Ty into the sergeant major. The two soldiers landed in a heap and the dire wolf ran into the night and the forest behind him. The soldiers rushed over to Captain Ty, guarding the man in a semi-circle in case the dire wolf returned. He was bleeding from his mouth, a sign of either internal bleeding or biting his tongue, and he was unconscious. The two picked him up by the shoulders and feet to bring him back to the command tent. Screams erupted throughout the camp as wolves howled and men shouted in return or screamed in terror.

* * * * *

The Council of Twelve that ruled Vorclaw was based mostly with who had the most influence, wealth and seniority. Some of the councils were not native to the Vorclaw' s capital of Sedgedunum, and one wasn't even native to Vorclaw. However, all had been domicile in the city. How many were present during the attack, no one could say. Nor could anyone locate the city mayor. Therefore, General Blackpool took command of the City Watch and declared martial law until further notice. He set up a base of operations along the harbor at an inn called the Dead Cat. It was a place he frequented before, as did his son. It was also not too far from where Disa Foehammer set up her infirmary with the aid of her husband Magnus and other clergy.

The retired sergeant major, Magnus Foehammer, was thrust to the forefront of the military once again, even though he had retired several years earlier. He was back at the side of his former commander, General Blackpool who granted him special privileges and made him an aide to the cause of ridding the scourge of arch-goblins and lizard-goblins from the city. Magnus provided the general and his men, including the general's estranged brother Anthon, with tales of his encounters. Just as Magnus was about to engage privately with Baltus about his estranged brother, another brother, Baltus had confided in Magnus about his previous disapproval of Anthon.

"What are you doing here?" asked the wizard pointing at Anthon. The wizard obviously knew Anthon and possibly of his jaded past.

"It is good to see you Horatio Mercutio," replied Anthon.

"You know you're not welcome in Sedgedunum," said Horatio. who looked tired. His purple robes were torn and covered in soot, likely from battle or being near the fall of the Wizard's College tower from then night before.

"Anthon is here at the request of the Council of Twelve or what remains of us. As Commander of the Military, I am declaring martial law over Sedgedunum. And with the unwanted destruction of the Wizard's College, I called upon what resources I saw fit," said General Blackpool.

"Who supports such a notion that you can declare military law over the city?" asked Horatio. "Where is the mayor?" Where is the City Watch?"

"Good wizard," began Admiral Drake Kahee. "I support him and I am a member of the council," he replied sounding annoyed by the wizard demanding answers.

"And I," said Lord Handle Nightingale, another council member and ally to the general for many years. Both Horatio and Handle were familiar with one another; the two were sent as envoys on behalf of the ruling council to apologize to Baltus when his wife Merriam was accidentally killed during an unauthorized wizard duel in the city.

"To prove myself in your eyes Horatio," began Anthon, "I have already helped the city relieve itself of several arch-goblins and rendered aid to our soldiers. I only wish I could have helped prevent this" replied Anthon. Two wizards, a male and a female, loomed closer to Anthon and it did not go unnoticed by all present in the inn. "Tell me, Horatio. Why was your Wizard's College attacked? Did you lot do something to offend the arch-goblins?" he asked slyly.

"Enough!" said Baltus. "Our first priority is to rid ourselves of the arch-goblins. Then we'll establish motive. For now, Horatio, I know you to join us and let us all pull together to solve this." General Blackpool had an undeniable pull on Horatio's senses. Horatio did not like it. He was suspicious of it all in fact, even General Blackpool's uncanny ability to convince him of what was right. But the wizard certainly could not deny that the general's actions and plans made sense.

"For now, I agree, let's set aside any issues and concentrate on the matter in hand," replied Horatio.

It was Anthon who extended a hand in friendship to Horatio, who reluctantly accepted.

"Excellent." said the general ending the discussion. "Now, Magnus, tell us more of what you encountered with the arch-goblins."

"Do we want to inform the wizards about the vampire?" asked Magnus.

Baltus froze in his tracks. He did not want the Wizard's College to have too much knowledge about Queen Ooktha, especially since Admiral Kahee's idiot pirate-son revealed to Queen Ooktha that what stayed her hand was the recognition of Leif Foehammer. Now Magnus was suspicious of the invasion and why his name meant anything to the vampire. Discussing it now may beg too many questions about who started this coup.

"I will brief him," said Admiral Kahee, also alarmed by the mention of the vampire. "Continue Magnus," said the admiral.

Magnus seemed distant. His eyes were fixed on the windows of the inn, and he saw people running from the direction of his wife's infirmary. "What goes on out there?" said Magnus as several soldiers trooped out closely followed by Magnus.

"Rats!" screamed one lady.

"Hundreds of them!" shouted another.

Several priests were running from the boathouses, storehouses and dry docks, where the infirmary was situated. Some of the townsfolk had biting rats hanging from them. They were covered with the little rodents. As Magnus made his way towards the infirmary, screams erupted from the place. Many people jumped into the water to escape the rats. Magnus could also see fires rising from the infirmary. Bright lights also shone from one of the boathouses. Magnus charged forward rounding the docks with his sword unsheathed. "Disa!" he screamed. Several soldiers joined him in the rush and entered the boathouses.

The rats and those injured in battle were engulfed by flames as they struggled to reach the water. Then an icy cold blast of air came from an unseen source that burned the soldiers' eyes and skin. Once Magnus opened his eyes and removed the ice from his own hair he could see his wife had collapsed. She was bleeding.

A mage came onto the scene and cast the *wind of frost* to extinguish most of the flames. It hurt people in the process but undoubtedly saved everyone from burning to death. Magnus went to Disa, crying as he saw blood over her chest and face as if a great claw mark had ripped through her clothing, across her bosom and over her face. Her skin was burned along her arms and legs. Rats scurried around her, dead ones beneath her.

Magnus scooped her up from the floor crying while the companion soldiers swatted and kicked away the rats. Other men wailed and moaned from the fires and the sudden freezing of their skin. Many were recovering from earlier battles.

"It was her," whispered Disa. "It was the vampire. She started the fires; she knows magic!"

* * * * *

After the assault on the infirmary, Baltus pulled Anthon to one side where no one could hear. "You have one task now my brother and you are to not to stop until she is no more. She has gone too far."

"I have the resources to protect me and defeat her but not hunt her, brother," Anthon replied. "I thought she was going to attack me as she presumed me the greatest threat."

"What more will this cost me?" asked Baltus, angrily.

"I don't know honestly, but I can ask my counterparts. They are watching this closely, waiting for their opportunities to profit on the restoration as you know. However, with them, everything costs," said Anthon referring to his Shadow Company connections.

"Find out what it will cost to hunt this bitch down. In the meantime, I have several more chess pieces on the board, and I intend to use them."

Moments later the general pulled in the wizard Horatio Mercutio, Admiral Kahee, and Major Goldwater who he recalled earlier from the Northern Gates. They quickly devised a plan to attack.

"Take back your college, Horatio," said General Blackpool. "Then instead of turning to the west, head straight north. I will give you the remnants of the City Watch, some one hundred strong along with an additional hundred city-folk and your twenty-five wizards. You should have no problem cutting a swathe north midway to the North Gate."

"We will be decimated once our spells are used and the City Watch is no match for the hundreds in the northwest," said Horatio defiantly.

"Not so," said the general. "To cover your assault, Major Goldwater will send word up the lines to engage full-attack before you begin. If we are lucky, it will draw their reserves into the battle making it easy for the City Watch and the wizards to attack anyone in their path going north and at the backs of the reserves."

"I am also going with you," said Admiral Kahee to the wizard. "I am also bringing my sailors and marines as sure as we speak. They will protect us."

After thinking about it for several moments Horatio merely said, "Agreed,"

"Good," said General Blackpool. "We will initiate this assault at first light."

Chapter 5
Are We Safe Yet

Three humans, a lizard-goblin, an arch-goblin and an elf ran through the night until they were exhausted. Leif took watch on the high ground along with Sker while the party rested under an overhang of rock. Sker simply collapsed within moments and fell asleep. They all had wounds to lick from the previous evening's events. All night they travelled, with no light to guide them. Dru, Damon and Bjorn all had twisted ankles, scraped knees or shins from the rocks in their hasty retreat through the mountains. Everyone also had suffered some from fire damage during battling with Rom-Seti. All received cuts and bruises from either the undead encounters or their battle with the flesh-golem. Everyone took a hit to their pride having been run off like they were. They had stunk from sweat and undead remnants upon their armor or weapons. But all were alive, for now.

Bjorn looked the worst. His colour was still pale, save his neck that was red. He was constantly scratching his neck and moving his hand around his sore throat.

"How are you holding up my friend?" asked Dru of Bjorn. "How's your neck?"

"It is akin to a terrible sore throat. It hurts to swallow even," he said.

"We need to get you to a healer," said Dru.

"I am a healer," said Bjorn with a laugh but it visibly hurt the man to laugh.

"Don't speak my friend," he replied, smiling. "Take rest."

Moments later Dru moved up to see Leif.

"How is he?" asked Leif who was worried about Bjorn.

"He is strong but were it not for the elixir I gave him and his own prayers, I am not certain he would have survived," replied Dru sitting down. The small trek up to see his childhood friend was tiresome given Dru's exhaustion. "I know I am stating the obvious, but we need to get him to see a priest, any priest."

Leif nodded in agreement. Several moments of silence passed between them while Leif scanned for any undead in pursuit.

"What the hell are we doing here my friend?" asked Leif after he ensured no followers were in sight. "How did we all come to be on the roof of the world?"

Dru didn't even open his tired eyes when he responded. "Something to do with arch-goblins near Fort Adamant?" responded Dru. "Who can say anymore? How are you holding up my friend?"

"Terrible," said Leif dryly, still scanning the cracks, horizon and hills for pursuers.

"You look well, considering what you've been through," said Dru with his eyes still closed.

Leif then looked down at his childhood friend. "You're not even looking at me, Dru," said a smiling Leif. When Dru did not respond, Leif continued to talk. "I have several sore bones and muscles from this evening, but I will live to fight on."

"I wasn't talking about today's battle Leif," said Dru. "I am talking about what happened to Leif Foehammer many weeks ago." When Leif did not respond, Dru continued to talk. "You are doing surprisingly well for someone whose whole company was killed around him. And you being the only survivor. Then being forced to serve the arch-goblins all this time. How did you survive all this time with them? I mean, clearly you made friends given how much Lorez seems to respect you. But did you make friends with just him or are there others?" he asked nodding off.

Leif presumed Dru was inquiring about Queen Ooktha but didn't want to engage in conversation about his lover and wouldn't take the bait. He merely scanned the horizon. Nor did he want to reminisce about that horrific battle where his commanding officer and company were killed. In fact, Leif consciously tried not to think about it. Those thoughts were indeed painful.

"You best to get some sleep my friend," said Leif. "We'll talk more on the matter another time."

Dru opened his eyes but instead gave him a smile and said, "It is good to see you again, Leif." Then Dru lowered his head to sleep.

"It is good to see you too my friend."

* * * * *

It took some time but the flesh-golem slowly broke down the massive city gate to the necropolis. As it did so, undead creatures too were able to escape as the door slowly fell apart. Several emerged through large cracks in the door that appeared from the golem smashing it open. Then larger multitudes of undead went through. Some undead themselves became casualties of the flesh-golem's destruction of the door by getting in the way. Eventually the doors broke open and albeit slowly, the flesh golem and the undead minions went off to take back their master.

* * * * *

"The soldiers controlling the north gate of Sedgedunum were harassed by wolves and bats throughout the night," said Captain Tyto Major Goldwater.

44

Captain Ty was seated on the ground, covered in bandages, having narrowly escaped the maw of a dire wolf. "They all had been awake throughout the night, barely in a condition to fight."

"They have to be ready to fight!" said the major. "We already started our offensive."

Major Goldwater looked around at the sight. While there was a decent enough barrier to delay if not hold back the arch-goblins from exiting out the north gate, a large enough force could eventually get through. The soldiers themselves, he had to admit, were clearly exhausted. Dead wolves including a few dire wolves lay about.

"Why didn't you send word using one of your mages?" asked the major.

"We have two of the three wizards left and they used up their spells to help rid us of the wolves, rats and bats."

"Well, it is dawn now," said Major Goldwater. "I think we're safe for now."

Captain Ty sat back down and coughed. "How can woodland creatures such as those mass an assault like they did unless the arch-goblins hold sinister magic, maybe even a demon?"

Major Goldwater saw blood spray from the man's mouth. The major knew what organized the rats, wolves and bats. He knew of Queen Ooktha and therefore studied up on the powers of vampires. He also realized that Captain Ty was now wondering what else was afoot. Already the sounds of battle could be heard from within the city.

"Captain, you have done well here. I am sending you back to General Blackpool to brief him and get healed. You're in no condition to fight." Captain Ty was about to argue but could barely rise without pain. "The road travelling south on the eastern side of the city is safe for travel. I well send you with anyone too injured to fight. Brief the general on what happened here and tell him I believe the arch-goblins are planning a breakout in the north. Tell him I believe the creatures were only used to soften up our forces."

Major Goldwater was somewhat of an opportunist, even sinister at times but he was a soldier nonetheless; a smart one but also proud of it. He truly believed a breakout was coming and if it did come he would either die in a great battle or live to tell a tale of heroism. Either one might make him a legend.

$$* * * * *$$

Admiral Kahee and the wizard Horatio Mercutio came armed with twenty-five wizards, twenty marines and three dozen sailors. It was early morning and fog still grabbed hold of the city.

"It seems General Blackpool's plans to draw out the arch-goblin reserves worked," said Horatio.

The naval and mage forces trekked out from the ruins of the Wizard's College and encountered barely a lizard-goblin. In fact, they were able to take on several refugees caught on the wrong side of the college. The fallen wizard's tower fell to the west and created an area of rubble that trapped many citizens. The sounds of battle came from the east several streets over.

"The plan is going too well," said the admiral. "Either this too is a trap or there aren't any reserve arch-goblins behind their lines." He said as much as asked.

"Well then, where is everyone?" asked Mercutio.

"Corporal," said Admiral Kahee. "Take three men down that alley to the east and report back what you find. Lieutenant, take three sailors and go down the alley to the west."

Horatio sent a wizard with each party as well. When both sets came back the parallel roads seemed devoid of resistance, so the admiral decided to break his team up into three, walking up parallel roads to the north. Admiral Kahee and Horatio took the centre road. It was the road in the east that first encountered arch-goblins fleeing. The wizards took them down easily with *lightning strikes* and were finished off by the marines. A few more refugees were found by the team in the west. They all got to the point where they had been assigned very quickly and had no losses. Their party had grown thanks to them finding refugees. Eventually the line in the east broke near the south and several Vorclawean soldiers shouted out to the marines and wizards there. It appeared the southern part of the occupied area of the city was clear of arch-goblins and lizard-goblins. However, the closer they got to north the more fighting they heard. There was something else they noticed: smoke. And where there is smoke, there is fire.

* * * * *

When the arch-goblin breakout began, it wasn't just at the northern gate. It was all along the northern walls. They lit fires to cover their rearguard with several buildings ablaze to act as barriers from Vorclawean soldiers within the city. As soon as the main battle force started coming out the gate to engage the tired Vorclawean soldiers, over the walls came the remains of the arch-goblins and even lizard-goblins.

"Archers!" shouted Major Goldwater from upon a bluff. "Get archers attacking those coming over the walls," he directed. It only took moments to get the archers turned and prepared to fire but many arch-goblins were down from the wall running for the cleared path in the northern forests. When the archers did notch and release only a handful of the enemy were hit. Most arrows bounced harmlessly off the wall. Already many of the free-running creatures were too sparse or too far to hit.

"Idiots!" shouted Major Goldwater. "Aim for the tops of the wall. Scare them off the tops!"

While the major directed fire, his front lines were collapsing. Captain Ty's construction of a pen to bottleneck the arch-goblins during a breakout was designed to also allow the Vorclawean archers to rain arrows down on them.

It could have worked were the arch-goblins not tacticians themselves; they didn't allow too many arch-goblins out at once. The arch-goblins hooked ropes around some of the fencing taking down some of the pen. Other arch-goblins attacked the pen and soldiers around it. They kept close to the walls to render the Vorclawean archers ineffective. As several arch-goblins fell, several more ran out of the gates to replace them.

Chieftain Gutter was directing them since most of these arch-goblins were his own out of Ironhold. He brought out crossbow teams and fired them at close range to help the breakout and slaughter unsuspecting soldiers. He sent in small arch-goblins to attack low while the arch-goblins attacked high. Finally, the pen was broken open at several spots and Chieftain Gutter sounded the full-scale breakout with the blow of a horn. Outran the rest of the arch-goblins through the north gate.

It was Chieftain Gutter who saw a somewhat organized retreat by the Vorclawean soldiers. "They fight well but they retreat even better!" he shouted to his arch-goblins, laughing. "No mercy my brothers! No prisoners! This victorious battle will be won for the honor of Ironhold!" The chieftain's words echoed with excitement and battle lust among his brethren as they chased the soldiers up the small bluff outside the north gates.

* * * * *

A retreat was called by Major Goldwater. Vorclawean soldiers withdrew up the bluff to where Major Goldwater was. His beleaguered wizards used spells read and stored from scrolls to provide support in the form of *lightning strikes* and *fireballs* but they too were becoming exhausted. The wizards were eventually down to the simpler spells of *mage's darts*, *spider's webbing* and *orb of light* spells to blind the approaching mass. The few priests available were overwhelmed with the injured and had to instead become fighters themselves. Screams of men, lizard-goblins and arch-goblins filled the morning air. However, many of the arch-goblins were also escaping into the forest.

Major Goldwater decided to send his signal flare into the air and play his next card, his reserves. While many of the arch-goblins and lizard-goblins made for the forest, others continued to fight the overwhelmed Vorclawean forces. However, the sound of hooves gave them cause for concern.

* * * * *

Out the west gates poured the remains of the arch-goblin forces. Chieftain Blist led them. Everyone who came out that gate held a bag of plunder! Into the western edge of the forest the remaining forces went. With the city burning behind them to cover their escape, their plan was to turn north and eventually to Ironhold. The journey may take several more days going this route but it was safest.

Chieftain Blist stopped to listen to the sounds of battle the arch-goblins were making. Too many were lost he realized. Foolishly, he and his fellow chieftains wanted war but what all it got them was a tremendous loss of life.

While they got plenty of plunder and a taste of battle, Chieftain Blist had to wonder if it was worth the losses.

"Warriors!" he shouted. "Halt and rally to me!" Once he gathered a large amount of his warriors, he turned towards the city. His arch-goblins, like him, dropped their bags of plunder and pulled forth their weapons. He led them to the edge of the woods and then heard the hooves.

* * * * *

Major Goldwater hid his cavalry in the forest. It was the same cavalry that decimated arch-goblin caravans from the day before. Now they emerged rested and on the charge. They came out of the forest, along the paths made by those same arch-goblin caravans, running down whatever got in their way. The small lizard-goblins were run over easily enough. Many were trampled to death or even tossed about by thundering hooves. Many arch-goblins however had to make a choice. Some chose to dodge or dive for cover. Others tried to defend themselves, not from the horses but the Vorclawean Dragoons, the elite cavalry units cut, killed and ran down many arch-goblins this morning. The dragoons broke into two columns eventually and then ran right around the bluff freeing the trapped Vorclawean soldiers.

Some arch-goblins caught between both the dragoons and now the advancing foot soldiers from the bluff, began to throw down their weapons in surrender. Chieftain Gutter was among them. The chieftain who smelled a victorious route just a moment ago, was now facing utter defeat. The chieftain did understand the common tongue and when he heard his own words echoed by the commander of the Vorclawean forces said, "No prisoners, no mercy!" he feared for his life.

* * * * *

Chieftain Blist's arch-goblins emerged from out of the west gate and were already into the forest. From the forest's edge, he watched his fellow arch-goblins fall in the morning light. He believed he saw Chieftain Gutter behind the circling swarm of horses. "No!" he shouted. The arch-goblin leader wanted to rush out and lead his own tribe in a great battle but realized that by the time his warriors travelled the open ground, they would be under threat of cavalry.

"Chieftain!" shouted one of his kin. "Do we advance?"

After many moments Chieftain Blist replied with a simple, "No. There is nothing now we can do for them." He turned his arch-goblins around, reclaimed their spoils and they began their roundabout travel back to Ironhold.

* * * * *

They were able to sleep several hours before Leif woke up Dru to keep watch.

Leif was barely into his rest when he heard Dru jump to his feet during his watch and pull out a small telescope.

"What do you see?" asked Leif. When Dru did not answer Leif stood up and peered in the direction of Dru's gaze. "I see it," said Leif.

"It is just a single skeletal warrior," said Dru. "I will dispatch it. You get your rest."

"Wait," said Leif. "With all the winding paths we took through the night, what are the odds of this one finding our exact path?"

"Well, he is about to wish he hadn't," said Dru.

"Look again my friend," said Leif. His keen elven eyes were far sharper than any humans.

Dru peered once more through his telescope and this time he saw that the single warrior was not alone. Several more lumbered behind.

"I count ten," said Leif.

"Twelve," corrected Dru. "And they are headed this way. How do they know?" asked Dru.

Leif held up the small Jade Tower that imprisoned Rom-Seti. "Because of this," he said. "I believe he calls to them."

Chapter 6
The Trek

They had been wandering the mountains for three days. The heat from the sun was penetrating during the day while the cold of the mountain air at night chilled them all to the bone. For the three days they had been periodically attacked by roaming undead creatures. Every time they sat down for more than a few hours, they eventually encountered undead creatures, mostly following them from the north. However, as they progressed further south, Leif's theory that Rom-Seti could call to these minions seemed more a reality as they soon encountered undead in the south as well.

All the members were still in good health considering, all except Bjorn.

"I think the only thing keeping him alive is his prayers to his god," said Damon Crag callously to Dru.

If Bjorn heard Damon's comments, he gave no indication, Dru thought to himself. The man just continued to trek. Dru, although irritated by Damon's comments, could not disagree. Bjorn's strength had about left him. The illness caused by Rom-Seti's evil grasp was worsening. The large man's neck was turning as red as his hair. The large priest abandoned his shield a day ago but Lorez, of all creatures, decided to carry or drag the shield for him.

Leif tried to be optimistic and keep Bjorn's spirits up. It was all he could do, he thought. "Do you remember father's proverb of pain?" asked Leif smiling. Bjorn wasn't acknowledging. Leif asked again to attract his attention.

"I do," responded Bjorn in a groggy voice.

"Good, what is it?"

"Do you mean to quiz me or lecture me, brother?" asked Bjorn garnering a smile.

"I mean to pass the time is, that's all," said Leif.

"Endure or die," he responded dryly.

"Well, that's not the proverb exactly," said Leif smiling.

"What is this proverb?" asked the arch-goblin Lorez.

"It's a saying our father used to preach to his soldiers," replied Leif.

"Endure the pain that achieves success. For if you do not, then you invite the pain of failure or disappointment," explained Dru.

"Ah!" said Lorez, understanding.

The arch-goblin drew forth his mace and scimitar at the sight of seeing another undead coming straight at them. "I have this one!" It was a skeleton wielding a rusted and broken sword. Lorez dispatched it easily enough. "Now more come from the south," said Lorez. "The undead from the mountains answer the call of the creature inside the little tower.".

"It's possible," replied Leif.

"Of course it's possible, elf," said Damon irritated. "There isn't any way a lumbering undead creature got around and flanked us. We should consider getting rid of that thing."

"How then can we prove that we completed our mission?" asked Leif.

"Your arch-goblin friend of course," responded Damon. "He will vouch to your master or whatever she is. We can bury it in the mountains and they can come back for it later."

"And if the undead dig it up and they free him somehow?" asked Lorez. "What then? You would have ensured our death."

Damon rolled his eyes in response and decided to let the matter drop seeing as there was no answer to the matter, not yet anyway.

"This undead is different than others," said Sker. "Covered in dirt," he said. Sker was much lower to the ground and better able to inspect the undead.

"What does that mean?" asked Damon.

"It means," interrupted Leif. "That you are correct, Damon. The Revenant's call goes out to other undead. This one likely came from the ground, perhaps in a shallow grave. More will be coming our way likely from all directions it seems."

"We should climb to the highest peak and leave it there," said Dru.

"I like that idea," said Damon.

"No," said Leif. "We will continue until we find a way back to Vorclaw."

"There is no turning east over the mountains and back to Sanctuary," said Dru looking at the enormity of the cliffs and frozen peaks. "Due south it is then until we make our way east. Lovely," said Dru.

* * * * *

"I am unable to locate them," explained the Revenant Pallentine, in the elvish language, to Revenant Niss. "They are either within Rom-Seti's necropolis and if so presumably dead. Or, they have deviated from the path back from whence they came. Perhaps they're lost in the cave network somewhere."

Revenant Niss sat on a bench across from Pallentine who continued to stare into his crystal ball searching the path back to the mountain refuge known as Sanctuary. It was the rally point for the ones invading Rom-Seti's lair. "Or, perhaps they had taken another route out of the necropolis?" she said in elvish.

"Perhaps," said Pallentine. "No matter, I am pleased the monster was attacked and suffered for it. My compliments to you and your lessor on striking a blow against Rom-Seti. Tell me, how do her other endeavours progress, such as this Ooktha?"

"I have not consorted with her of late as I have been more preoccupied with this endeavour."

"I above all appreciate your anger towards him, my friend," began Pallentine. "I appreciate you bringing this opportunity to me, to join in Rom-Seti's demise. Rest assured; we will eventually snuff this devil out of existence."

"I am actually now concerned with the success and whereabouts of the soul sucker!" she announced, now standing. "I want to know where it is," she said angrily. "I spent years creating it and now that it was unleashed, I want to know of its success or failure."

After several moments of silence in the dark room, Rom-Seti asked, "What else would you have me do?"

If she had eyes she would have rolled them. "Find them!"

Rom-Seti looked up immediately but said nothing. After a moment of both revenants staring each other down, Rom-Seti called out, "Teodor!"

In entered the elf Teodor. He seemed quite at home in the presence of the two undead revenants.

"No doubt you're eavesdropping, my friend," said Pallentine. "How do you feel about infiltrating Rom-Seti's necropolis?"

"I have done it before but only in the catacombs below," he responded.

"No," said Pallentine. "I don't mean there. I mean look around the necropolis."

"That, I can do."

"Good," said Niss. "I want you to find them and find my Jade Tower."

* * * * *

"I see you are keeping us to the mountains," said Lorez to Leif.

"Aye," said Leif.

The two had taken up the lead of worming their way through the mountains.

"Why is that?" asked Dru.

"Isn't it obvious?" said Damon. "He is looking for a path over the mountains."

"I thought it was…" began Bjorn. "To keep us away from the cold winds from the west," he said straining with each breath.

"I see someone is regaining his sense of humor," said Dru of Bjorn.

"I am trying," replied Bjorn.

After several more hours of travel and steadily climbing Leif decided on a halt and Lorez agreed. "We'll make camp here," said Leif. "It has a good view of anything coming up the hills and secluded from the winds above."

"Well," began Damon. "We will definitely spot anything coming out of the south and north," he said. "But it lacks visibility from anything coming down upon us from the mountains on either side of us."

"Aye, but I feel the threat is more from in front and behind us than above," said Leif.

Bjorn let out a sudden cough.

"And I think we travelled enough for today," Leif finished.

Damon stared at Leif whose eyes were gazing at his brother Bjorn and his failing health. The man rolled his eyes and was about to say something to his apprentice Dru about his frustration with the location but caught himself remembering that Dru was the Forehammer's childhood friend.

Damon spotted a small number of undead coming up the hillside. Leif tried to mount an ambush but was stopped once Lorez realized they could throw large rocks and drop small boulders on them. They were able to cripple all six approaching undead, all skeletons coming out of the south. Leif handed the Jade Tower over to Sker for safekeeping. Then Leif, Lorez, and Dru went to finish off the undead.

"Make yourself useful, lizard-goblin," said Damon to Sker while the undead were being dispatched. "Go find us some eggs or squirrels or something."

Sker growled slightly but Damon kicked some dirt at the stunted creature and off Sker ran but not before he let off a hiss.

After several minutes, Leif, Lorez and Dru returned.

"Well, that was the easiest encounter yet," said Dru. He, Leif and Lorez, all returned to the campsite overlooking their own ascent path.

"Where is Sker?" asked Leif.

"I sent him to try and find us some food," replied Damon relaxing under one of the small trees.

Bjorn coughed which drew Leif's attention. "Did you see which way he went?" he asked of Bjorn. Bjorn nodded no in response.

"Don't worry, he will return," said Dru. "I dare say the little fellow loves you!" finished Dru with a chuckle. Lorez agreed with the joke and bellowed.

"He has the Jade Tower!" said an irritated Leif.

Leif called out for Sker.

"Are you mad?" jumped up Damon. "You just announced our presence to anyone or anything else nearby. He is just up the woods getting us some food."

Leif started off, alone.

"And Leif," said Damon. Leif turned towards him. "If you value your life, you would do well not to give away our position, again," said Damon coldly.

"I will do my best to keep you safe then," said Leif as he rolled his eyes.

Lorez sat down and ate the last of his dead squirrel. His huge maw ate the thing whole.

"I guess it is too late to ask you if you're interested in sharing?" asked Damon of Lorez who just smiled with a mouth of fur. "Yuck, never mind." Damon just rolled his eyes, shook his head and sat down, irritated as usual.

* * * * *

53

Sker was loyal to Leif Foehammer, without question. Saving him from his own race and the arch-goblins had indeed brought the lizard-goblin a sense of friendship and belonging he had never known. However, he was not pleased in the way Leif had, in his mind, put him in harm's way. Sker held the Jade Tower during the assault and now he held it once again. Then Leif left him with that callous man, Damon Crag. And now Sker was doing that horrible human's bidding.

Sker came across a pine tree where he heard a squirrel. He didn't see it, lizard-goblins' eyesight was poor by human standards during the day. He did hear it however. As luck would have it he also heard some birds chirping in the same tree higher up. The lizard-goblin easily scaled the pine tree. He cursed the tree however, for his padded toes encountered pine sap in the ascent thanks to his clawed toes. Higher up in the tree he could now smell different scents. Sker's instincts took over suddenly as he sniffed the air. He froze in place as his eyes eventually confirmed what his nostrils had alerted him too. Sker wanted to jump down and run back to Leif but it was too late for that.

A group of tall humanoid creatures with jackal-like heads appeared. These lycaons were the same creatures they had encountered at Sanctuary and eventually killed during their trek to the cave, days ago. They had tall, pointy ears that went above their heads. They had some leather and cloth material for clothing covering below their waists while their bodies were black with dark fur covering over their shoulders, necks and faces. They were led by an unusual creature. It was tall like the lycaons, but Sker thought this creature's body was golden and was in staunch contrast to its darker kin.

They were moving silently on padded paw-like feet and were obviously stalking his friends. Sker watched the lycaons take up ambushing spots among the rocks and pines. Sker's heart sunk as he watched Leif coming forth up the hill following his own tracks. What could a runty lizard-goblin do? If he alerted Leif then he would be killed. If he didn't then he may yet survive. Also, this party of lycaons outnumbered his own three to one.

Sker watched Leif helplessly succumb to the lycaons. They started with several blow darts. Only one of the three pierced Leif's neck. Sker wanted to scream but could not out of fear. The runty lizard-goblin began to tear.

Then the lycaon hidden above and behind a large boulder threw a net over Leif as the elf drew out his weapons. Leif shouted an alarm that surely alerted the rest of his party and Sker took heart that Leif might be rescued as it was too late for him to escape on his own and he was captured.

Dru, Lorez and Bjorn all arrived to see Leif under the cover of a net, looking groggy and a small dart protruding from his neck. He was held in place by two lycaons. To the left of the lycaons was the golden lycaon.

"Well, well, well," said the blond lycaon in the common tongue but with a growling accent. "I see you lost your elf," said the creature as the rest of the lycaons emerged from their hiding.

"What are you? Who are you?" asked Bjorn.

"I am Rreebish, chieftain of the lycaons," he said with a rolling accent on the **R,** akin to a growl. "I lead this clan," Rreebish said walking closer to the three. "And you all took from me, four souls back near Sanctuary."

Leif then appeared to collapse from the poison.

"What have you done to him?" demanded Bjorn.

"He is sleeping, that's all," said Rreebish, hands on his waist. "He may prove to be the lucky one. If he dies, he would never see it coming. And keep in mind, I can easily have him killed, unless you tell me what I want to know."

"And what's that?" asked Bjorn.

"I first want you to tell me why!"

"Why what?" asked Bjorn.

"Why did you take four of our kin, outside Sanctuary? Jorak here tells me you ambushed them and are in league with orcs."

"Nay," said Bjorn. "I walked into their camp and demanded they release a lone orc."

"The human lies!" announced Jorak the lycaon in the common tongue. Jorak himself was some distance off to the left of Bjorn. "Kill them master and be done with this so we can be gone from this haunted land!"

"Silence!" barked Rreebish in the lycaon tongue.

"His counterpart here, holding your friend says the same. You ambushed them with orcs, three of them, and it all started at Sanctuary with the fourth member of your party who is undoubtedly sneaking around as we speak."

"They're lying and we can prove it," said Lorez.

"Oh, am I to trust the word of a warmongering arch-goblin?" asked the lycaon leader.

"No, not my word," said Lorez. "The daughter of the Mistress of Sanctuary can vouch for my lord here. She was our escort bringing us to the mountain gate."

"Ha! Now I know you're lying. She would never participate nor approve."

"I never said any of that," announced Lorez. "I said she was there. She warned us against it but we or he…" Lorez said pointing at Bjorn. "My large priestly friend and his elf companion under your feet have a righteousness about them and attempted a rescue."

Rreebish was mulling the words over and did not speak.

"And two orcs survived and passed us on their way saying that they were ambushed by the same six lycaons who harassed us at Sanctuary. They will corroborate our story as well. Isn't that true, lycaon?" asked Lorez looking at the Jorak who was the actual instigator of the events at Sanctuary.

"If they released that orc to us instead of killing him," started Dru, "you might not be facing…what did she say, a shattered peace?"

"Interesting little human," said Rreebish.

"I am not that little. Just skinny," responded Dru.

"So the Mistress of Sanctuary or at least her daughter will vouch for your tale," responded the lycaon leader looking at Jorak.

"May the goddess Matronae, my deity, the mother goddesses, strike me down if I am lying to you good sir," said Bjorn.

"And what say you Jorak?" asked Rreebish. "To the human priest who swears by his god?"

Jorak did not respond.

"When I ask the Lady of Sanctuary, what will she say?"

"No, my lord! She would not dare because she was not there."

"No what? No, that you did not lead us up here due to your own folly? And what of her daughter, did you know the daughter of the Mistress of Sanctuary was lurking in the wood when you two ran away?"

Jorak did not respond, merely growled.

"Will her story be the same as yours or this human's?"

Jorak now began to look frustrated and growled some more. He even bared his teeth to the lycaon leader. "Lies, my lord. All lies!" the lycaon responded with a growl.

"And what of the two orcs he claims you let escape? Will the orc's chieftain tell me a tale similar to his or to yours? Or worse, will the orcs be on the warpath upon my return?" he asked, teasing.

Rreebish now shouted at the lycaon Jorak in the lycaonish tongue, "Did we come up here because you were too frightened to tell me of your defeat?"

The other lycaon looked downward and shameful. He stared at the ground, then at Leif. His body language spoke volumes to all present even though Dru, Bjorn and even Lorez didn't know what was being said.

Jorak, on the other hand, responded with a fierce growl.

"Or was it your own cowardly ways you were trying to hide from me? Did you turn and run or is what they say all lies?" said Rreebish in lycaon.

Jorak did not answer. He did not need to when the other lycaon that was Jorak's counterpart at the battle and present at Sanctuary bent down before Rreebish's large pawed feet whimpering and begging forgiveness.

Rreebish then put his footlike paw upon the back of the lycaon grovelling and yelling at it. Several other lycaons gathered around the one called Jorak, weapons drawn.

"Look out!" shouted Bjorn who jumped back from the incoming giant missile.

A lycaon was somehow tossed into the air from afar and landed in a heap atop Rreebish, the lycaon under his pawed foot and the other lycaon guarding Leif. They all rolled in a pile before Bjorn, Dru and Lorez.

"Monster!" shouted Lorez seeing now what threw the lycaon.

The flesh-golem caught up to them.

Chapter 7
Undead Follow

Another lycaon fell to the flesh-golem by a swat of its mighty fist. The flesh-golem had only one working arm, the other dangled broken with an even more dangling hand by the wrist. It also moved without grace as its legs were both damaged from its fall in the great chasm. It wasn't alone either. Several undead zombies, skeletons, mummies and ghouls lumbered behind. Once the ghouls got sight of living flesh, the three jumped at the nearest lycaon.

The lycaon was able to bat away one ghoul with his flail but was unable to get away from the other two. The ghouls bit into the lycaon's flesh at the throat and wrist. The battered ghoul then recovered to bite at the lycaon's ankles. Skeletons armed with various weapons came past the mummies feasting to engage the remaining lycaons. The flesh-golem however made its way directly for Bjorn, Lorez and Dru.

"Damon, we need you!" shouted Bjorn.

Bjorn ran over and past the lycaons that lay at his feet. The man was not concerned with them; he was concerned with Leif's safety. "May the power of Matronae end you!" shouted the pale and weakened Bjorn. The man charged forward to meet the flesh-golem. The large man was still flexible and able to avoid the swing of the monster's fist. Bjorn landed his powerful overhead strike upon the creature's chest, knocking it backwards several steps and cracking the flesh-golem's chest.

A skeleton warrior was crushed beneath the behemoth but two more rounded it, coming for Bjorn. They froze suddenly at the sight of Bjorn's holy mace as it began to glow.

"Be gone unclean!" gritted Bjorn between is teeth. To Bjorn's surprise, the two skeletons crumpled to a pile of bones. Bjorn realized his power was growing but did not have time to contemplate as more skeletons emerged from the rocks and around the few trees in the area.

The ghouls however, were not so easily caught off guard by Bjorn's holy symbol. The semi-intelligent undead launched surprisingly from behind the rocks, knocking Bjorn to the ground. Claws raked across the back of Bjorn's chain mail. Were it not for Lorez, the maw of a ghoul would have bitten down on the back of Bjorn's neck.

Lorez landed a heavy boot to the face of the open maw. The arch-goblins kicked shut the maw closed forcing the ghoul to snap off part of its own tongue. The arch-goblin continued to counter with assaults from his mace.

Dru engaged the other ghoul. His two short swords danced over and around in circular motions. The ghoul struck with clawed fingers but took a hit from Dru's sword. The ghoul struck again and again taking hits to its arms and hands. Bits of flesh and digits broke off but the ghoul was hungry for flesh. Dru tracked its gaze to Leif lying entangled in nets unconscious. Dru went on the offensive and began to push back gaining the attention of the ghoul. Dru swiped and stabbed and swung until he got a hit across the chest of the semi-intelligent creature who then backed off.

Some of the lycaons engaged with skeletons while others ran from the scene, including Jorak. Several of the lycaons assaulted the mummies while they closed in.

Rreebish stirred and tried to get up and out from beneath three of his lycaons. All lied in a heap above him. The lycaon leader could taste blood in his mouth from biting his own tongue after he was attacked by the thrown kin.

By now Dru gained the full attention of the ghoul. Much taller than Dru, the ghoul decided to launch itself upon Dru believing its height and lust for flesh gave it the advantage. Dru got both swords swinging and come up into the stomach and chest. The ghoul reached forward with its maw and hands. The maw snapped wildly and Dru pushed back on the creature trying to pull forth his swords by spinning the creature round and round, but to no avail. The claws made their way up to Dru's shoulders and it tried to pull Dru closer to the hungry mouth of the ghoul. The creature suddenly stopped as a gloved hand came across the forehead of the ghoul and a blade protruded suddenly through the neck of the creature, severing its spine. It fell limp and Dru could see Damon Crag standing behind the ghoul helping to pull it from Dru's blades.

A skeleton armed with a rusty axe made its way above Leif. Neither Dru nor Damon could get to the skeleton to stop that axe. Up came a fur-covered hand to catch it though. Rreebish got out from beneath the pile of lycaons and save the unconscious elf from certain doom. Then a spiked flail came across the face of that skeleton crushing it to powder and extinguishing the undead creature. Next came the zombies through the rocks and trees.

"I hate zombies," said Damon. "Slow, stinking and rotting."

* * * * *

The flesh-golem returned to its feet thanks to the ineffective skeletons trying to assault Bjorn. *"Kill the intruders, and follow them until they're all dead!"* That was the command the flesh-golem followed. Bjorn was the closest target and again the flesh-golem went for the large man swiping at him with his powerful fist. Bjorn was able avoid the blow.

Lorez ran at the flesh-golem and sliced at the right leg of the creature. It showed no pain but it did acknowledge Lorez's presence with a backhand swing of its right broken arm. The limp-wristed hand caught Lorez by the face, sending the arch-goblin backwards and tumbling to the ground.

Bjorn used the distraction caused by Lorez as an opportunity to send a powerful swing to the back of its left knee. The flesh-golem fell on that knee but a backhand by the creature landed across Bjorn's face and sent the man to the ground.

As the flesh-golem began to rise, an axe landed squarely at its chest. Rreebish's enchanted axe was one he confiscated from a dwarf long ago. It sent the flesh-golem backwards as it rose. It stumbled backwards near a tree and fell. The enchantment gave the blade increased cutting ability and dug deeply into the flesh-golem's already cracked ribs. The creature though did not cease, it merely landed on its back and began getting back to its feet.

"How do you kill the beast?" asked Rreebish now only armed with his spiked flail.

Lorez didn't answer. The arch-goblin warrior got back on his feet and ran at it. With both his scimitar and small mace in his hands, Lorez hacked at the thigh of the flesh-golem with his scimitar. It did little damage to the magically enhanced bone of the abnormal creation. He alternated between swipes with the mace and scimitar. Screaming in anger and frustration, Lorez hoped to cleave the leg or damage it permanently.

Bjorn too didn't answer Rreebish either. He went on the offensive following Lorez's lead. Bjorn readied an overhand chop of his rose-mace and brought it down upon the opposite shin, hoping to cripple the creature's other leg fully. But Bjorn barely connected as the same leg kicked out unexpectedly and sent a massive foot to the open midsection of the large priest. Bjorn tumbled backwards in a heap.

Lorez swiped twice more with his scimitar and even one with his mace but did little damage to the flesh-golem. Lorez then smelled an overpowering aroma. Two zombies made for the arch-goblin. The arch-goblin backhanded one with his mace and shoved his scimitar into the other. While one fell to the ground with a busted face, the other tried to continue to come at Lorez while the scimitar was still within the undead. Two surviving lycaons ran past Lorez, trying to escape the undead as several more zombies advanced.

As the flesh-golem attempted to get back up on its busted legs and broken arm, Bjorn too struggled to gain his bearings. Bjorn instinctively looked to his brother, still netted but safe. Luckily, Dru and Damon dispatched their undead and moved into cover for Bjorn. Some mummies came at Bjorn but another zombie came at Lorez.

"Come feel the wrath of Matronae, foul creatures!" shouted Bjorn in a frustrated rage. The man's divine mace beamed a brilliant pink and white *divine light*. It forced the undead mummies and any zombies in the area to turn away. The closest mummy caught fire! Their undead flesh burned and sizzled as they departed.

Lorez used his weapons to turn his attacking zombie towards Bjorn and watched it catch a flame, struggle and collapse. The remaining mummies turned and ran from the scene. Bjorn breathed heavily, exhausted but he had no time to relish in the small victory.

The flesh-golem got back up, its head in the tree branches and magical axe still protruding from chest. It pulled forth the axe and threw it at a passing lycaon, killing it.

Skeleton warriors now came at the party from behind and up the hill. The two remaining lycaons had no choice but to engage them. Rreebish followed after them, to either retreat or assist. No one but Rreebish knew.

"They will buy us some time to flee up the hillside and regroup," shouted Damon.

"We are not leaving Leif," said Dru sternly to his master and charged at the flesh-golem shouting.

Bjorn and Lorez followed Dru. The three stabbed at the legs, hands and torso. They all took swipes from the creature as well but remained elusive around the rocks and trees. It was almost like a game of deadly tag.

Damon had no time to either argue or join the fray. He had to take on the third mummy that materialized from off to his left. It was wounded from the lycaons attacking it but did not feel the *divine light* from Bjorn moments before. The mummy attacked wildly with its fists and releasing some unholy blasts. Damon, unafraid, dodged the assaults and parried those attacks with his sword. Although he had to backpedal with each swipe by the mummy, it was Damon's ruse. He wanted the creature to gain confidence and lunge at him. It eventually did so. Damon spun around to his left allowing the mummy to pass him and miss him entirely. The mummy's back was exposed and the assassin sliced it open with his right short sword and magically enhanced strength. As the mummy turned in protest, its head was cut off by a backhand of Damon's other short sword.

Bjorn, Dru and Lorez were becoming exhausted from the continuous melee with the flesh golem.

"We cannot kill it!" shouted Bjorn.

"And it doesn't tire!" said Lorez.

"Keep it here near the trees so it doesn't see Leif," said Dru.

It was then that a runty lizard-goblin leaped from the trees and landed on the bald head of the flesh-golem. Sker's claws dug in and stabbed down with his knife, tearing at the eyes of the creature. The flesh-golem could only get one arm up to swing at the little lizard-goblin, the other arm was too broken and mangled to reach for Sker who was knocked off but landed safely.

The flesh-golem was now blind, with one eye cut open and a knife protruding from the other.

"Sker, you magnificent creature!" shouted Dru.

Bjorn was now able to get a perfect two-handed swing of his enchanted mace upon that large knee of the flesh-golem. He finally shattered it forcing it to the ground. The flesh-golem's hands flailed about trying to swing and grab at what it could. Dru slowly came up behind it and put his sword through the back of the neck, ending the creature.

With the flesh-golem defeated, Lorez went after the lycaons and lycaon leader to aid them. Damon had no intention of helping the lycaons. In the end, the undead were defeated but only one of the lycaon leaders remained. The rest were either raked to death by the undead or ran off.

"I will check the perimeter for more undead," said Damon. "Keep watch, all of you, there are two mummies out there still, at least."

Dru went looking for Sker and saw the lizard-goblin kneeling next to Leif. Sker was cutting the nets away from his master and was trying to rouse the elf.

"He is only sleeping," said Rreebish. The lycaon leader dug into a pocket and produced a small vial. "Here, put this under his nose and let him breathe it in.

Sker did as instructed and Leif roused slowly. "Master Leif, you're alive!"

"What happened? Where am I?" asked Leif.

* * * * *

Leif tended to Bjorn's wounds. The large man's face was a bloody mess from the cuts and bruises he received from the battering by the flesh-golem. As Dru explained what happened, Leif hardly listened. Leif took out a sewing needle and began to stich Bjorn's cuts above his left eye. The priest's lips were swollen and his neck was still red. His breath was labored and Leif feared that the man's strength that would have sustained him was just spent saving him.

"You look like you got your tail-whooped, brother," said Leif.

"I didn't want to disturb your nap," he responded with a bloody smile.

"Gross, don't smile," said Leif.

Lorez was equally gnarled. The arch-goblin bled from his nose, cheek and mouth. However, he hardly seemed impacted by the damage. Both Lorez and Bjorn were solid, both capable of taking and giving whatever they got. However, the staunch difference in the two told Leif that Bjorn was not healing from his battle with Rom-Seti.

Leif helped Bjorn out of his armor. Bjorn's ribs were badly bruised from sustaining a direct kick by the flesh-golem.

"You need to rest here for a few days my brother," said Leif. "I will be the one protecting you so you can rest," said Leif looking at Rreebish. "What are you and why did you attack me?"

"Fair enough," said Rreebish, his breath still labored from the fighting. "My name is Rreebish, and I lead the lycaons. I followed you lot up here to find the truth of the matter."

"The truth?"

"Two of my tribe claimed you lot ambushed my lycaons, along with several orcs," said Rreebish.

"Ambushed with orcs?" asked Leif but did not give the lycaon a chance to answer back. "Did your lycaons tell you about the part where they began instigating hostilities at Sanctuary?" asked Leif. When Rreebish did not answer, Leif continued. "Ask the Mistress of Sanctuary's daughter. She was there. In fact, they attacked the orcs, three of them in the mountains. Two escaped and passed us on their retreat. My brother here went to ask them to release the orc but he was already dead at the hand of your kin," said Leif, somewhat irritated. Leif was more upset that he missed the battle by being drugged and at the sight of his already wounded brother who was now more wounded than he remembered.

"Everything you said is what your friends said," responded the lycaon leader.

Leif rose from tending to Bjorn. He looked around at the scene. "I am sorry for your losses," he said. "I know what it is like to lose soldiers in battle."

"What are you lot doing up here anyway? And what business had you in Rom-Seti's necropolis?" asked the lycaon leader.

"What did you say?" asked Dru.

Rreebish did not answer, but merely looked at Dru.

"You know of the revenant by name?" asked Lorez. "How?"

"Rom-Seti's city was once known as Milothia. He rebelled from the rulers of a land known as Anubia, decades ago," said Rreebish.

"I never heard of Anubia," said Leif.

"Nor I," said Lorez.

"Nor should any of you," replied Rreebish. "Long ago, us lycaons too were banished along with Rom-Seti, for worshipping the god, Set. It was considered sacrilege but my people repented. Still, the god Osiris banished Milothia to this place to live out the rest of our lives but Rom-Seti and his followers were transformed into undead. We were only exiled because we repented. So we left the city to seek out life in the mountains while Rom-Seti remained, bitter."

"Interesting tale but helps us, not," interrupted Damon.

The assassin wanted to leave them all behind. He wanted to return to Vorclaw, no to the nine hells with that—to be away from here, anywhere. However, the logic of safety-in-numbers outweighed his own desires. "Dru, you are with me," said Damon. "We must do what we can before this evening sets in. We will set traps and snares throughout the perimeter," he explained. "And I am certain the two mummies will return along with more undead from the necropolis."

Everyone nodded in agreement.

Chapter 8
A New Sedgedunum

General Baltus Blackpool, the Mage Anthon Blackpool, Admiral Drake Kahee and Major Isaac Goldwater stood at the most northeast tower of the Sedgedunum city wall. It gave them a good view of the damage to the city. Before them were the burnt-out buildings of the northeast and northern sections of the city. It took two days to extinguish all the fires within the city. From their vantage point they could see the smouldering Wizard's College in the distance. The only things truly burning now were the pile of dead arch-goblins to the north of the city just before the forest. It was where the general decided to dispose of the invaders.

"The count of dead arch-goblins so far is over five hundred," said Major Goldwater.

"And what of our losses?" asked Baltus.

"Soldiers, we just broke over a hundred dead, thrice that wounded but most will be able to fight on. For the citizens who fought, or were caught in the fall of the Wizard's College that is over two hundred thus far, and counting," replied the major.

General Blackpool nodded but not at the results of lives lost. Although he expected more loss of life, he was truly pleased with the results and admired the damage he had helped to create. His major goals, to remove the ruling council was next but the toppling of the Wizard's College for his brother was complete; he found it strange how little thought he gave to the invaders or citizens of Sedgedunum.

"Hang the arch-goblin chieftain's carcass over the north wall facing the forest," said General Blackpool. "Don't burn him just yet. I want any spies or scouts they have lurking to see him. Hopefully, they will recognize him."

The four continued to survey the damaged city in silence. After another view of the damaged city, Admiral Kahee said, "More soldiers arrive from around the nation daily. We are ferrying the wounded to the nearby village of Sedgefen.

"We garrisoned some soldiers there," said Major Goldwater. "It's the home of your friend Magnus, if I am not mistaken. I sent Captain Ty to supervise."

"Good choice," replied the general. "It will give the man time to heal."

After several more moments of viewing the scene, the general asked, "And what of Magnus and Disa Foehammer?"

No one answered as no one considered it. That irritated the general and he wore it on his face.

"I will send word to Captain Ty and ensure that she receives special attention," said Major Goldwater.

"Very good, major," said the general. "I want you to know, all of you, that Disa Foehammer cared for my son when my wife was killed. While I was away," he finished. He then turned to Major Goldwater and said, "Make sure she is well cared for."

"As you wish, my lord," he responded. "I will send word in the next hour."

"And what of our sons?" asked Admiral Drake Kahee. "Have you heard word yet, Anthon?"

"No and I admit he is overdue," said Anthon.

"And what are you going to do about it?" asked the admiral.

"After the council meeting today, if it goes without major incident, I will scry Sanctuary to see if I can track them down."

"And we still have no word of the arch-goblin queen?" asked the admiral.

"No," said General Blackpool who began to descend the steps of the wall. "But I have the perfect agent to get us her intentions and whereabouts," he announced to everyone while eyeing a man on horseback who was waiting below the steps. Mimdrid, the shape-changer, was in the guise of General Blackpool's aide, a slender man once known to him as Nigel Newman, a former merchant from Dubravna.

"Ah, Major Newman!" began the Baltus. "What news have you for me?" asked the general.

"Mr. Night has informed me that all had gone according to plan, sir," responded Mimdrid in the form of Nigel. The fact that Mr. Newman and Mr. Night were the same individual brought a smile to the face of Baltus. When Mimdrid was in the guise of Mr. Night, the man wore no rank, no uniform. Major Goldwater only met him a few times and Admiral Kahee even less. Neither of them knew of Major Nigel Newman's nor Mr. Night's true identity, only that *they* served as aides and informants to the general. The only other person who knew the identity of both men was Anthon Blackpool.

"I want you to ask if Mr. Night can gain access to the arch-goblin stronghold. I want to know the whereabouts of their queen," said the general bluntly.

"Ah, she lives then, if one might call being undead, alive," said Nigel.

"So it would seem," said Anthon, mounting his horse.

"Mr. Night could get access my lord. But it may take time now that our relationships are no longer amenable. Shall I use our friends at Fort Adamant?" asked Nigel. "They should at least grant him passage into the city."

"No," said Baltus mounting his horse. "I want your ally to get into Ironhold. I want an update on their present manpower situation and to know if their queen is nestling there or back in their underground city of Skulls-thorpe."

Mimdrid did not like the sound of that. He had been to Ironhold before. It was his exit point from the arch-goblins before he arrived in Sedgedunum. "As you wish my lord," replied Nigel. "But why cannot mage Anthon simply scry?"

"I tried," said Anthon. "It seems she is a wizard of sorts herself or she has allies that placed scrying shields over her cities. I must admit she never took interest in my work and I dealt mostly with the chieftains. If she is a mage, I am surprised by it but should not have been unexpected as many with strong elven blood have a magic capability."

"In the meantime, we have more pressing matters to attend to," interrupted the general. "Let us move on to our next course of action."

* * * * *

Led by General Blackpool, the five made their way to meet with the remains of the Council of Twelve.

Not all members were present for the meeting. Boyd Draconian, headmaster of Sedgedunum's Wizards College, was identified among the dead. Sea Captain Taywin Ray, a wealthy shipbuilder and maritime entrepreneur who represented Cairnloch, sailed out of the city shortly after it was invaded. Lord Singeing Anglewood, a wealthy warrior from the frontier town of Exbury and Lord Dremil Dissmee the retired half elven rogue of Wrexbury escaped, both presumably returning to their respective country homes. Archbishop Storm Evander a priest of Dagda who took part in the defence, was moved to Sedgefen for recovery after sustaining injuries. Lord Igor Frothbeard, the dwarven arms dealer from Irons-by-the-Sea, was not in the city at the time of the celebration. Therefore, he was also not present at the council meeting.

Lord Nightingale whose family of a wealthy bricklaying and construction firm was also present as was there was Lord Evan Ester, the leader of the miners' guild in Cairnhold. Of the clergy leaders, the Archbishop Zelana Spool, a high priestess of Matronae and Archbishop Elman Wisemind, a priest of Ogma were present and remained to help the sick in the city.

General Baltus Blackpool and Admiral Drake Kahee commander of the Navy, entered the room with their aides.

"Gentlemen," began Archbishop Zelana Spool before the two military leaders even sat down. "Let me begin by saying how appreciative I am of both your bravery and quick reactions to this horrid invasion."

"Here, here!" announced Archbishop Elman Wisemind. "Your actions likely saved the rest of us from further deaths and suffering."

"We didn't come here to hear your praises and thanks," interrupted the admiral, which was out of character for him. "We came here to deliver a report of the findings and best courses of action. Therefore, I yield the floor to General Blackpool," said the admiral in a show of solidarity.

"To begin with, let me say we are *not* victims of recklessness," started Baltus. "I believe this was a provoked attack."

"What? Who provoked the arch-goblins in the forest?" asked Lord Evan Ester.

"No one in particular," replied Baltus. "However, the arch-goblins near Fort Adamant were indeed provoked."

"So what?" responded Lord Ester. "They're many miles away. And what on Vana do you mean no in particular provoked the arch-goblins?"

"It is all are connected," said Baltus throwing down a map that showed the three arch-goblin cities. This was recovered by some arch-goblins in the Fort Adamant region. It showed their three cities and connecting routes through underwater passages."

"Rubbish," responded Lord Ester. "You would lead us to believe that this arch-goblin map proves the arch-goblins attacked Sedgedunum in retaliation for the building of Fort Adamant."

"The map shows the connection between the arch-goblins in the city they call Blood-helm and the city in the forest they call Ironhold."

"Fort Adamant itself pushed them into conflict," said Admiral Drake.

"Quite right," responded General Blackpool. "Or better still, members on this council pushed them into conflict with us."

"That's preposterous!" said Archbishop Elman Wisemind.

"Is it?" asked the general. "You archbishops, along with you Lord Evan Ester and my predecessor pushed for Fort Adamant for the sake of the jewels the fort is named for. It even resulted in the untimely death of my predecessor, Lord Brisbane," lied Baltus. It was he who had Lord Brisbane killed.

"General, I understand your frustration," began Archbishop Zelana Spool. "But now is not the time to point fingers," she said trying to calm the room. "I suggest we concentrate on shoring up our defenses in case of another attack, here or elsewhere," said the archbishop.

"My frustration goes a lot deeper than the council knows," said General Blackpool. "The reason why I was able to get here so quickly and muster forces with Admiral Kahee was because had received word of the attack and had to empty Fort Adamant, which is now no longer under our control. The arch-goblins have taken that as well."

"Surely not," said Lord Handle Nightingale.

Lord Evan Ester stared at the general and was about to blame him for incompetence after abandoning Fort Adamant but even he knew the damage to the city would've been ongoing had the general not abandoned the fort. Lord Ester was still frustrated as he knew the general was pinning a lot of the blame on his guild; he lobbied to have the fort built there to garner the riches in the mountains. He could divert some of the blame to the deceased Lord Brisbane but all present knew the reason for Fort Adamant was indeed to provide safety to the miners' explorations into the region. But then it dawned on him and he asked the question that might mitigate some of the blame.

"Question," began Lord Ester. "Are you to blame me solely and the miners' guild for this or are you forgetting that the arch-goblins fashioned an iron-golem. That it did make right for the wizard college did it not?"

"That it did," said General Blackpool.

"Certainly, this attack could have been equally provoked due to interfering from some disgruntled agent from our wizard college then, could it not?"

"Yes, and I have an answer for that as well," said the general. "We have captured a female wizard who said she conspired with the arch-goblins at Ironhold. The arch-goblins gave her up during their retreat. Her male counterpart was killed she said. We have her in custody."

"Where?" asked Archbishop Wisemind. "I wish to interrogate her!"

"I have her jailed presently at the Academy of Arms. I also have several wizards from the college that claim she was dismissed from the college for numerous infractions."

"Seems she wanted revenge," surmised Lord Nightingale. "What now general? What courses of action do you have planned?"

"I am glad you asked," said the general. He then dismissed Major Newman. "Ladies and gentlemen, I intend to leave the city's care in the hands of Admiral Kahee. He has drawn up plans already to incorporate the City Watch with his marines and sailors for security and plans for a curfew. I trust this is agreeable with you all?"

"Do you intend to take back Fort Adamant then?" asked Lord Nightingale.

"No," the general responded. "I intend to take our forces out of the city and follow the arch-goblins into the forest and bring the fight to their own doorstep."

It was then that three dozen soldiers and two wizards entered led by Anthon Blackpool.

"As for all of you, I hereby place you under arrest for incompetence, political conspiracy and exploitation of the people of Vorclaw."

* * * * *

Sea Captain Taywin Ray sailed for Cairnloch. He left Sedgedunum behind while it was being invaded. He made port in the seaside town of Cairnloch where he intended to muster forces and spread news of the Sedgedunum invasion. Once ashore he made directly for the city mayor's office. He removed his wide brimmed hat and walked up to the clerk whom he never seen before and demanded to see Mayor Shellbee.

"Ah Captain Ray, the mayor is expecting you," said the clerk.

"Expecting me?" asked Captain Ray.

"Yes, please come around the desk and go into see the mayor. He is very anxious to hear of the news affecting Sedgedunum and how he can help."

"I should not be surprised I guess, important news travels fast," he said to the clerk following him into the room.

When Taywin entered Mayor Shellbee's office, a place he was very familiar with, there were unfamiliar faces present. The mayor sat nervously. His round, white cheeks were flush red. The soldiers in the room stood up at the man's presence which was not uncommon given he was a council member.

"Shellbee," nodded Taywin. "I see by the presence of the soldiers, you're aware of what befallen the capital?"

"Taywin Ray, you are under arrest," said Major Ickingham. Who was prepositioned in the area by General Blackpool to round up any escaping members of the Council of Twelve. The rest of the men went for the man who tried to turn and run but the clerk pushed Taywin forward into their grasp.

"What is the meaning of this? I am member of the Council of Twelve. I will have your heads for this?"

"Under the orders of General Baltus Blackpool, I hereby place you under arrest for incompetence, political conspiracy and exploitation of the people of Vorclaw," said the major.

* * * * *

Lord Igor Frothbeard, a dwarven arms dealer, made the sea voyage to the capital once a month. It took about four days. He stayed for about a week to deal with council matters and occasionally met with his nephew, the dwarven ambassador. Then he would return to his hometown of Irons-by-the-Sea. The bald headed and white bearded dwarf sat comfortably sipping a mug of ale and eating a robust steak on his terrace. He owned one of the most respectable estates in the city. His terrace was within a compound of his own design that included tunnels beneath it. He garrisoned twenty bodyguards. His compound also hosted servants and smiths of all kinds. In all, his miniature stronghold housed about fifty people at any one time but no one knew for sure how many people the dwarf had in his compound.

Igor refused to be summoned by the Mayor of Irons-by-the-Sea or anyone else for that matter. Therefore, he found it no surprise when the mayor of the city, a female elf by the name of Dominika Gildedwing, showed up at his door. She was the only one allowed in the compound without an invitation.

"I can smell you mayor, from the moment you entered the compound," announced Igor with a laugh. "Your love of lavender gives you away. What brings you to me?" he asked biting into another piece of juicy steak.

The tall, blond elf didn't sit down. She stared out from his balcony overlooking his compound.

"Tell my councilman, truly, how much is your compound truly worth? Not the weapons mind you, I mean the structures and facilities?" she asked.

Igor chewed his steak and looked around. "Not certain really. Why do you ask?"

"I want to know when I confiscate it from you," she said.

"Ha! You wish," he responded as she handed him a notice sent magically to her from the capital. "What be this nonsense now?" he asked.

"Seems you have been recalled to the capital. It's under siege you know."

"I am to report to appear before General Blackpool to discuss allegations of incompetence, political conspiracy and exploitation of the people of Vorclaw," said the dwarf.

"You!" she said. "Exploit-no?" she joked.

"Bah," was his response and he crumpled the paper and threw it over his terrace.

"You don't find this concerning?" she asked.

"What should I? You know I don't like to be summoned."

"I advise you to answer the general's call and sign me over as the executor of your holdings," she said laughing.

"You think this is funny?"

"No, this is very serious. He is backed by the entire Vorclawean army and seems to have Admiral Drake Kahee in his pocket as he co-signed the letter."

"You were a soldier in the army here, what is he like?" the dwarf asked eating another piece of steak and washing it down with some more ale, seemingly unafraid.

"I am told he runs a secret society as well, called the Black-masks," she responded now turning towards the dwarf.

"Never heard of them?" replied the dwarf downing his cup of ale.

"If I were you, I would send a reply with your resignation from the council to keep him away from here," she said with a smile. "But maybe include a reminder of your importance to the weapons trade, your friends in the miners' guilds, the dwarven clans, and whatever else you can think of."

"You are not really helping and you are being very democratic about this," he said.

"Well, I did tell you the capital was under siege by arch-goblins about a few days ago and you did nothing," she replied.

"It wasn't to my benefit to take a boat to the capital," he said as if unconcerned. "I did however, instruct you to ready a force to sail for Sedgedunum so you could become a hero to these, people-humans," he said cutting some more steak and taking another mouthful.

"A novel concept that I was already undertaking when you told me to do so," she responded.

"See, great minds think alike," he said with a mouthful.

"Perhaps," she said walking over to the dwarf, looking at his food at first but then coming around behind him.

"No, I did nothing wrong," the dwarf continued while talking with his mouthful of steak. "And Igor Frothbeard answers to no one especially a human. By the Terra's tits, it's the main reason why I joined this bloody Council of Twelve, so I could be my own boss and be left alone. No, I think I will sit here and wait for the general to come to me if he dares."

"I guess great minds actually do not think alike," she responded.

"Eh?" was all he could muster before he felt the blade go through the back of his neck.

"You know, us Black-masks answer to no one as well," she said as she stuck a dagger into the dwarf's throat.

Chapter 9
Saving Grace

Two more days they walked with sore ribs and muscles. They were out of food and water for an entire day when they finally spotted a large forest of green trees in the distance. However, it was too far to traverse now that night was upon them.

"We haven't seen any undead in the last half-day," said Dru. "Do you think it is safe to camp here for the night or do we march on?"

"We would not arrive at that copse of trees until late night so I think it's best to camp here in the rocks under this lone pine until morning," said Damon.

"I will take first watch," said Leif.

"Fine," said Damon.

Leif, Dru and Damon established a perimeter of snares and some minor traps that would alarm them of anyone sneaking around. It served as a warning, nothing more.

"You are very good at establishing a perimeter, Damon," said Leif. "They're very simple and effective but I never would have thought of them," said Leif.

"Simple traps may have saved my life once or twice but also allowed me enough warning to take others," he said without remorse.

"They have definitely proven effective over the last few days," responded Leif trying to pay the man a compliment. Damon, if he heard or cared, didn't show it. "Where did you learn your particular set of skills?" asked Leif.

"Where does anyone learn?" replied Damon. "On the road, in the company of others, experience is the best teacher," he said.

"Sure, I agree with all of that," said Leif. "I am more curious about where you garnered your skill sets, how you came into the service of Dru and the army. Where did you come from?" Leif asked.

Damon turned suddenly on Leif. "Why do you want to know where I am from?" he asked in all seriousness.

Leif stared back. "Where does your confrontational nature come from? Why can I not ask you questions without you being defensive?"

Damon resumed setting his trip wire. Leif was about to engage the conversation further but Dru shook his head in an effort to stop Leif. The elf acknowledged and walked away to set up another trip line.

"I was a slave once," said Damon aloud. "I was sold into slavery in Karthia by my uncle when he fell on hard times. I escaped eventually and joined the army in Uden and became a knight of Uden only to be thrown out once they learned I was an escaped slave. I was pardoned but released anyway so I joined the thieves' guild there. Now, I am my own master."

Damon turned to look at both Leif and Dru. Leif nodded in response. "I will finish these snares and trip lines. You two look in on our wounded. Make sure that lycaon leader doesn't eat them."

Leif and Dru did so and saw that Bjorn was already asleep when they arrived back at the camp. The large man's face was no longer swollen but his breath was labored. His neck was burning red with pain still from Rom-Seti's touch and he had not said a word all day because of his pain. Bjorn was able to pray and cure some of his wounds but insisted on healing the rest of the party first.

Lorez was on the mend and busy removing his bandages.

Rreebish, the lycaon leader who was also wounded from the battle, was also recovering. He was also eyeing Sker who undoubtedly was considering the lizard-goblin for its next meal.

Sker was safeguarding Bjorn, not that anyone of them would attack him but knew how much Leif valued the man who he called brother.

"What does a lizard-goblin, an arch-goblin, a human, an elf and a lycaon have in common?" asked Leif.

"Insufferable jokes from an elf," said Dru.

Lorez laughed while the lycaon leader looked at him with a crooked head wondering what the answer was.

"Ah, no," said Leif. "The answer is everything. We are all not so different after all."

No one agued and it was Rreebish who nodded in agreement.

"Tomorrow we will be at that greenery and hopefully be out of the elements. We can find some water and possibly even food," said Dru.

"How do you know?" asked Rreebish,

"It is likely water seeps down from the mountains during melting, allowing trees to grow. We should see better days ahead."

That night Dru took first watch. He found a high rock but stayed low peering through the night. He was tired, incredibly so but remained determined. Again, the sleepiness hit him. He decided to stand and shake his limbs. In doing so he lost his balance. Very uncanny but he must have been more tired than he realized. His eyes were very glassy then. They were eventually unable to pierce the night so he sat down and decided to listen for the alarms Damon had set about the area. However as soon as he sat down, it was too late he realized. The *sleeping* spell took him as it did all his friends, except for one; that person was awake and being charmed away from the camp.

* * * * *

Bjorn could not explain it. He was being summoned away from his friends. He somehow knew or believed he knew his friends would remain safe in his absence and under their protection. But who were *they* calling to him? He had to know whose sweet calls bade him to the distant copse of trees. The large but sickly priest of Matronae still held his mighty rose-mace. He held it out like a torch lighting the way in a soft light that came from the four rose-crystal stones embedded within it. It lit his path in the night.

It also brought unwanted attention as the two trailing mummies saw Bjorn on his own from a distance. The pair moved in on him. It took some time but they were going to reach him before he would get to the copse of trees from where the calling came.

"You must first defeat the mummies, my dear," said one soft melodic voice by a lone pine. "They are almost upon you."

"Where are you?" he begged. "Who are you?" his voice strained. Bjorn was in a panic now. How did he get here? Where was he? The warning he received broke the link he had with the copse of trees. His rose mace shone brighter and his holy symbol within the hand guard radiated white hot light that burned the mummies as they came towards him. The two undead creatures lumbered to a stop, hissed and screeched at Bjorn. Their undead wrappings and flesh burned, almost to their bones.

Bjorn pulled away the holy mace and said, "Come at me filth and let us finish this."

The two mummies, seeing the holy symbol no longer emitting *divine light*, obliged and ran lumbering at him. Their clawed hands reached out and forward, savoring the flesh to come. When they were within several strides, they again found the burning white-hot light of that holy symbol. The priest's ruse lured them into a false sense of confidence and began burning them once again. Their inertia had them eventually crumpling at Bjorn's feet. Only the outline of bodies made of ash and bone remained.

Within moments he again felt the charm of the female voices calling him to the copse of trees and another suggestion to hurry to a loving embrace within the trees. It was too far to turn back now.

Bjorn eventually arrived at the trees: pines, oaks, spruces, cypress and water! He made a dash for the small stream he chanced upon in the night. By lying prone to the ground, he cupped the water in his hand.

"Drink great warrior," came a soft female voice but was accompanied by the laughter of another female voice from somewhere in the woods. "For too long you have gone with thirst," said the voice.

After splashing water on his face, Bjorn eventually came to his senses and suddenly felt very vulnerable. "Who are you? What do you want from me?" Only female giggling came back in reply from the dark woods.

"Fear not priest of Matronae, for we worship the same goddess," said the woman.

A bright light suddenly appeared. It came from some object held by a female form. It was a rod, no a small mace that gave off the bright white light.

The woman before Bjorn was beautiful, smooth brownish skin, naked and violet colored hair with purple flowers blooming throughout. Other women came up behind her, all with slightly different shades of brown skin and different coloured hair, the colours of green, brilliant red, orange and yellow. Again, they too had flowers of the same shade blooming through their hair.

"You are now under our care!" said the violet-haired creature.

Bjorn suddenly collapsed and fell asleep.

* * * * *

Leif was the first to awake. "Why did no one wake me for my shift?"

"Nor me?" said Damon.

"Where is large human brother?" asked Sker.

"Where is Dru?" asked Lorez, now awake.

Damon drew his sword and headed to Dru's location and Lorez followed. They found Dru sleeping soundly, snoring in fact. He was splayed over a large rock.

"Get up!" demanded Damon. "You fool. You slept through your shift."

"My word, I did? It was an enchantment I am certain," said Dru as he struggled to his feet. "I felt it last night during my watch. An overpowering sleep hit me."

"Whatever," said Damon who walked back to camp. "Arch-goblin, go with Dru to check and collect the traps."

Leif ran up to join them, "What happened, where are they?" Damon didn't answer and merely pointed back towards Dru. "Dru are you all right?" asked Leif, "Have you seen Bjorn?"

"I tell ya Leif, it was an enchanted sleep. I tried to fight it."

"I believe you," said Leif. "I should have awoken but did not. Have you seen Bjorn, he was not in camp when we awoke?"

"I have not."

"Let us check the traps to see if one is tripped," said Lorez. "It may give us an answer."

All traps were still in place when they finished looking. It was Sker that found Bjorn's trail.

"He headed off towards the trees," said Damon. "He took his weapon but left his shield."

As quickly as possible, the two humans, elf, arch-goblin, lizard-goblin and lycaon leader gathered up their kit and made their way following Bjorn's trail. Leif and Lorez went on ahead. The party caught up to them at the site where Bjorn had turned the two mummies to dust and bone.

"Do you think it was the two mummies?" asked Damon.

"Looking at the remains and tattered rags," began Lorez. "I think these were the two we encountered with Rreebish and his lycaons."

"Good!" spat Rreebish. "Glad the priest ended them."

"No sign of Bjorn?" asked Dru.

"His tracks seem to lead to the forest up ahead," said Leif pointing the way.

"What do you think awaits us there?" asked Sker seeming frightened.

"Hopefully a large priest sleeping under a shady tree next to a babbling brook," responded Leif with a smile.

"Me hopes so Master Leif," replied Sker, "Me hopes so."

* * * * *

Bjorn was in a haze. He was naked. That much he knew unmistakably but was covered by soft flowery petals of different colours and was resting on soft, cool soil. He could not move for ropes, no roots, held him still to the ground! The brown skinned ladies with colourful hair kneeled around him, chanting softly. Their brown faces looked hardened and determined, their eyes shut. Suddenly he felt as though he might be sacrificed to some pagan god. He tried to move in his panic but was held firm. The little movement he was capable of only tired him. He realized he was truly helpless. So, he did all he could do, he prayed to Matronae and passed out.

Either moments or minutes or hours later, Bjorn could not discern how long, he awoke with a sudden shock. He felt cool water washing over him. The brown skinned maidens stared down at him. The sun now beamed through the tree tops blinding him. The cool water pooled around him and he sank, slowly into what became mud. Bjorn screamed in terror as he felt the roots pull him tighter and down into the soft mud.

* * * * *

They all drew their weapons as they approached the forest.

"If anybody was a lookout, they know we're coming," said Damon.

"We should spread out," said Lorez. "Less chance of ambush."

All did so without saying another word. Rreebish went with Lorez and Dru off to his left while Leif and Damon went to his right. Sker walked just behind Leif. The birds suddenly jumped from the trees.

"Crows," said Rreebish. "Sending warnings to their masters."

It was then they heard a man's scream, followed by a gurgle of sorts.

All of them ran forward except Damon. "Careful!" he shouted, "There could be traps."

As they ran forward, they could see a pink light up ahead.

"The light, it's his mace," shouted Leif.

As they moved forward the brush in the woods got thicker and thicker and it became hard to advance.

"The forest, it's cursed!" shouted Lorez, hacking at the vines that were moving to connect to each other. "It creates a barrier of roots and vines." It was then a root lashed out at the arch-goblin's feet. Lorez tried to free himself but then another jumped at his leg. "Run back! It's a trap!" It wasn't long before they were all ensnared by vines that eventually held them all either in place or prevented them from moving forward, save for Damon Crag who was nowhere to be seen, and Sker.

Sker could jump around the vines and roots or perhaps was not seen by whoever was controlling them. The lizard-goblin cut Leif's legs free eventually. Lorez was next for Sker while Rreebish was cut free by Leif. Sker eventually moved to Dru. They heard Bjorn scream again.

"We have to break up and go around," said Rreebish. "Attack from all sides. I believe a creature or creatures are controlling the woods but I didn't see your lizard-goblin. If we break apart we may be more than they can handle," explained the lycaon leader.

No one could argue with that assessment and what choice did they have?

"I believe Rreebish is correct," said Damon coming from the north. "I was up there," he said referencing northward and a slightly more elevated landscape. "The way was clear, sort of. I saw through the woods a shrine of some sorts. Great stones in a large circle and several slender figures kneeling around something. I could not tell what. But I could see Bjorn's mace resting next to one of them, glowing like you said Leif."

"Did you see Bjorn?" asked Leif. Damon shook his head.

"By the gods, look!" shouted Dru!

They all turned to see a large black creature coming towards them. Even its hair was black. The vines and roots parted at his feet. It had the semblance of a man. All the party ready themselves, weapons trained on the approaching creature. Behind it walked several others with bright hair of different colours and skins of different shades of brown. The black creature leading them was well muscled, tall as Bjorn and had water blue eyes.

"What's the matter, my friends, do you not recognize me?" asked the creature.

"Bjorn?" asked Dru.

"What in the name of Matronae are you doing covered in black mud?" asked Leif lowering his weapon.

"Hold fast!" shouted Damon. "It could be Bjorn or it could be a creature possessing him or it could be a demon of the wood."

The creature then scraped off some of the wet mud and flicked it at Leif and smiled.

"It's him," said Leif. "Who are your friends?"

"I don't know really but by the grace of Matronae, I know they healed me."

"They are forest-dames!" said Rreebish. "Beautiful ones at that," said the lycaon.

"We worship Matronae," said the purple flower-haired forest-dame. "Just as this great man here does. Matronae, the mother goddess guided you to us so that we might save you from his affliction."

"And I thank you great ladies, but I seem to have misplaced my clothing and am in need of a bath." said Bjorn.

"In the common tongue, I am known as Violet," said the purple flower-haired forest-dame. "My sisters and I will allow access to our grove except for those two," she said pointing to the arch-goblin and lizard-goblin.

"They have done nothing to you," said Leif.

"They have or at least their kin has. And to your own family as well. You will see firsthand if your path continues past our grove," said Violet.

Leif nor anyone else knew what Violet was referring to by that statement but paid it no mind.

"On my honor, these two saved my life," said Leif. "What their kind has done to you has nothing to do with these two souls, we are all far from home and not from this region. We are all on the same quest, to rid this world of an evil," said Leif.

"On my honor as well," said Bjorn turning around to face his saviors, hands on his hips, covered in mud and naked.

Violet looked him over and smiled and her fellow forest-dames giggled.

"Can someone get Bjorn a towel?" exclaimed Dru.

The purple flower-haired forest-dame walked right up to Bjorn, marveling over his form. Suddenly she made eye contact and said, "The mother Matronae said we were to save you and we did. Will you protect us from any evil that comes with you then? It is a small price to pay for entry, for your friends."

"That is easy enough. None of my friends will harm you my forest-dame, um-er-my good lady," responded the naked Bjorn.

"Very well but there is one more thing you must do for me," she said as she ran one of her hands over his chest.

"I ah, think I can help you with whatever you might be thinking," said Bjorn.

"Please, someone get Bjorn a towel!" shouted Dru.

Chapter 10
Master Sergeant Saltclaw

On his release from the brig at Fort Adamant, the now unceremoniously retired Master Sergeant Dunkin Saltclaw made his way down the hills towards the coast from Fort Adamant. He was asked by Captain Ty at the behest of Bjorn Foehammer to seek out Magnus and Disa Foehammer and tell them the tale of Leif Foehammer as he knew it.

Dunkin was trained by Magnus when he first joined the military and held the upmost respect for him. Dunkin also knew both Bjorn and Leif Foehammer, having served briefly with both. He was present at the battle where Leif Foehammer was captured. Therefore, he considered this task an honorable thing to do.

Dunkin Saltclaw's mind was tied up in knots though. For many weeks, he thought he was the sole survivor of the ambush by the arch-goblins in the mountains; the same ambush where Leif Foehammer was captured but also claimed the lives of his entire company of soldiers, his battalion commander and Lord Ethan Brisbane. Dunkin had been sickened with remorse and guilt. His whole company was dead, his commanding officer dead. He often had nightmares involving the events where he relived the screams of his lost young soldiers. He had nothing but those thoughts to sustain him while rotting in a garrison cell. He was further mystified over what he witnessed the night of the Fort Adamant evacuation.

Dunkin Saltclaw saw something he could not shake from his mind. He witnessed a red-haired arch-goblin, one he swore he saw in the battle with Leif Foehammer, following General Blackpool's evacuating army out of the fort. He himself was trailing but not trying to keep up; he was no longer in the army. Dunkin had settled down on the hillside and made a camp but his nightmares prevented him from falling completely asleep. The creature however, was gaining on the departing army by using an elongated run; the creature's legs stretched to abnormal lengths and strides, too long for any arch-goblin! Then, to Dunkin's amazement, he watched the red-haired arch-goblin change form into that of a man. That man Dunkin knew as Mr. Night, the supposed expert on arch-goblins in the mountains. It was the same man Dunkin punched in retaliation when his company was ambushed. That incident put Dunkin into the garrison prison and forced his retirement.

Therefore, Dunkin decided to go back up to Fort Adamant to see what remained of the garrison manpower, hoping he might be of some use but also to inform someone about Mr. Night. He did know of the evacuation and heard rumors from among the shanty town folk outside the fort when he was originally released; all residents and adventurers were packing up, evacuating due to the garrison being recalled for an emergency of sorts in Sedgedunum. The mandatory evacuation was explained as necessary for safety reasons.

Dunkin didn't get very far upon returning, only as far as the shanty town outside the southern region of the fort. There, the arch-goblins were pillaging what they could. They had taken over the area in full. During the day and from a distance, he saw the arch-goblins manning the walls of Fort Adamant. In addition, they were using some of the stonework from the fort to put up an additional wall at the narrowest point between the mountains thereby sealing the only road into the fort and thus sealing off Vorclaw from the entire region. He wondered how they could have done it so quickly or how they even knew the fort was emptied. Dunkin departed back down the hills before nightfall, or else the arch-goblins' night-vision would have been able to see him.

Oddly enough he was glad for the images of an arch-goblin turning into Mr. Night. He welcomed the knowledge of the arch-goblins taking over the fort. It was a welcome break from where his mind was previously stuck. He ended up in confinement and forced to retire, all for hitting the man or creature that should have provided his men with some warning. Mr. Night was supposed to be some expert on the arch-goblins in the mountains, after all. Dunkin now presumed Mr. Night, the so-called arch-goblin expert, was behind the ambush. He concluded the man must be a mage of sorts or a demon. Either way, after the terrible ambush in the mountains and now this unorthodox takeover of Fort Adamant by the arch-goblins, Mr. Night was clearly not who or what he claimed to be.

Dunkin's thoughts during the descent out of the mountains allowed him some measure of respite but his mind did wonder back to that day of the battle. It often did.

They would have won the day, he knew, had not been ambushed. Surely the explosion was meant for both his battalion commander, Major Titus and the leader of the armies of Vorclaw, Lord Brisbane. Those two were the most well armored and excellent swordsmen. Surely the tide would have been turned were they not killed in the beginning. Only a wizard or alchemist could create such an explosion, he mused. Who would have known Lord Brisbane was going to be there other than the army or the Council of Twelve? Were the miners guild involved? Weren't they the ones who requested the army build Fort Adamant or was it the council? How would the arch-goblins know his company was going to be there to ambush them? What kind of mage would be powerful enough to magically disguise such a large arch-goblin force? These questions and many more haunted him during his time in confinement. Did someone want Lord Brisbane or his commander Major Titus killed? Who would gain from either death?

In addition to the demoralizing and even embarrassing loss of his comrades, he was forced to retire and put into confinement for striking Mr.

Night, who may not even be human but Dunkin Saltclaw was the sole survivor of the battle that day and for his efforts, he was slapped into the garrison reformatory the very next few weeks. None of it made sense. Now it appears Mr. Night was in league with the arch-goblins the whole time. That made him angry at the army, even Major Goldwater, the garrison commander for being so blind. Yet, did Major Goldwater know about Mr. Night? Is Major Goldwater like Mr. Night? So many questions were jumping in the man's head, it was so confusing. And as soon as his mind was beginning to wrap around it all, the faces of his fallen soldiers popped into his head. Perhaps his mentor, Magnus Foehammer could make some sense of it all.

Dunkin Saltclaw made his way to the crossroads where one could go west to Sedgedunum, Sedgefen was along that way, or go east and head to Seaforth. However, most of the hoof tracks and footprints oddly went directly south towards the coast. Dunkin followed them until the coast was in sight. Based upon the abandoned rubbish from food, horse droppings and a few bits of fallen items from soldiers, Dunkin surmised ships were waiting for General Blackpool's men. Again, more questions jumped into the man's head Why would ships be waiting? What crisis was waiting in Sedgedunum? Would Magnus even be in Sedgefen while Sedgedunum was facing a crisis? Another question filled Saltclaw's mind; would it not take a lot of planning to get enough ships to carry such a large number of horses and men to Sedgedunum?

Dunkin arrived only with a knife on his person but in the debris, he found a small spear left behind. He now had a weapon. It was not his traditional fighting weapon, the glaive, but it would suffice. He decided to use some of the debris to his advantage and make camp at the embarking point for General Blackpool's forces. He made a small shelter from some wood and torn tents left behind. He built up a fire and ate the remainder of his fruit and vegetable rations that night. Now that he had a spear he could hunt. But he also set out a few snares to try and catch some prey to help sustain him for the next leg of his journey.

That night he lay down in his shanty and for once, he felt relaxed. Instead of thinking about the pain of his devastated company of soldiers and leaders, he thought of the questions he formed over the trek out of Fort Adamant and the mountains: Did Major Goldwater know about Mr. Night? Was this attack on Sedgedunum known well enough in advance to get sufficient ships to ferry the soldiers and cavalry? Did someone want Lord Brisbane or Major Titus killed? Who would gain from either death? Who was the wizard or wizards involved? How did Bjorn know his brother Leif was alive?

Dunkin hoped his mentor, Sergeant Major Foehammer could help him through these questions.

Part II: The Unexpected

Chapter 11
Licking Wounds

Queen Ooktha watched from her perch within the confines of the mountain stronghold of Ironhold. Her allegiance to Revenant Niss and her scry-shield spells, allowed her to rest comfortably. It gave her time to marvel at the booty being placed in piles and the slaves chained to one another. The booty piles favored the city of Skulls-thorpe while slaves favored Ironhold. What outweighed the spoils was her dead and missing. It was night when Chieftain Blist arrived and the vampire flew down in the form of a bat to greet him.

She transformed suddenly before him and his beleaguered soldiers. "Greetings, cousin," she said, reminding everyone present of her false relations to the arch-goblin tribes. It was of course untrue but gave her the way in she needed to become their queen. Only the chieftain before her and Leif Foehammer knew the truth of the matter. "How fares you and your warriors?" she asked.

"A hard march but the clan of Skulls-thorpe will survive on," replied Chieftain Blist.

"And what of Chieftain Gutter?" she asked.

"Dead," he said bluntly. "I saw his carcass strung up along the city wall." That statement left a concerned look on Queen Ooktha' s face and the arch-goblin knew why: a new chieftain would have to be named and many of Ironhold' s best warriors were killed or wounded. "But more importantly, we were not just betrayed, we were used by the human," he said.

"Speak no more of this cousin," she said. "Recover from your hard march and revel in your spoils. We can speak again once you have tended to your wounds."

"Yes, my queen but I have one more concern," said the chieftain. "Do we know how Chieftain Merka fares in his campaign at Fort Adamant?"

"I sent a request up the river yesterday. We should hear back in the next several days," she said. "Go now, rest my friend," she said and he nodded in reply as did other arch-goblins in her presence.

Queen Ooktha, the elven vampire who posed as part arch-goblin to rule over the three arch-goblin tribes, should have been happy. She gave her arch-goblins the war they wanted, albeit not the outcome they had intended. Spoils and slaves were plentiful regardless of her intent to have twice the amount before her. Overall the campaign was successful in purpose but why was she not happy? She had been betrayed by Baltus and Anthon, used to get what they wanted or so she believed. The war was something they both wanted but to have been expelled so quickly, that could only mean betrayal.

Additionally, the loss of a chieftain was no small matter. There would be a contest and factions could form. She would have to get this matter resolved soon or else there would be too much chaos for her to control. Then again it could be amusing to watch these filthy beasts pummel themselves for her favor. She smiled at the thought. The next order of business was she needed to eat and a nice crop of slaves had just arrived to pick from.

* * * * *

Chieftain Blist was concerned about nothing more than the loot he gained. He wanted to be gone from Ironhold with all his warriors, earnings and slaves before something happened. He could sense something was coming for what all had been done. As he took off his armor, he wondered if Vorclaw was going to retaliate. A sizeable force had never come to Ironhold, it was too difficult, too much forest. The terrain was unknown to the Vorclaweans. However, a trail existed that led to Ironhold and that worried him.

During his own retreat, he watched mounted troops run down arch-goblins and lizard-goblins in the forest and knew Vorclaw could follow that path they created to Sedgedunum back to Ironhold.

He let out a sigh of relief when his armour finally fell free from his massive shoulders. He decided to allow some reprieve and shake off all notions of defensive preparations for Ironhold, for now. The massive chieftain instead marveled at the hoard of items he had captured. He needed a bath, water and food; he wanted to take some time to enjoy his spoils.

* * * * *

Queen Ooktha drank the blood of the young man dry, right in front of the captured Vorclaweans, arch-goblins and lizard-goblins alike. Then she broke the boy's neck and ripped out his heart to make certain he would not return as an undead vampire like her. Then she ordered him to be cooked and served to the lizard-goblins as reward for their efforts.

She then flew up to her perch within the Ironhold cave network to begin the scheduled meeting with her Union of Undead. She enjoyed Ironhold. It had a forest outside. She could see the stars and the moon. She almost felt, elven at times when out and about. Her arch-goblins here, who not only hung her mirrors on the wall for her, made her a throne of iron covered in fine animal pelts.

The union itself was a confederacy of powerful undead forces whose members were vampires and revenants of different races. Rarely did any meet in person but all could view one another through mirrors that projected one's image through another mirror. She had her mirrors transported to her location and given safe, guarded and quiet accommodations.

When she arrived, the meeting was in its infancy with small discussions among pairs. She noticed Rom-Seti was not present. His mirror was just the reflection of her room, standard when it was not activated. Lord Drim, the undead revenant, the most revered and feared of the Union began the meeting. He was their informal leader.

"Have any of you recently been in discussion with Rom-Seti?" asked Drim. The mirrors were silent even from Revenant Niss and Queen Ooktha. "Then let us begin without him. Would anyone like to open a discussion?" Drim asked but cut everyone off from answering when he said, "I am curious to hear from you, Queen Ooktha. How fares your campaign?"

Queen Ooktha was surprised. Lord Drim had rarely addressed her directly before now. It took her a moment to gather herself. "Thank you, Lord Drim," she began. "My campaign that began several days ago is now coming to an end. We have sacked the city, taken prisoners and a multitude of precious goods," she explained. "My arch-goblin forces are now returning!" She was careful not to say retreating, as they in fact, were.

"Returning already?" asked Lord Drim with his loud booming voice. "You mentioned you were to have several more days of plunder."

"Circumstances, Lord Drim, have changed," she replied.

"Curious," said Lord Drim.

Queen Ooktha didn't know if she was to reply or say nothing so she divulged some more information. Her campaign was a success but not as it could have been if she were not betrayed.

"I have lost one of my three arch-goblin chieftains to battles. Therefore, in order to turn the situation into needless chaos, I felt best to return to the safety of our keep."

"Interesting," said Lord Drim.

"I, for one, congratulate you Queen Ooktha," intervened Revenant Niss. "On how you took advantage of this opportunity to retain control of three arch-goblin hordes by a common goal. It is unfortunate that Rom-Seti is not attending to hear of your successes." That last statement produced a few undead laughs or better yet cackles and coughs since much of the muscles needed for laughter were decomposed or turned to dust. Many of the Union knew that Queen Ooktha disliked Rom-Seti. The same could be said for Revenant Niss.

"What will be your next move?" asked Lord Drim.

"To count my spoils," she said with a smile. More harsh laughs and simulated laughs escaped from the union.

"Very good," announced Lord Drim. "Next topic!" he announced closing the subject.

Queen Ooktha sat proud and pleased with herself. She had gained respect among the Union of Undead and almost wished Rom-Seti was present to see it, almost.

After the meeting, she conversed with Revenant Niss. "I was betrayed by the Vorclawean general. He attacked me soon after the wizard's tower fell. We were only able to hold out for barely half the prescribed time."

"I wonder what changed his mind or was that his plan all along?" replied Revenant Niss.

"Perhaps, I don't know," she replied. "What of Rom-Seti and of the elf I sent with them?"

"You mean your lover?" responded Revenant Niss. Queen Ooktha bowed respectfully wishing to know. "Truthfully, I cannot locate any of them thus far. I have an agent to look into it and I am due an update soon."

"Any information you can provide would be appreciated," said Queen Ooktha.

"Of course, however, now you must be mindful of the future. You face danger on many fronts," Revenant Niss said. "General Blackpool undoubtedly has many allies and now knows well the network between your three strongholds. He could strike at you through his wizards or even attack your city in the forest, perhaps even in the mountains. How fared your battle in the mountains?"

"I sent word for an update and expect to hear in the next day. I could have travelled there myself but thought my attention was best placed at this battle."

"And yet you still lost the chieftain closest to the city you attacked. You should be shoring up defenses and naming a new chieftain," she scolded.

Queen Ooktha respectfully bowed. "That, I am already beginning to do."

* * * * *

"There will be no fires here," said the orange haired forest-dame who cuddled up next to Rreebish. Her name was Marigold and she stroked his furry arm. The lycaon leader seemed to enjoy it. "The light this evening will by magic," she said, smiling.

Rreebish enjoyed the attention. The lycaon leader revealed that the losses he endured on this expedition could not be replaced. They have only a small number of females and none have been able to conceive. Marigold, who looked somewhat elven, save for the flowers that bloomed in her hair, did not seem to mind the differences in their species. And neither did Rreebish.

The other forest-dames circled around the newcomers from behind trees and rocks. Four large stones stood protruding from the ground. Each had a unique symbol to it. In the middle was the muddy bath water that Bjorn was bathed in. They were all brought food, apples, berries and pears.

Violet then arrived, accompanied by Bjorn who was clean and looked well rested and healed. Violet brought out her rod which gave off a great light, illuminating the circled grove.

"What is this place?" asked Leif.

"You are in the grove of the Sisterhood to Matronae. We forest-dames worship the goddess."

"We thank you for your hospitality," said Leif. "We have been without food or drink for days. You saved our lives."

"But how did you get Bjorn to come to you in the middle of the night?" asked Damon.

"By the grace of Matronae, we used our innate abilities to call to him to bring him to us," responded Violet.

"Then why not simply ask us to come to you directly?" asked Damon suspiciously.

"Do you think I would have submitted to a naked mud bath on my own accord?" asked Bjorn.

"Fair enough," said Dru. "But it was you lot who cast a *sleep* spell over us all?"

"It was and we can do it again, instantly," she said in defiance.

"We mean no offence great lady," said Lorez.

"Please do not speak to me arch-goblin," said Violet. "Your kind has killed and tortured plenty of my sisters over the years. And elves too," she said looking at Leif.

"None of us mean to offend," said Leif. "We are merely curious, nothing more. It has been a long and perilous journey for us and we did not expect to be this far north for this length of time. As I said before, we are all foreigners in this land. Therefore, we are unaccustomed to your ways and the region."

"Yes, no more talk of this," said Bjorn. "They have cured me from the revenant's curse and I am in your debt," he said staring at Violet.

Damon and Dru were unconvinced.

A green and yellow haired forest-dame emerged with wooden flasks, one per person and forest-dame alike, to include Sker and Lorez.

"Nectar from our apple trees," the yellow haired forest-dame said. "I believe the common word for it is sitter?"

Bjorn took a swig of the drink before Dru could protest his concerns that it was poison.

"It's cider!" announced Bjorn.

"Yes, that's it, cider!" laughed the yellow haired forest-dame who sat next to Dru.

Dru shared a laugh with her as she leaned against him. Dru winced slightly at the pressure she put upon his arm.

She looked at him curiously and asked, "Do you have wounds warrior, from your adventure?"

"I do my dear, sore muscles bones and cuts," said Dru.

Bjorn interrupted, "Come Dru, let me try to ease your pain, it is the least I can do."

"No, let me tend to his wounds," begged the green-haired forest-dame. "Come with me warrior Dru, I have healing herbs and medicines that can ease your suffering and clean your wounds," she explained, leading him away from the circle of stones.

Dru looked to Damon who had a serious look on his face, "Don't worry, I won't go far," said Dru.

A yellow-haired forest-dame crept closer to Leif who asked, "Have you any wounds I can tend to?" she asked the elf sheepishly.

"I am sorry my dear I do not but I do know my grumpy friend over there has many a wound that needs healing," said Leif referring to Damon standing with his arms crossed.

Bjorn decided to join in the taunt, "If you could heal his grumpiness, we would all be in your debt once more," said Bjorn laying in in the soft grass and opening his arms inviting Violet into his large arms. She of course smiled and obliged him.

Two forest-dames walked over in a seductive manner to Damon who surprisingly unfolded his arms and became less defensive. No one was more surprised than himself by his less defensive nature. One forest-dame of green hair, another of brilliant red moved towards him and ran her fingers over his leather armour.

"May I wash your wounds and apply healing medicines to your body?" asked the red-haired forest-dame.

Damon suddenly felt at ease with the forest-dames, too much at ease. "That depends," said Damon. "Are you both going to heal me? Because I need a lot of healing," he heard himself say. The two giggled and whisked him away.

Leif saw Sker and Lorez looking up at the stars, discussing something in arch-goblin. It was a language he didn't understand, not yet but Sker did. Another useful talent of Sker's, Leif realized. Leif asked to join them. He lay down next to them and said, "Sker, I never properly thanked you for saving my life, the lives of all of us."

"That he did, all of us" said Lorez.

Sker had guilt though. When the lycaons surrounded him, he could have warned Leif but did not for fear of his own sake. The lizard-goblin felt shame.

Leif looked over at Sker whose lizard-goblin face was traditionally expressionless, but Sker usually answered Leif. The elf suspected something was amiss and Leif thought he might know what it was.

"Sker," said Leif. "You were right to keep silent in the tree when the lycaons attacked."

Sker looked over at the elf he called master but also considered a friend. Lorez did the same.

"They would have killed you had you spoken," said Leif. He then smiled at Sker and winked at Lorez. "What? You didn't know that I knew you were hiding when I approached? My eyesight is far better than most," said a smiling Leif.

"Oh Master Leif, Iza so ashamed," said Sker who got on all fours, face down in the dirt. "Please forgive me master, Iza was too scared," he said shaking.

"Sker, the ambush is my fault. I was worrying about you instead of being made aware of my surroundings. But you are my friend and I did not want to see you killed," explained Leif, helping the creature back to his feet. "You did the right thing by remaining silent. I would have been deeply saddened if you were killed. Nothing to be ashamed of."

Lorez rolled his head back to stare at the stars. "I think I shall sleep well tonight providing those forest-dames don't kill me," said Lorez. "Sker, if you do see them come for me, please do say something," he said with a chuckle. Leif too chuckled as did Sker. The elf, the lizard-goblin and the arch-goblin laid back as they sipped cider.

Chapter 12
Ironhold

Queen Ooktha sipped on a cup of blood that was extracted from her last victim. As she watched the wrestling spectacles going on around Ironhold, she felt confident in her decision to hold a wrestling competition to find the next chieftain of Ironhold. She believed it would save countless dead arch-goblins that otherwise, would have fought to the death to replace Chieftain Gutter, the same chieftain who hung dead from the Sedgedunum city wall. Therefore, she tried to lift the spirits of the arch-goblins by ensuring food was plentiful for them. Captured livestock was slaughtered and even some of the slaves were provided as both entertainment and food.

"Too many of Ironhold were lost," she said to Chieftain Blist who sat next to her.

"Perhaps my queen," he replied.

She seemed unconvinced. "They know it and so do you," she said.

"You hope to ease their losses with food and drink purchased from Skagsnest and our spoils?" he replied sarcastically referring to the trading city that sat along the underground waterways between Skulls-thorpe and Blood-helm. Many subterranean races traded there.

"I want the Ironhold arch-goblins to enjoy some measure of victory for their hard-fought battles, even though it was extremely costly," she said. "Yours slowly trickle away back to Skulls-thorpe," she added smiling, and closing the matter.

She frowned at the sheer number of wounded creeping around the wrestling pits though. Had some of them been undamaged or whole even, they might have competed as well, even succeeded. However, she thought it best to find a successor immediately. Ironhold was nearest to the city she'd just sacked and she did not want it to go without a leader, especially since she intended soon to retreat to her own citadel in Skulls-thorpe. It was where her home was. It was where she kept her crypt, her own haven and she wanted to return to revel in bringing the three arch-goblin cities together in one purposeful action, regardless of the cost.

"You heard that the mountain city of Blood-helm had indeed taken Fort Adamant," she said to Chieftain Blist changing the subject.

"I suspect it was taken easily in the wake of the early arrival of General Blackpool's troops in Sedgedunum," he replied.

"That matters not though to me. Our three cities walk away in victory, provided Vorclaw does not retaliate against Ironhold. Regardless, Ironhold will recover from its losses over time."

* * * * *

Mimdrid the shape-changer, in the guise of a red-haired arch-goblin, infiltrated Ironhold easily enough. It took him several days to get there but the ring Anthon gave him would teleport him back quickly. He inquired why the ring could not teleport him there directly and then back again but discovered you could only teleport to a place the wearer had already been to. That was the limitation of the ring and it could only be used once. After that it was worthless.

Mimdrid revelled in the chaos he helped create. Shape-changers enjoyed making a mess of things; by pulling the strings of others in their guises they prided themselves on how much they could influence. Joining with the Blackpool family had been quite an adventure for the shape-changer and he had yet to regret any of it. In fact, he originally intended to kill and replace Baltus Blackpool back when the man first took over the Academy of Arms but the resilient brothers thwarted that plan and captured him. However, instead of killing Mimdrid, they employed him as an agent. The shape-changer helped orchestrate the attack on the White Eagles in the mountains and broker the deal between the arch-goblins of Blood-helm and General Blackpool. He even had a major part to play in the meeting between Queen Ooktha and Baltus by passing correspondence to her guards. Those notes eventually made their way to Queen Ooktha thus the rest is history. Now he would be able to take pride in the meddling of the arch-goblins.

The shape-changer had been to Ironhold briefly long ago but this was a new adventure to be had. He was also armed with knowledge of the installation from Anthon Blackpool who built the iron-golem there.

Ironhold, as the city was called, had an exterior that appeared as a fortress from the outside. It budded up against a great sheer wall of rock that connected to a vast cave complex that existed beneath and behind the fortress. Ironhold was a rectangular keep on the outside. It was made of thick stone and iron. It was very wide and very deep.

There were farms and cattle outside the keep, tents for wounded and dead also. In and around the fortress, arch-goblins prepared their defenses. Siege weapons, ballista and racks contained an assortment of spears, pikes and swords. The smiths were working as well. It was surprising to Mimdrid how easily it was to simply walk in. Perhaps the arch-goblins had no fear of reprisal. Not yet anyway.

While the stronghold was a pure defensive structure, in the rear, along the sheer cliff wall were two recessed iron doors nearly twenty feet high. Both were swung open as many were going in as out the entrance. This led to the inner city that was truly Ironhold.

When Mimdrid entered through the doors he walked into a giant carved out cavern. Stone and wooden bridges crisscrossed the cavity. It was lit by flames amplified by reflections of golden discs and multicoloured glass of red, orange and yellow. The smell was akin to various incense to counter the stench of sulphur from the forges and dung from different animals. Drums were beating, slaves were being whipped and wrestling, for some reason, was taking place at various pits around the cavern.

Mimdrid's missions were simple enough. He was to assess what was taken, what was the current manpower at Ironhold and if possible to locate Queen Ooktha. His plan was simple too. Slip in as one of the beleaguered arch-goblins from battle and garner as much information as he could. He was able to speak their language after all and was familiar with their customs. However, Mimdrid was not expecting to arrive during an assentation ceremony.

"It be wrestling," said an arch-goblin whose face had a fresh wound from his right eye or lack thereof to the opposite side of his maw. "Why not combat, to the death?" he asked a small crowd.

"We're depleted enough," said another missing an arm. "So Queen Ooktha decrees it this way."

The one-eyed arch-goblin spat in response watching the competition. "Queen Ooktha," he said in a sarcastic response.

He also spat in agreement. "We have lost our way with this quarter arch-goblin queen. And Ironhold has now lost its chieftain."

That notion of dissention gave Mimdrid his means to garner some information and an idea.

"I hear she is not even arch-goblin," interjected Mimdrid disguised as an arch-goblin.

The two turned to look at the red-haired arch-goblin, a persona that Mimdrid wore.

"You from Skulls-thorpe?" asked the one one-eyed arch-goblin, not recognizing the arch-goblin.

"Nah," said Mimdrid, "I am from Blood-helm," he lied.

"I heard no arch-goblins from Blood-helm were joining us. Had some battle in the mountains," responded the one-armed arch-goblin.

"Aye but some volunteered anyway," responded Mimdrid. "I heard that rumor on my passage through Skulls-thorpe." Mimdrid used his key magical item, an earring, that allowed him to read the surface thoughts of a nearby person. He could sense their frustration with their queen and satisfaction with his simple story. "How depleted is Ironhold?" he dared to ask, changing the subject. But did not get a response.

Mimdrid tested the waters using his psionic capabilities to see if more dissent could be found and it didn't take long to find the dissidence he sought.

"Then what she be if not?" asked the one-eyed arch-goblin allowed referring to Queen Ooktha, ignoring Mimdrid's question.

"Isn't it obvious?" Mimdrid responded after no one else did.

"You mean to say she be all human?" asked the one-arm.

"You fool," said the one-eyed, "pointed ears humans do not have."

"Then what she be you think?" asked Mimdrid.

"She cannot be elf," said the one-arm. "The chieftains would never allow it."

"Perhaps," responded Mimdrid noticing others were now listening to the conversation. "Quarter elf, half elf or all elf, methinks our vampire queen bewitched our chieftains to do her bidding?"

"How so?" asked another arch-goblin whose arm and hand were bandaged with bloody rags.

"She wanted war, she wanted control, she wanted the blood of slaves and booty, who knows?" said Mimdrid. "But does she care about what happens to Ironhold and its traditions?" Then it dawned on him. "I wonder how many arch-goblins from Skulls-thorpe were lost compared to Ironhold? And me wonders who gets a great share of the plunder? Slaves and all?" he said. "Not the city without a chieftain. And not the arch-goblins closest to the city we just sacked," he said. Sowing that seed, Mimdrid walked away satisfied that the Ironhold arch-goblins were now doubting this war and their queen.

Mimdrid worked in the cavern where the wrestling matches were being held. It was easy for him to change his hair, wounds and even size to plant the same seed and discussions among the spectators. He stopped peddling dissent though once he got all the way around and back to where he started.

He asked about how many arch-goblins *we* lost while posing as an Ironhold arch-goblin he met on the other side of the wrestling pits. After a couple of hours, he discerned that Ironhold lost half of its fighting strength while Skulls-thorpe lost a quarter of what they sent.

It was then Mimdrid felt a sense of unease. He saw Queen Ooktha in the distance, sitting on an iron throne covered in pelts, watching the spectacle. Mimdrid really did not like that creature. Although he enjoyed pulling the strings and creating anarchy, he did not like the undead nor their kind of trouble. To Mimdrid, there was something fundamentally wrong with the notion of undead. His mindset was once you're dead, you should stay dead instead of meddling in the lives of the living. That thought made him smile cynically given the nature of his upbringing and enjoyment shape-changers tend to get from manipulating those same living races.

Next to her stood the giant arch-goblin Chieftain Blist, who looked undamaged from the campaign on Sedgedunum. However, he also noticed some of the arch-goblins, Chieftain Blist's arch-goblins, making their way out of the city cavern.

Again, Mimdrid saw Queen Ooktha in the distance on her fur-covered throne smiling and enjoying the wrestling. To him, there sat an elf by all accounts. Save for her being covered by black makeup across her eyes and baring pointed teeth at times, she indeed looked more like an elf than anything else. Sure, her skin was pale and yes almost blue like the noses of these beastly creatures but no real resemblance or passable relation to the arch-goblins could possibly exist, he believed. It was then he thought that arch-goblins were very stupid indeed.

She was a mage of some descript, or so he heard. Perhaps she charmed the lot or merely the few chieftains and brought them into subservience. Mimdrid really didn't know for certain but Queen Ooktha did not boast any traits that he could equate to arch-goblin heritage. No, he was certain it was a ruse by the undead creature.

* * * * *

"Good!" said Chieftain Blist. "It is down to the last round of wrestling," he said drinking a strong brown ale.

Queen Ooktha gave him a disapproving look at the comment. Then she stood up and put up both her hands to quieten the crowd and the drums.

"Today, my arch-goblins, we celebrate many things," she announced. "The victory of the sack of Sedgedunum!" she shouted. However, no one returned her enthusiasm.

"And, you all have captured slaves and treasures" she said trying to build excitement. However only a few cheers and fists rose in respect came back her way. Chieftain Blist then stood behind her, his muscular arms crossed across his massive chest. His scowl though may have been more intimidating. A few more cheers rang out.

"I loved Chieftain Gutter," she began again. "And he would have wanted you all to celebrate your battles, your victory with food and ale and drums and slaves."

Chieftain Blist let out a loud celebratory roar. His intimidation sparked some arch-goblins to show some praises to Queen Ooktha but the majority were unenthused.

"Chieftain Gutter will live on in your memories and songs of this victory," said Queen Ooktha. "But now we must let our new chieftain rise to the occasion. Let the final match begin!" she said. The cheers rose from the crowd but may have had more to do with her no longer speaking.

* * * * *

As the final two arch-goblins wrestled for control of Ironhold, Mimdrid was certain arch-goblins in this city did not share in their queen's enthusiasm. To Mimdrid, these arch-goblins were keenly aware that their victory wasn't as sweet as she had promised. There were far too few spoils to go around, too many losses and Queen Ooktha' s attempt to soften the blow with both food and drink did not go unnoticed.

Mimdrid continued to sow more seeds of doubt among the arch-goblins. As he did, he inquired about the preparations for retaliation. He knew it was not at the forefront of things when one of the arch-goblins he shared a drink with, asked him for his own ideas on defence.

At last a winner was announced; a new chieftain by the name of Skraw stepped forward from the wrestling pit. His opponent was dead. Mimdrid took note of the creature. He was broad at the shoulders and missing part of his left ear. He was also covered in fresh cuts, either not healed from the recent battles in Sedgedunum or from wrestling. Mimdrid could not tell. He was tall but he also looked exhausted. He did not speak to that arch-goblin, not yet anyway.

He made his way up to Queen Ooktha and Chieftain Blist and kneeled before them. She placed a crown of bones upon his head.

The arch-goblins and even the lizard-goblins began to shout, "Skraw, Skraw, Skraw!"

Chapter 13
Debts Mounting

Having taken up residence at the Academy of Arms, Anthon used his scrying pool to view Sanctuary and the surrounding area, to no avail.

"I did not see any sign of my apprentice nor any of his companions," he said to his brother Baltus when he entered his quarters. "However, when I tried to peer inside the buildings, I was blocked," he finished, frustrated.

"And you already searched the area around Skulls-thorpe and Bloodhelm?" asked Baltus. Anthon nodded in response confirming so.

Anthon didn't need to say it but it appears his nephew, apprentice, assassin and the Foehammer-brothers were lost to this world. He could see the look on his brother's face that he was thinking something similar.

"Don't despair yet, brother," said Anthon. "Once Mimdrid returns, we might discover the whereabouts of Queen Ooktha. And her being unharmed might prove Rom-Seti is unaware of her involvement and therefore, they might all still be alive."

"Perhaps," said Baltus. "I still need to tell the admiral something."

"Tell him the truth," replied Anthon.

"Before I tell him anything, I want you to go to this Sanctuary, find out what you can," said Baltus.

"What? No! I have enough to do with trying to locate and destroy a vampire, let alone deal with my own--superiors."

"Your superiors will benefit soon as we already agreed. If they would like to ensure they profit here, they should see their way clear to allow you freedom to take care of our outliers," responded Baltus coldly.

Anthon was not impressed. Baltus did not know who or what his superiors were at the Shadow Company. Anthon believed caution was always the best course of action when it came to dealing with higher echelons of the Shadow Company.

"Can't we send one of your soldiers or a young wizard in my stead? It would actually make my life easier."

"No of course not, no one else knows of their mission and I do not want anyone else to know we were once in league with their queen," replied Baltus, referring to Queen Ooktha. "No, it must be you," said Baltus.

"I see your point, brother, but there is another option."

"I am waiting," replied Baltus.

"We could ask the admiral to send his other son to Sanctuary. The man is well informed and resourceful. I am certain he would be willing to go on the hunt being it's his brother that is missing," concluded Anthon.

"You want to send a seafaring pirate into the mountains?" asked Baltus.

"Well then we will wait until Mimdrid gets back and then see what he knows. I am certain the admiral would be satisfied with that," said Anthon.

"Why didn't you just give one of them a ring of teleportation so he might return on his own and report like you did Mimdrid?"

"Funny you mention that, I did give one to Dru and one to Erik," replied Anthon. "And that means…"

"I know what it means," snapped Baltus. "They are either unable to use them because they are dead or unwilling. Either one does not bode well."

"Why did you not give more of them out?"

"They are expensive and not easy to come by. Brother, we are mounting in debt you know to the Shadow Company. Spells, information and magical items all cost money. They are heavily vested in us and not forgiving on debt."

"I know this," he replied. "That's why I released that fop, Handle Nightingale, to his aunt so that her company might start rebuilding and using Shadow Company shipping and supplies to rebuild the city. I already started to satisfy their need for money. And to keep the wizard's guild at bay I strongly recommended Horatio Mercutio be the next Archmage of the Wizards college," he said.

Anthon chuckled at that, knowing that he was a better mage than Horatio but Anthon did not want to become the arch mage, He wanted revenge against that institution and he got it.

Baltus paid his brother no mind to the chuckle. "So, our options are to wait or ask Admiral Kahee to send another of his children into the mountains because you will not go until Mimdrid returns. Is that what you are saying?" asked Baltus, frustrated. Anthon merely nodded in agreement.

"Good then, you tell the admiral when he arrives this afternoon. I will be busy planning my invasion of Ironhold," he said and walked out of the room.

* * * * *

"What do you mean?" asked Admiral Kahee angrily. "You cannot or will not find my son?"

"Both actually," replied Anthon who winced at his own reply. "What I mean to say is wait until I hear back from Mimdrid. That is all."

"And he too is overdue, is he not?"

"I expect him back in the next day or so," replied Anthon.

"I will give you two days to provide me with some answers, wizard," responded the admiral. "Know this, you are not the only one with ties to the black network. My other son has his own lines of communication and they will hear about how the fog of war may be too much for you to handle," he threatened.

Normally Anthon would send *lightning strikes* at the man's face but he was not that clumsy with his own pride and knew all too well not to cite rivalries that both hampered the promotion of the Shadow Company nor fighting among other factions. That would lead to being counterproductive. The admiral's son, Ruko Kahee, was deeply tied to the Black-masks and would not be in the best interests of the Shadow Company to kill the admiral.

"Report if you must," said Anthon trying to appear calm and unafraid, "but I think the best course of action is to wait until Mimdrid returns with more information before we pour too many resources into searching and thereby turning more heads in our direction," he said. The admiral though seemed unconvinced.

* * * * *

The Kahee family and the Blackpool families were close and both steeped in military traditions, one navy, and the other, army. Admiral Kahee was viewed as a naval genius. The man's tactics and naval knowledge led the now defunct ruling council to praise the man. Shortly after his appointment to admiral, he was able to reduce pirating and smuggling almost overnight. While that was true, his genius in reducing the damage done by the running of illegal trade and attacks had more to do with his partnership with one pirate than the man's knowledge of naval combat.

Like the Blackpool's, not all the Kahee-family members were in professions dedicated to the betterment of the nation. Erik Kahee resented the Vorclawean Navy. The sea kept his father away much of his life and therefore he applied to the Wizard College instead. Seeking a career away from the sea was difficult given the nation's large coastline; his schooling was geared more towards magically engaging the elements of water and air. Eventually, Erik Kahee sought out the Shadow Company where he became the apprentice to Anthon Blackpool. However, it wasn't through Anthon that he engaged into the service of the Shadow Company. No, it was Ruko Kahee, his older brother, the privateer or as others might refer to one of his profession, the pirate!

Ruko Kahee was incredibly valuable to the Kahee family. It was he who loved the sea and who was fascinated by the aspects of a professional navy career. The man began his sea life simply enough. Ruko began as steward aboard Vorclawean naval ships, thanks to his father's influence. However, when the ship Ruko he served on was besieged and eventually sunk by pirates employed by the Shadow Company, he was forced into a new way of life.

Ruko was captured and survived long enough to climb up the ranks of a pirate's life to captain his own ship. As luck would have it, years later, all changed once he encountered his own father on the seas. Unknowingly, the two engaged in battle and then Captain Drake Kahee defeated his pirate-son. All pirates were executed save Ruko who pleaded for an audience before the commander of the vessel. It was a shock when the two met; the admiral could not kill his own son so he struck a bargain asking his son to help bring piracy to an end in the area.

Drake Kahee got his son back and the intelligence needed to thwart other pirate networks and got him promoted to admiral. Ruko, however, had to continue working discreetly for the Shadow Company; it was the price they both had to pay as the company would not allow such an act go uncontested nor unavenged. The Shadow Company agreed and the Kahee family gained substantial wealth from the partnership. Admiral Kahee though never quite got accustomed to his son's pirate life but endured it for the sake of getting back the son he thought lost to the sea. Thus, it was Ruko Kahee who connected Erik Kahee to the Shadow Company wizarding guild.

Admiral Drake Kahee stepped aboard one of his son's smuggling vessels known as the Sea Maiden. Anchored outside the port of Sedgedunum, the craft housed both legit and smuggled products. The man was not in uniform but wore his black mask to both hide his face and notify the crew that this was indeed a man that should be treated with respect. A young man led Admiral Kahee to the private quarters of his son. The admiral sent word that he wanted to meet via the magical scrolls they both possessed; writing from one piece of parchment would transcribe on to the holder of a paired parchment piece. Ruko never had his father come aboard one of his own vessels before. Often they conversed through the scrolls. Therefore, Ruko thought it of great importance and had a meal planned with drink in his private quarters, presuming it would be a long meeting.

"A meal!" said the admiral. "I had no idea a pirate's life was privy to such delicacies."

"I know you're fond of shrimp and crab but wasn't certain what you would be in the mood for. Am I to presume my brother has returned and his mission fruitful?"

"No, you are not to presume such. In fact, your brother is why I have come to see you," he said reaching out for some boiled shrimp. "He is long overdue and I fear now that he is in trouble."

"Where is the Blackpool wizard, Anthon?"

"He wishes to wait until his shape-changer spy returns with news from the arch-goblin stronghold," he replied. "When that will be who knows as the shape-changer is also overdue."

"Relax, father," said Ruko filling his plate with backed squid. "Erik, is resilient enough and surrounded by multiple allies. Bjorn Foehammer is quite a powerful young priest and Damon Crag a very capable assassin. Besides, I could never believe the general would send forth his only son into harm's way without some serious magical assistance."

"I don't care what you think," said the admiral. "I didn't come here for your opinions!" he said raising his voice. The admiral regained his composure. "I came here to ask you to use your contacts to try and locate him," said the admiral. "You do have contacts still do you not?"

"I do but mine are not of the wizardry persuasion," he replied.

"What about that priestess-lover?

"Her name is Shanna," replied Ruko.

"What does she worship? I am certain she has more value to you than keeping your bed warm."

"Shanna is a priestess of Lir but a priestess would be little help in locating him. And the scrying sensor Erik used, was returned after Erik left my pirate isle," said Ruko referring to his own island base of operations.

"I am surprised Anthon doesn't have one at his disposal," said the admiral.

"That was his but it was not his. It was a device owned by the Shadow Company," said Ruko chewing on an octopus tentacle. "Nothing is free with them, unless you're making them some money," he said smiling with the tentacle hanging. "Not to worry father, I have my own connections or two that may be able to help find Erik."

"And bring him home," inserted the admiral. "Not to Anthon, to me," he said.

"I think you are being a bit paranoid, father," responded Ruko. "Paranoid about this glorious event and about Erik's mission. Stop worrying, we are going to become so rich from the rebuilding in the aftermath."

"How much?" asked the admiral.

"Well who can say, at least twice as much as we are making now," responded Ruko.

"No you fool!" shouted the admiral. "I want to know how much it will cost to find your brother that you so easily dismiss!"

Ruko swallowed hard on the octopus tentacle.

* * * * *

After dinner, Ruko had his crew clean his room and eat whatever he and his father did not finish. His father always unnerved him. Part of it was because he knew he was a proud navy officer who was torn between his naval code of ethics and his love for his privateer son.

In fact, Ruko was surprised his father even agreed to the coup concocted by the Blackpool brothers and their shape-changer ally. However, Ruko also knew his father grew up with the Blackpool family resulting in his father and Baltus Blackpool being close friends even before being in the military. Did the two military leaders see eye-to-eye on the state of the nation even or was it out of friendship or respect for the loss of Merriam, General Blackpool's wife? Ruko then had a thought that Baltus Blackpool seemed to have some sway over his own father. Was it because of his own affiliation with the Shadow Company? Was it out of fear that if it was revealed that his son was a pirate that bolstered his father's career to a seat on the ruling council? Maybe his father was manipulated by a spell by Anthon Blackpool or perhaps the shape-changer's psionic capabilities?

The next morning, those guilty and devious thoughts hadn't vanished much. He had to cast them aside for now; there was work to do now for his father. Ruko locked the doors to his private cabin and sat at his desk. In one of its many hiding places, he pulled forth a small ring given to him by his brother Erik. It was set with a pearl in its centre. He placed the ring on the index finger on his left hand. He then pulled forth a lock of hair he was given by his brother. "Just in case." he said referring to the ring his brother gave him, in case he did not return and needed to be found.

Ruko then turned the ring upside down so the pearl when squeezed would be in his palm and ignite the magic. Ruko then closed his eyes and thought of his brother. His mind drifted to when they were younger. Then he thought of their early teenage years together, before Ruko joined the navy. Next, his mind moved to their adulthood. Ruko felt the hairs in his right hand, his brother's hair. The pirate's next thought was of when he last saw his brother and his face; it was when he departed from his island to Vorclaw's mountains. With the connection of Ruko's memories and the lock of hair from his brother connected to the magic in his ring, Ruko opened his eyes. Although he knew he was still seated at his desk, his mind's eye was transported to Erik's location.

Ruko could see and hear the water although he was not there. He could sense it was cold but not freezing. His senses were trying to adjust to the vision he was seeing but his body felt as if he were in the warm cabin of his ship. It was dark, almost night and he stood at the base of some small waterfall and instinctively looked up. He could almost feel the water cascading down upon him. Green mosses covered the walls. There was a large passage to the side of the falls but it was completely dark.

Ruko looked around to see what was behind him. It was a lake but ruins of some buildings fell into it from high above, at the far end. Ruko yelled even though he wasn't certain his voice would be carried through the projection within his mind. He tried to walk and astonishingly he could but it was sluggish and slow. He need not walk far though. He could see his poor brother dead and bloated body in the water, just below the surface.

Ruko, the pirate captain, wept as he reached down for his brother's body. He tried to pull him out of the water but like his walking being sluggish moments ago, so too was everything else. Even pushing his hand through the water to grasp his brother was more difficult that it should have been. With much difficulty, he was able to get his brother to the surface on a rock. He saw that Erik was not wearing the ring of teleportation. His brother already had three rings one his fingers. Anymore could cause a ring's magic to falter with disastrous consequences. Ruko padded him down looking for the ring of teleportation. Ruko could not use it there with his brother, for Ruko was only there ethereally. But Ruko could take small items back to his corporal form, back at his desk. Once Ruko had the ring, he returned to his desk. As painful as it was he had to use the ring to concentrate on his brother's bloated corpse next to the waterfalls. Then he set the *teleportation ring* into motion. Once back at the falls, he again used the ring to teleport back to his ship, along with his dead brother Erik.

Chapter 14
Another Elf

None of them had ever seen one of these fantastic beasts. It was winged and taller than a horse at the shoulders. It had the head of a bird of prey like an eagle but had the body of a lion. It was covered in golden fur all over its body but that gave way to gold and white feathers over its wings. The creature was beautiful and powerful.

Upon the griffin sat an elven male. He was dressed in brown leathers that included a helmet of the same material. A short sword was strapped across his back and two wands hung from his waist. He was a slender elf but one of many years. When he made eye contact with Violet, he showed he possessed an aura of importance.

"Greetings, Teodor," she began. "It has been sometime since we last met. What brings you to our grove?"

The elf dismounted without an answer. He took off his leather helmet revealing short brown and gray hair. He stared at the scene before him and said, "I come for the humans, the arch-goblin, the lizard-goblin and what are you? You resemble a lycaon," he said pointing at a golden lycaon leader.

Rreebish puffed out his furry chest and crossed his furry arms over in response.

"Who are you?" asked Bjorn. "And why have you come for us?"

The elf put his hands beneath the folds of his leathers and produced a piece of paper. The initial movement resulted in Damon Crag unsheathing a sword.

"It is a map," replied Teodor noting the human's movement.

"To where?" asked Damon.

"To my benefactor, of course. He awaits you all," said Teodor. "I cannot carry you all but I can carry the one who holds the Jade Tower."

"How do you know of it?" asked Leif, eyeing him suspiciously.

Teodor moved closer to Leif studying his facial features. He shook his head as if returning from absurd thought. "I am the one who delivered the map to the Mistress of Sanctuary, so you might find Rom-Seti's layer. I am well aware of your mission."

"You were the other person hiding in the room when the Mistress of Sanctuary gave me the map?" asked Leif.

"I am, but I saw no need to reveal myself because I never intended to meet any of you. However, your circumstances seem to have changed, forcing me to find you," replied Teodor handing Leif the map.

"Why do you want the Jade Tower?" asked Dru.

"I don't, my benefactor does," replied Teodor.

"Well, don't think we're going to just hand it over to you," said Bjorn.

"No one is flying with you my friend." said Dru.

"And who is your benefactor?" asked Lorez.

"I forgot you speak common tongue?" was Teodor's response to the arch-goblin.

Leif looked over the map. "Why would we follow your map, it does not take us back to Sanctuary?" asked Leif and passed it back to Bjorn. Everyone huddled around to have a look.

Teodor turned to remount his griffin and said, "You cannot go over the mountains and you cannot go back. The place is crawling with undead and a few lycaons are about as well. Or there were lycaons at least."

"You saw lycaons?" asked Rreebish.

"Yes, but I vanquished them," he responded.

"You what?" growled Rreebish.

"They were wounded by the undead and likely to die anyway or turn undead from their wounds."

The lycaon leader then dug his paws in and made for the elf mounted on the griffin. The lycaon leader's assault was cut short by Violet and Marigold who put their hands on his furry body to calm him. The elf either did not notice or perhaps didn't care.

"Who is your benefactor?" asked Lorez again.

"Yes, who is your benefactor?" asked Damon.

"Is that all you people do is ask questions?" responded Teodor. "Last chance for a ride, anyone with the Jade Tower is welcome. No? Suit yourselves, then. Just follow the map and we can return you from whence you came," he said. Then he said something in elvish and the griffin spread his mighty wings and leaped into the air.

"Leif," began Dru. "Please don't end up as an elf like that."

Leif laughed. "I make no promises," he replied.

"Yeah, he was about as considerate as Damon usually is," said Bjorn laughing.

Damon stared hard at Bjorn.

"Who was that elf?" asked Bjorn of Violet and paid Damon's look no mind.

"That was Teodor. And yes he is about as superior as elves can be but ultimately, he has a good heart. We did not wish you to battle him," she said to Rreebish. "He is very powerful and we owe our existence to him and his benefactor. If he said your kin were to die, he was being truthful."

"Who is his benefactor?" asked Damon.

Violet didn't answer immediately. "He is even more of a condescending elf, of a sort," she said looking unsure.

"Oh great, perhaps I should stay here," said Lorez.

"What do you mean you owe them your existence?" asked Leif.

"This grove, us forest-dames, we are all here because of them," said Marigold.

"How so?" asked Rreebish.

"The grove was created for us and our trees, transplanted here for our safety. Our lands were invaded by lizard-goblins, orcs, arch-goblins and dark-elves," said Violet looking at those races present. "Teodor, his master and their army defeated the invasion but not before the damage was done, to our forests."

"What does Teodor and his master want with our Jade Tower?" asked Dru.

"I don't know what that is?" she said.

"Show her, Sker," said Leif.

Sker revealed the small green item carved into the small tower that trapped Rom-Seti within.

"Inside there is a trapped being called Rom-Seti," said Leif. "We were to deliver it to…" Leif continued but was cut off by Violet.

"You must go immediately, all of you. Be gone!" She spat on the ground looking at both the lizard-goblin and the Jade Tower. She than began shouting in her own tongue, and all other forest-dames began to moan and hiss at the lizard-goblin. Leif instantly went to his side and Sker clung to his leg.

"You may have been brought to us by our goddess but the presence of that thing, the lizard-goblin and arch-goblin must be gone at once!" she demanded. "We have healed your priest, go now!" she said pointing at everyone around.

"Why must we go all of a sudden?" asked Bjorn. "We mean you no harm."

"Rom-Seti is what brought the hordes to our lands. That thing your lizard-goblin carries must be the reason why the undead now roam. They are searching for their master. I am certain of it now," she responded angrily.

"Who is this elf-master of Teodor and savior of the forest-dames?" interrupted Damon.

"His name is Pallentine," responded Marigold. "He is the war mage of the ruin of Archangel, our old home," she said with sadness. Violet and the other forest-dames, save Marigold who clung to Rreebish, walked to the nearest tree and vanished inside it as if it were nothing more than air.

"Where did they go?" asked Rreebish of Marigold.

"They are here but want nothing more to do with you all," said Marigold. "Violet is right though. You must cast out the lizard-goblin that holds the evil relic. It will bring danger to our grove," she said staring at the lizard-goblin. "The power of Matronae protects us for now but eventually the undead will stumble upon our grove in search of their master. Take it to Pallentine. He and Rom-Seti are sworn enemies and will know what to do with it," she said to all.

* * * * *

After much deliberation, they all agreed to follow the map. The forest-dames swore by the elves of Archangel and Teodor said they could return them home. However, during packing Rreebish broke the silence. "I will not be joining you my new friends," said Rreebish. "I will make my way home at some stage, the way I came or up over the mountains."

"No!" came a cry from Marigold rubbing her brown hands through his furry body.

"I will come back and often, my flower," said Rreebish nuzzling her. "But I should make right this new feud between my lycaons and the orcs," he said to her.

"How do you intend to do that?" asked Leif curiously.

"I will ask their chieftain for a meeting at Sanctuary," Rreebish responded.

Leif gave it several moments of thought. "Understood," nodded Leif. "I have met the Mistress of Sanctuary. She and her daughter seem just and should be helpful if you wish to evade a war with the orcs," he said.

"I never met her, only her daughter," replied Rreebish. "It is my hope that she will aid me in preventing any more hostility."

"If we make it back before you, we will vouch for you at Sanctuary," said Dru.

"If you get to speak to the Lady of Sanctuary, tell her of our encounters and what we told you about our encounter with the orcs. Her own daughter was there and will lend credibility to you in your quest to keep the peace," added Leif.

Rreebish nodded in response. Then he dug out a small totem from the folds of his garments. "I wish you all well on your journey," he said as he handed a piece of wood to Leif that fitted the elf's hand. It was carved in the shape of a lycaon and some runes down the back. "If you find yourselves in the land of the lycaons, show my totem and speak my name. It may provide you with safe passage. He then turned from them all to pack his things near Marigold's tree, taking her with him, his arm over her shoulder, comforting her.

"This has been an interesting year for me," said Leif watching Rreebish walk away.

Sker and Lorez then came up next to Leif also watching the strange creature from another world walk away. Sker though, only came up to Leif's knee.

"Master Leif," said Sker. "You know Sker is not like other lizard-goblins. Iza would never invade your home," he said referring to what Violet said earlier about lizard-goblins invading her homeland.

"I know my friend, I know," said Leif looking at his lizard-goblin friend. "But, it seems we are headed for more uncertainty," continued Leif. "These elves we are going to meet do not know you Sker, my friend nor you Lorez, my friend. And this place we're headed for is not my home," said Leif. "Stay close to me, the both of you," he said.

* * * * *

"Where did you find them?" asked the Revenant Pallentine.

105

"They were with the forest-dames," said Teodor.

"The forest-dames?"

"Yes, somehow they ended up there?" responded Teodor.

"And the Jade Tower? Do they have it? Was he in there?" asked Pallentine.

"Honestly, I don't know? I didn't ask."

If the revenant had eyes to roll, they certainly would have. Instead the undead being shook his head in his bony hands. He then held out his hands and said, "And you did not think to ask?"

"You asked me to find them and I did," was his response. "But I did offer to transport the bearer and they declined. So I gave them a map to here. At least now you can scry and monitor their progress. And if they do not head here, I will fly back out to change their minds."

Pallentine sat back seemingly satisfied with that. "Niss will ask me soon about the Jade Tower's whereabouts. If they leave today how long till they arrive here?"

"They all seem healthy so probably in two days if they stick to the map," responded Teodor. "What are you going to tell Niss?" asked Teodor.

"She doesn't need to know you found them just yet and so we shall keep this between us," responded Pallentine.

"You play a dangerous game my old friend. Please don't implicate me in what has the potential to become a great feud between you two," said Teodor.

"You worry too much, Teodor, you always have."

It was now Teodor's chance to roll his eyes, and he did. He then said, "I will be out harvesting for a meal. I wager we will have guests soon," and he turned and walked out of the dark room.

"Make sure you tell our forest vermin to expect guests," said Pallentine as Teodor departed. He hoped he heard him but didn't really have a concern. If these interlopers were able to escape Rom-Seti then surely they could handle what lurked in his forests.

Revenant Pallentine was more concerned with how he should handle Revenant Niss and the Jade Tower. If Rom-Seti was in there, Pallentine wanted it for himself. He wanted to gloat, to hold it and to bury it in the deepest, darkest hole he could find! Revenant Niss however, wanted to know if her creation worked but also promised it to her own pupil in the Union of Undead. Even if Pallentine confiscated the Jade Tower, he would never know if Rom-Seti was in there, not unless he broke it open. Could that even be done?

Rom-Seti was especially eager to find out the status of the Jade Tower, for indeed it was Rom-Seti who brought the dark-elves, arch-goblins, orcs and lizard-goblins to ravage his homeland.

"By all the gods, I hate Rom-Seti!" he said aloud.

Chapter 15
Family Matters

Baltus was more than a little apprehensive, a feeling he was not used to. He did not love the sea and riding in a rowboat at night out to Ruko Kahee's ship was more than a bit unnerving. He also knew who would be present and why.

Anthon was also aboard. He would have preferred using his magic to get there but had mounted some debt presently with all the magic components he was using up and decided to take the cheap route. He did however plan to teleport himself and his brother out there if the Kahees intended to revolt, in light of the recovery of Erik Kahee. After all Erik Kahee was his apprentice and this war was concocted by the Blackpool brothers. It would be easy for the admiral to blame them for his son's death and bring Vorclaw's armies and elite to bear down on them.

The brothers were briefed by Ruko earlier that day and told he would send a boat to bring them aboard at night. Ruko also explained how he recovered his brother's remains but no other members of the expedition were present when Erik was recovered.

When the boat arrived the general, wearing his black mask, was greeted by Admiral Kahee and his privateer son Ruko, also dressed in their masks. "Permission to come aboard," he asked.

Drake Kahee, sneered, turned and walked away. Ruko, extended his hand to help the general aboard, but remained silent.

"How is your father," asked Baltus of Ruko.

"His son is dead. How do you think he is?" responded Ruko.

"Where is your brother?" asked Anthon.

"Follow me," said Ruko, seeming somewhat irritated.

Anthon and Baltus looked at each other, acknowledging the tension but neither could blame them. Ruko led them to the steps going down into the bowels of the ship. The brothers stopped and looked down wondering if an ambush was awaiting them below. Ruko turned to see them still at the top of the steps and sensed their apprehension.

"We're not going to kill you," said Ruko, as if reading the expressions on their faces or their minds possibly. "Our families have known each other too long for that nonsense."

Anthon went first, followed by Baltus. The scene they came upon was eerie to say the least. A dead Erik lay in the centre of a large oak table. He was covered in clean white sheets and two gold coins were covering his eyes.

Candles lit the entire innards of the ship. Scented candles were abundant to hide the smell of the decay. Ruko excused his sailors and the only ones remaining were the Baltus brothers, Admiral Drake Kahee, his living son Ruko and finally a priestess of Lir dressed in her blue and white robes.

"I am very sorry for your loss, my friend," said Baltus.

Drake merely nodded. Baltus approached his old friend but Drake put up a hand to halt him. It was clear Drake was in mourning and unsettled.

Anthon walked up to the remains to inspect his pupil. "Was he wearing any rings when you found him?"

"You mean this?" said Ruko and he tossed the teleport ring to Anthon. "He was not, but not that one."

Anthon frowned and reached out to touch his apprentice's cold dead hand. "You were a great mage my pupil, my friend," he said. "We shall avenge your death."

"Before we make promises we cannot keep," began Ruko, "let's find out what happened," he said slightly agitated. "Shanna, are you ready?" The priestess nodded.

Shanna, the priestess of Lir, walked to the head of the deceased. She raised her hands, closed her eyes and began her chant. Her body swayed from her fingertips to her hips. Her calling went out to Lir, the water god. After many minutes, Shanna felt the power of Lir within her. She laid her hands out over Erik Kahee and grabbed his cold shoulders. The body convulsed as if still alive. The flames of the candles also jumped as if alive, startling everyone in the room. The convulsion only lasted for a moment but Shanna did not let go. Erik's corpse rested back on the table. It was enough to send the admiral reeling backwards against the hull of the ship, seeing his dead son move so. The unexpected movement shocked him to the core.

The corpse of Erik illuminated slightly and a mist began to swirl around him. That mist coalesced into a shape of a person and formed parallel over the body of Erik. It sank within Erik's corpse. Erik's dead eyes opened and the coins over his eyes fell to the floor. There was no breathing and no air escaped from Erik's lungs as his chest did not rise.

Shanna kept her eyes closed and put her arms around her own body as if trying to contain Lir's gift. "Speaking with the dead is fickle," said Shanna. "You may ask three questions maybe four. Begin!" She started to chant.

Ruko asked the first question. "Tell me, who or what killed you?"

Erik's corpse opened its mouth. A soft cryptic voice escaped. "Flesh-golem."

Everyone in the room looked perplexed, save Anthon.

"At least we know they made it to Rom-Seti," Anthon said quietly.

"How do you…" began the admiral.

"Do not speak!" shouted Anthon. "Any questions might be answered by the—by Erik," said Anthon. "Besides, powerful mages create golems and we knew Rom-Seti to be a powerful mage. It must have been one of his guardians."

The admiral walked up to Anthon and said, "Good. I am just pleased he was not killed by one of the members on this ridiculous expedition." The admiral looked at Baltus, and then walked up to his dead son whose eyes were still open. He put a hand on his cold cheek. "Goodbye, my son," he said and walked out, up on deck.

General Blackpool walked up and looked at Ruko. He didn't ask a question but using his hands he gestured to Ruko if he may ask the next question. Ruko obliged.

"During the journey that led to your untimely death, who else was killed among your party?" asked the general.

Erik's corpse opened its mouth and again with his soft cryptic voice, he said. "No one."

The general slowly let out a sigh of relief that his own son might still be alive.

"Now that you have your answer about your son, ask you next question of my brother carefully," said Ruko.

The two Blackpool brothers looked at each other and Anthon nodded to his elder brother to ask the last question.

"Before you died, was Rom-Seti captured?" asked Baltus.

"Yes," came the cryptic response.

The candles flickered one last time and then dimmed. Erik's eyes closed and the illumination around the dead body faded away.

Shanna stopped swaying and her eyes opened. She looked at Ruko. "I must rest and give thanks to Lir for this gift," she said and collapsed to the floor. Ruko went to pick her up. When Baltus moved to help, Ruko motioned for the general to leave it to him.

"You have what you needed, your son is alive for now," he said holding the weak priestess. He moved past the Blackpool brothers to his private cabin. "I wish Dru the best. Do not let him befall my brother's fate," he said looking at Erik on the table. "I make for my home in the morning and will bury my brother at sea along the way," he said walking to the back of the ship to a private cabin and closed the door.

* * * * *

The Blackpool brothers returned to shore without incident. They didn't speak until they were back on their horses and the boat was back out to sea. "What is our next move, brother?" asked Anthon.

"I have the men assembled so I intend to march on Ironhold," he responded.

"No, I meant about Dru and the rest of the party," said Anthon.

"You gave Dru the same ring, did you not?" asked Baltus.

Anthon nodded. "But you know he won't use it, not unless it means certain death."

"Yes, I know. He loves the Foehammer brothers as do I and so I don't expect to...," said Baltus but was interrupted.

"No, I meant he won't leave Damon Crag if the assassin is alive still," said Anthon. "If Dru was to leave Damon while still alive, the assassin may seek vengeance for leaving him on his own to face whatever untold dangers they encounter."

"So even if the Foehammer brothers were killed, Dru would not teleport home immediately," said Baltus.

"I only gave rings of teleportation to your son and the admirals," said Anthon, "Anything more would cost so much more."

Baltus contemplated the information but too much was unknown regarding his son. He didn't know if he was alive or dead or undead. He had to hope Dru would teleport out of trouble if his life depended upon it. Oddly enough, Baltus was less worried about his son than he should have been. Baltus was estranged from his own son and at times even favored the Foehammer brothers over his own son, especially Leif. Part of the distancing was due to Dru's chosen profession. Where Leif chose to be an officer in the army willingly, Dru only did it as a means to an end.

As a boy Dru Blackpool was getting into trouble, causing embarrassment to the general. Dru's talents included but were not limited to theft and breaking and entering. Dru developed these talents ever since his mother was killed by accident during a wizard's duel. Baltus was away at the time and returned to Dru living with Disa Foehammer in the interim. Dru of course resented his father for not being there and blamed him, in part, for Merriam's death.

Eventually, it was Anthon who encouraged Baltus to allow the lad to embrace his talents of theft and sneaking around. After Dru graduated from the Academy of Arms in Sedgedunum, Anthon retained the thief and assassin, Damon Crag via the Shadow Company, to fine-tune Dru's capabilities. It may also have given the Blackpool family a seat at the table at different thievery guilds. None of that would matter if Dru did not return and that thought brought Baltus back to the present. It was what this whole endeavour was about in the first place.

"I now have control of the city and soon the country for that matter," began Baltus unimpressed at Anthon again penny-pinching. "Finding the funds to help pay for your debts should be trivial," said Baltus. "Once I take the arch-goblin stronghold of Ironhold and destroy it, it will secure my claim to Vorclaw and your debts. Our debts will be paid in full by the nation's coffers."

Anthon merely nodded in response. The wizard was banking on his brother's capability to take the nation and help absolve the debt the wizard himself mounted in creating the Iron-golem. All the spell components and magical assets were lent to him by the Shadow Company.

"In the meantime, let us hope our spy returns from Ironhold with some news that is beneficial to our cause."

* * * * *

110

Skraw, the new Chieftain of Ironhold was put to the test about the security of Ironhold's clan the very next morning. As drink cleared from the heads of the clan, many remembered the discussions of their vulnerability. His broad shoulders did little to quell the claims that Chieftain Blist's clan had already departed on the long road back to his city of Skulls-thorpe. Blist did leave behind some of his warriors but now that sobriety was kicking in from the night of celebrating the war, it became clear that Blist left those too wounded or weak to travel and the very young as well. He claimed the young were to help compensate Ironhold for its losses in manpower.

Ironhold did however have a large number of new slaves. Skraw started his reign by ordering them to work on securing the outskirts of the stronghold and forage for materials. While it was told to the residents of Ironhold that magical protection and the devastation of Sedgedunum would prevent any worry of Ironhold falling into serious danger, Skraw did not wish to take any chance that Sedgedunum would traverse the forest to retaliate. And the so-called magical protection was not going to happen due to the betrayal of Anthon and his wizards.

Mimdrid, the shape-changer relished that he sowed the seed of mistrust among the clans so well. He worried that he may have done it too well now that Ironhold was beginning to mobilize itself to prepare for a siege, albeit lazily. The shape-changer was long overdue but didn't want to leave, not yet. He wanted to see and understand what protections were being initiated and where they might be exploited.

He took on some of the duties of handling the slaves. He was given a whip and made some of the slave's harvest tree branches for fletching arrows and pick berries for consumption. He had them pile everything centrally. Other arch-goblins were with him as well whipping away at their own slaves. Others Sedgedunum slaves were digging defensive positions around the stronghold.

The next morning the slaves were tasked with cutting down trees and collecting large stones. They were taking the materials inside the stronghold. Eventually, Mimdrid realized they were building a trebuchet. Normally used for attacking forts, the arch-goblins intended to use it in defence against General Blackpool's soldiers, if they came this way.

Mimdrid took mental notes of how many slaves were employed in the stronghold, the number of capable arch-goblins and the strongest defensive positions to include the weakest. Finally, when he again took out another detail of women to the treeline to search for branches for arrows, he decided to make his escape. However, he decided to kill the other two arch-goblins escorting him. Then he simply went deeper into the forest, turned his ring of teleportation and disappeared.

The small herd of female slaves quickly realized they were alone. Some even saw the one arch-goblin, who was Mimdrid, bludgeon the other two. The women grabbed the keys from the dead arch-goblin, released one another from their bonds and ran for Sedgedunum.

Chapter 16
Archangel Forest

It took two days of walking in the crags until a lush green valley appeared. Their aching bodies and tired feet found new life at the sight. The trek was relatively uneventful. Only a few wandering undead creatures appeared but not nearly the multitude they encountered at the beginning of their escape from the necropolis. The rocks gave way to a downward slope and eventually, over some more rocks, a large forest emerged.

It was surrounded by a small mountainous ring. The valley ran about ten miles in length and three in width. A ring of mountains protected the valley both from the cold western winds of the sea and the great snow-covered peaks to the east; a waterfall fed by the snow cover peaks in the east breathed life into this paradise. A small lake governed the centre of the valley..

Leif asked to be the one to guide using the map. "Well, I hope this is the correct valley?" he said loudly. Lorez and Damon, both tired, looked at the elf in irritation at the joke. Sker was perched on Leif's shoulder looking down at the valley, then down at the map and then back to the map. After several moments, Leif replied, "No, this should be it," he said with a smile. "The sea is on our right and a jagged row of mountains keeps the cold winds at bay." Damon and Lorez still looked irritated.

"He is teasing," said Bjorn coming up behind the pair. "My brother knows how to read a map." The large priest was a completely different person from days ago when he could barely speak. His throat was still sore but healing. He had vigour in his step as well.

Dru brought up the rear of the party, always scanning for stalking dangers. "You know, when we were younger, Leif used to joke and try to make us think he was confused. It was kind of a game to see how mad he could make Bjorn, for fun. But he is very intelligent, don't let him fool you."

Damon chuckled at the thought while Lorez followed the elf heading into the valley.

As they entered the forest, the foliage limited the light.

"These trees are tall and thick," said Damon. "This forest has been here a long time."

"The map says we will eventually come upon a trail or road that should take us to the lake," said Leif.

The further they went the darker it got.

"I see some faint game trails," whispered Dru. "Deer and maybe some type of dog." Damon acknowledged him and the two stopped to look.

"I see deer hooves but do you see the prints?" asked Damon of Dru.

"Barely," he responded as they stopped. Both knelt down to examine.

"Hey elf, over here," said Damon with a bit of irritation. Everyone gathered around Damon and Dru. "You recognize these prints?"

Sker recognized them immediately. "Those, ah lizard-goblin," replied Sker.

"Funny how the griffin rider failed to mention this," said Damon.

"It is one set of prints," said Bjorn. "Who cares?"

"Yes, just one," said Lorez amused by Bjorn's comment. "Sker, do lizard-goblins ever travel alone? I mean usually they live in large packs. Correct?" asked Lorez. Sker shook his head in agreement.

"From now on, I will lead," said Lorez. "And Sker you will stay in front of the elf near to me."

"I have a name," said Leif.

"Everyone else stay close," continued the arch-goblin. "If there is a large force of lizard-goblins, they may have another race of arch-goblins or even orcs leading them."

No one could argue with the logic. After about a mile into the forest, they came upon the remnants of an overgrown road which was more of a path but void of large trees. Their travel became easier and the sun was shining on them again.

"We are not going to make it to the lake before nightfall," said Lorez.

"Shall we camp off to the side of the road or keep going?" asked Dru.

"We must have another hour of daylight," said Damon.

"This road," began Leif, "has anyone noticed the large indentations about?" asked Leif referring to several crater-like dents along the current portion of the road on which they travelled. They were about the diameter of a man and about one to two feet deep.

Bjorn took a quick trot into one just off the side of the old road. "See Dru, I am still taller than ya!" he said with a laugh.

"Ha ha, very funny," said Dru.

"It is probably death from above," said Damon.

"What do you mean," asked Leif?"

"The craters are probably *fireballs*, reigned down by your griffin rider or his kin," explained the assassin.

Bjorn ran out of the indentation in the ground and up next to Dru. The large man was about to joke some more with Dru when he realized that Sker had held out his scaly hand to stop everyone.

"Me is sorry," whispered Sker. "I thinks we-zah in ah trap."

"I don't see anything?" said Bjorn.

Damon unsheathed his two short swords and Dru followed suit. Leif took off his shield and Bjorn did so as well. They began to form a circle around Sker and Lorez but those two remained at the front not moving. Lorez asked

Sker in the lizard-goblin tongue what he knew. Before he could answer, a hail of fist-sized rocks came at them from the left. Then another from out of the treetops on the right. High pitched war cries, similar to large birds, bellowed around them.

About twenty yards up ahead Lorez saw six small creatures dressed in red and black run across the road launching small arrows at them. Sker let out a warning but the arrows either fell short or were well off the mark. The archers quickly ran back to the trees.

They all took hits from some rocks, but the worst was Dru who took a rock to the chin.

"That's it?" asked Bjorn.

"Iza stops us well short of trap," said Sker.

"What are we up against here?" asked Damon facing the path they just came down. "Was this some kind of teasing or warning?"

There was rustling of the trees off to both sides and the small creatures came out launching more arrows that were again way off the mark. More rocks showered them but were blocked mostly by Leif and Bjorn's shields.

"Lorez," began Leif. "Why haven't you drawn your weapons?"

"Are you going to answer them Sker or am I?" asked Lorez.

Everyone then turned to look dumbfounded at the runty lizard-goblin who seemed unsure of himself. Then Sker walked out from the circle and let out a few bird calls back at the would-be attackers.

Lorez wore a huge grin of amusement and said to the group, "They're lizard-goblins."

There was a lot of yelping back and rustling of the trees from both sides, but no stones were thrown.

"Iza tolds-dem we on mission from far-zah away," said Sker. He then barked some more but now only one barked back. That lizard-goblin came forth from the brush down the road. It was with five others who were all holding notched arrows.

"Maybe show him the map?" said Lorez. He stepped forward and handed Sker the map. "I go with you Sker. Everyone wait here."

Lorez and Sker walked to the six lizard-goblins.

"They are fairly well armored," Lorez said to Sker noticing their leathers. "They have clearly taken some of the work from another race or are supported by such." Lorez stopped at the point where he felt the arrows could inflict some serious damage. He looked them over, clearly, they were nervous but he also noticed they were not alone. Several ones were watching in the distance to either side.

"This be our land, you be gone!" said the leader who folded his small scaly arms over his chest, bow and quivers hanging from his back.

"This is a path on a map we were given and told to follow. We only want to go there," said Lorez. "Show them, Sker," he said prodding Sker to show him the map.

Sker obliged, nervously. It had been some time since he seen his own kind and hadn't thought to meet any this far north. Sker handed it and the leader swiped from Sker staring down at runty-Sker who was just half a foot shorter.

"Whatcha wanna goes here for?" he asked.

"We-zah not wants to go but it be our mission?" replied Sker nervously fooling with his own paws.

"That place," began the lead lizard-goblin, "Death!"

"So we were told," lied Lorez. "I see this be your lands and out of respect for your tribe we will not hunt but may we at least rest here until the morning?"

After several moments and some discussion via whispering the lead lizard-goblin finally responded.

"What tribute?" asked the lead lizard-goblin.

Lorez stared down at the lead lizard-goblin but didn't want to argue. He was tired. He reluctantly handed over a dagger hidden in his boot by tossing it to the ground.

"You may rest here for one night. But no hunting food. It be ours, not yours," he said.

"I agree to that," said Lorez nodding.

"But kin come with us this night," said the lead lizard-goblin. "What be name, kin?" asked the leader of Sker.

"I am called Sker," he replied.

"Sker comes with us for the night. He may return at da sunrise," responded the lizard-goblin leader.

Sker looked up helplessly at Lorez. The arch-goblin looked down at the lizard-goblin. He never considered Sker a friend, a lizard-goblin was beneath him. And he didn't want to fight his way through this now expanded tribe of lizard-goblins. Therefore, he responded in what he felt was best for all. "Of course, Sker will join you."

Lorez nodded to the lizard-goblin leader and backed away.

He was taken by the hand by one of the lizard-goblins. A few more yelps were given throughout the forest. Off Sker went, reluctantly into the brush.

"Sker!" shouted Leif, now trotting towards Lorez.

"He will be back at sunrise," said Lorez holding out his hands not to proceed. "It is part of the peace settlement; we can spend the night without harm. But no hunting for food tonight, part of the peace. And we will likely be watched."

"What are they going to do with him?" asked Leif in a concerned voice.

"Feed him, question him about us and ask how he came to be here," said Lorez unconcerned. "Now let's start a fire."

"What else did they say?" asked Bjorn.

"Something about the place we are headed, is equivalent to death," responded Lorez cryptically.

Everyone looked at Lorez silently.

"Don't you humans and elf worry," said Lorez with a hearty laugh. "Lizard-goblins are just superstitious and easily scared is all."

Who could argue? Lorez knew more about lizard-goblins than any of them.

Dru and Bjorn had already started collecting firewood.

Damon selected a camp site just off to the right of the direction they were heading, just off the path. "I am going to create a perimeter," said Damon. "I will also look for signs of other more dangerous creatures."

"Come elf," said Lorez. "Rest, for once."

Leif was tired. Guiding for two days and enduring questions about his direction sense from Damon drained the elf.

Leif sat down by the small fire that Bjorn had created rather quickly. For once he dared to let his guard down, sit against a fallen tree and rest. The sun was setting, and the afternoon was beginning its eventual chill. The warm fire felt good already. "Why is it you think that Damon dislikes me?" asked Leif of Lorez who was sitting off to the elf's right, eating a squirrel he captured earlier, hair and all.

"Who knows? Perhaps an elf wronged him in his past," said Lorez. "Elves are not all good and friendly. Many are not friendly at all."

"I have heard such rumors," said Leif.

Lorez finished devouring his squirrel. "The dark-elves are the worst," said Lorez and spat. "I am glad you killed that one in the arena," he said to Lorez referring to Leif's encounter with a dark-elf during his time in the underground city of Skulls-thorpe. Leif had been forced to fight the dark-elf in the coliseum many months ago.

"That seems so long ago now?" said Leif. "I never understood that rage I had for that elf, why I mistrusted him so. I didn't even know him. But I know I regret it."

"Ah elf, you're too soft," said Lorez. "Did you know that dark-elf betrayed his own kin to save his own hide? So I heard. You were right to kill him, for he would have gladly killed you."

Leif didn't answer. He just tried to relax. His mind wondered. He had dared to hope that he had done enough to secure peace between the arch-goblins and Vorclaw. He was the reason peace existed between the arch-goblins of Blood-helm and the nearby orc tribe. Because he championed the arch-goblin army and defeated the half-orc half-ogre champion of the orcs, he was able to prevent that war from erupting by not slaying the orc-ogre champion even though he defeated him soundly. It was how Sker came into his companionship.

He had hoped Sker would be fine. Perhaps some time with his own kind would do him some good. He liked Sker, the lizard-goblin had a good heart and Leif felt he needed goodly souls in his life. Those thoughts led him to thoughts of Queen Ooktha, his vampire lover. When would he see her again and would Rom-Seti's capture finally secure his freedom and peace in the region when he presented her with the Jade Tower?

"The Jade Tower!" shouted Leif suddenly and jumping up. "Sker has it!"

"For pity's sake!" shouted Bjorn returning and dropped all his firewood in a heap. "Why does he still have it? If that revenant is released, we will be done for," said Bjorn

Dru had also returned and heard the conversation. "You know we only caught the revenant because surprise was on our side. That and the creepy old witch through the mirror helped a bit."

"We have to go get him," said Leif.

"Frankly, I don't care for the little lizard," said Damon. No one even saw Damon behind a tree when he spoke. The assassin was very good at stealth. "I have no intention of collecting him; my mission is complete as far as I am concerned."

Leif believed he knew where Damon was thanks to the elf's keen sense of hearing. "Good for you Crag," said Leif who was somewhat irritated with the man. "I will get him and none of you need bother," explained an irritated Leif.

"No!" said Lorez standing up. "I will go."

"Then I will go with you," said Leif.

"Fine, the rest of you stay here. If we are not back by morning we will likely be gone and left you all behind," said Lorez. "It is a joke, yes!" said Lorez with a big toothy smile.

Just then the sound of drums began to beat through the coming night. "Ah perfect, they should now be easy to find," said Lorez.

* * * * *

The beat of the drums fascinated Sker but also made him weary. There was a great fire in the middle of a small village of rounded huts made of dirt, wood and assorted stones. Most lizard-goblins lived below ground but these ones dwelled in an open glade within the forest. Sker counted several hundred kin but could not be sure. Their leader and the one who bargained for Sker to join his tribe for the night was pleasant enough.

"Come Sker, sit and tell me of how you and the arch-goblin come to be with the humans and elf," asked the leader in the common-lizard-goblin language. The leader was an older lizard-goblin. One of the oldest he had seen. The leader looked over the knife he was given by Lorez with the eyes of an experienced fighter. "The knife is of good make. The arch-goblin must hail from a dwelling of good ore, good craftsmen," said the leader.

Sker didn't know if the leader was asking him a question or merely talking aloud. Sker felt very vulnerable. He hadn't been separated from Leif in many weeks save a few precious moments. Also, many eyes were on Sker, whispering and giggling while this tribe of lizard-goblins sat around the fire; some danced while others ate small vermin they obviously raised for food.

"Tell me," Began the lizard-goblin leader, "What brings you to us this night?"

"We are on a mission sent by the arch-goblin queen," said Sker in the common-lizard-goblin language. "Her kingdom has three tribes of arch-goblins in three cities. Each has its own tribe of lizard-goblin kin. I am from the mountain home of Blood-helm."

The leader nodded at the answer but had more questions. "How did you avoid our trap?" he asked. "You or the arch-goblin clearly stopped short of it."

"In my tribe, I am small," said Sker. Many of the other lizard-goblins giggled but the leader raised a scaly hand to quieten them. "But I am good at making traps for our kin and arch-goblin masters. Because me, not good at fighting."

"So, you were sent to look for traps for the invaders?" asked another lizard-goblin angrily.

"Nah, we are not invaders," responded Sker. "I am squire to elf. I travel with him, Master Leif."

"How are elf, friends with you and arch-goblin?"

"He is good friends to arch-goblin queen," responded Sker. "And elf friend saved my life."

The leader nodded in response to all Sker's comments. He took the small kin to be telling the truth.

"Why you go to the place on map?" asked the leader. "That place, is forbidden for my tribe. I have not gone there for many moons. Some of my younglings have never been beyond the waters of lake."

"We were invited by the flying elf," replied Sker.
Do you know what lurks there?"

"What?" asked Leif standing from a distance but clearly listening. Lorez stood next to him.

The tribe exploded into a frenzy of surprise. Lizard-goblins grabbed spears, bows and arrows, pointing at the uninvited duo. Leif and Lorez held out their hands to show they meant no harm. The leader stood up shouting and pointing at the pair. The now armed lizard-goblins surrounded the two.

"Is-ah this how you honor treaty?" shouted the leader at Lorez.

"My apologies but the elf insisted on making certain his squire was well cared for," replied Lorez.

"What do you think wez-ah, savages?" questioned the leader.

"Sker is more than my squire, he is my close friend. And I would not rest the night not knowing he was safe," replied Leif.

"Master Leif, its-ah ok!" responded Sker from behind the leader. Sker felt a profound feeling of friendship. The runty lizard-goblin was overwhelmed by Leif's comments.

"I see that he is fine, but I would like one last word before we turn in for the night," said Leif.

The leader waved Sker to go over and the lizard-goblin warriors parted for Sker. Sker himself was overjoyed at the sight of Leif.

"You unharmed?" asked Leif.

"Oh no sir, mez-ah fine," replied Sker. "Iza am very happy you come to check on Sker, but Iza," said Sker but was interrupted by Lorez.

"Do you still have the Jade Tower?" asked Lorez and Sker nodded. "Then hand it over," said Lorez.

Sker did as asked.

"First light," said Leif, "I will come for you," said Leif but it fell on deaf ears, Sker was suddenly saddened, believing the Jade Tower was more important to Leif than Sker himself.

The exchange did not go unnoticed though by the leader nor the look on Sker's face. "What be this then?" asked the leader. "What you give to greedy elf?"

"Nothing that will concern your tribe and better if you do not know," said Lorez.

The lizard-goblin leader then shouted a command. All the lizard-goblins again surrounded the duo and now Sker who was nervously panting. The whole tribe now exploded in uproar. Ropes were being lassoed around Lorez and Leif's neck and wrists. The two were now thoroughly surrounded and lassoed from multiple directions. The lizard-goblins herded Leif and Lorez to the nearest tree and tied them to it. Small spears prodded and poked at the two.

"Bring that small green trinket to me Sker," demanded the leader.

"Iza have no choice, Master Leif," said Sker and he did as the lizard-goblin leader demanded.

"You don't know what that is," said Leif. "It is very dangerous."

"What be this then?" asked the leader. "You offer me worthless knife as tribute for entering my lands but hide this from my sight?" said the lizard-goblin leader in anger.

"Kill them. Then find their companions and kill them as well this night," said the leader in the lizard-goblin tongue.

A screeching sound of a bird came out suddenly from above the night. The lizard-goblins looked around at each other, suddenly frightened or unsure. A bright light suddenly burst forth before Leif and Lorez, blinding everyone nearby. Again, the screech came forth from the night and the lizard-goblins ran every which way to escape from both the light and the noise. No one could see but they could hear and then feel the crackle of lightning hit the ground followed by a cool breeze.

The light disappeared just as suddenly and in its place stood a wondrous beast, a griffin and the elf Teodor sat upon its back.

"Release them at once," said the elf in the lizard-goblin tongue. "I been watching you," said Teodor to the leader, pointing a wand at the old creature. "I been watching all of you!" shouted the elf. "These creatures are my master's guests," said the elf. "Unless you wish to incur his wrath yet again, you will cease hostilities. And you," Teodor said to the leader, "hand over that Jade Tower," he said with some venom. The leader complied and ordered his lizard-goblins to do as demanded. "Who do you think gave them the map?" asked Teodor of the lizard-goblin leader who was now on his knees. The rest of the tribe followed his example. "And this!" said Teodor holding out the Jade Tower. "This is for my master to have, not a filthy lizard-goblin."

Once Leif and Lorez were free, Teodor said, "They should not harm you from here on in. Leave your camp at first light and come to the palace at the top of the city. We will be waiting," he said and off the griffin flew high into the night sky.

"I think you two have some explaining to do when we return to camp," said Lorez to Sker and Leif.

Chapter 17
The Siege of Ironhold

"Thanks to information from your spy, general," began Major Goldwater from inside the war tent, "we were able to avoid the fire traps, ballista and trebuchet range but we have not made a dent in the compound. The first ram we built was covered in burning oil and we lost many men in that attack."

"That's why I called forth the remains of the Wizard's College to help sort this out," said General Blackpool.

"Sir, I ordered the engineers to begin building our own catapults," said Major Goldwater.

"Good!" replied the general. "Let the arch-goblins see you do it as well." They will either break out and attack or get comfortable in their hold and not expect a magical assault. Either one is a step in the right direction. What else have you done?"

"I was sending in troops to probe the walls but was unable to get anyone through or over the walls. I now send out regular patrols to get the arch-goblins to expend their arrows and bring in any intelligence. In the meantime, I have fortified our position and sent out scouts to ensure no creatures lurk elsewhere that may take advantage of our rear or flanks," said Major Goldwater.

"Very good major," said the general. "And no sign of the vampire?"

"None sir," responded the major. "Perhaps we could convince the jailed clergy council leaders to join us so they can see what we're up against? Maybe they might even see the error of their ways."

"No," replied the general coldly. "I am bringing in other faith leaders and if they see any battles then they might earn a seat on the council. Those degenerates already jailed will be exiled or remanded to their original holdings in Vorclaw. They will never set foot again in the capital. And you major will never again suggest giving them value or reprieve," said General Blackpool to his major who nodded in response.

It was then announced that the wizards had arrived. In came Horatio Mercutio and two other wizards, a human female of brown complexion with long black hair and in her late thirties, who clearly did not appear to be from Vorclaw, and an older male, bald and in his late fifties.

"General, it is good to see you once again," said the wizard Horatio and appointed headmaster of the demolished Wizards College. "May I present Mr. and Mrs. Archibald and Yasmina Smite. They have volunteered to participate in your campaign to restore order to our nation," said Horatio.

The general and major nodded.

"Something tells me Yasmina you are not from Vorclaw," said Major Goldwater.

"Ah, she is actually," interjected Archibald, her husband. "She was born and raised in Vorclaw."

"My family moved here from Karthia before the Karthian civil war," she said.

"You're clearly from Vorclaw," said the major referring to Archibald.

"Actually no, I am a foreigner. I've only lived in in Sedgedunum for the last ten years or so. I was born in Uden. I learned my trade there. My father though was a seafaring trader who retired locally and well, here I am."

"Well clearly, I am the fool," said Major Goldwater. "My apologies to you both," he said with a bow.

"The major oversees the siege," interjected General Blackpool getting down to business. "I trust you will both work with him to the best of your abilities to break the siege and vanquish these arch-goblins. And time is of the essence as we still yet might recover some of our inhabitants," said the general. The two wizards nodded to the general. "The major will bring you both up on current events. Horatio, we must chat, I have matters to discuss with you that do not pertain to the siege," said Baltus.

"Of course, general," replied Horatio.

"Let us take our leave of these three then," said the general.

* * * * *

"They are building siege weapons," grunted the arch-goblin lieutenant from the southeast tower. Several arch-goblins sat around a table in one of the rooms of Ironhold keep.

"They have been approaching us along the walls, seeing how close they can get before we fire arrows on them," said the lieutenant from the southwest tower.

"They have found the last of the oil traps and successfully burned it out," said the arch-goblin captain over the main gate.

"We have a traitor in our midst it seems," said Chieftain Skraw, the new Chieftain of Ironhold.

"Probably a result of the two dead soldiers and missing slaves that escaped a few days ago," responded the captain.

"Scribe!" shouted Skraw. A young arch-goblin, barely out of his youth responded ready to write. "Take this down and send it to Chieftain Blist," said the agitated new chieftain.

"The Vorclaweans are settling in for a siege. We expect them to be ready to attack with siege weapons in the next week. We are being probed along our walls in an effort that we will exhaust our supply of arrows. All our traps have been discovered and destroyed with no loss to the enemy. I can only presume

a traitor had revealed the locations of our traps. Therefore, I decided to take the initiative and open the gates this evening and begin a full-on attack. Please send whatever reinforcements you can."

"Send that lad, now," said the chieftain and the young arch-goblin was off. "How many do you think he will send?" asked the lieutenant from the southwest tower.

"He will send the bare minimum, he does not really care and nor does Queen Ooktha," responded Chieftain Skraw. "They got their war and spoils, otherwise she would have stayed along with the warriors from Skulls-thorpe."

"I heard from an arch-goblin out of Skulls-thorpe that she doesn't have an ounce of arch-goblin lineage in her. She is all elf," said the other lieutenant.

"I too heard that rumor but from an arch-goblin out of Bloodhelm," said the captain.

"If we all survive this, is it perhaps time to cut ties with her, given she lacks arch-goblin blood?" asked the lieutenant from the southwest tower. "I mean, I think she looks elf to me even with her war paint."

The other three arch-goblins all looked at the lieutenant from the southeast tower. That arch-goblin realized he may have gone a step too far and nervously meddled with a small ordinary ring on his finger.

"My apologies, I overstepped my station my chieftain," said the southeast tower arch-goblin.

The chieftain stood up from the small table. "We have been poisoned. Deceitfulness about our queen has been spread around our stronghold since returning from our plunder. Our traps and positions have been given away. If we are to survive this siege, we need to focus our efforts on what is outside our gates. If there is still a traitor among us, we must be quick in our actions before the traitor can act and give away our plan. Return to your posts and say nothing of today's discussions. I will muster our warriors this evening. I will form them up inside the mountain. I will lead them on an attack tonight."

* * * * *

It was just becoming dusk, and Chieftain Skraw was returning from a visit of the southeast tower to the main gate. A small entourage of five bodyguards accompanied him. The captain was there at his post as discussed, atop the main gate house, observing.

"My lord, I am ready to have the gates opened," he said quietly. "But I fear you are correct about a spy," said the captain.

"Explain!" demanded Chieftain Skraw.

"I been observing with my spyglass," said the captain referring to his telescope, one of two in Ironhold. "I can see they are no longer building siege weapons but preparing defenses."

Chieftain Skraw already knew this of course. He had the other spy glass and observed the same at the southeast tower. "I questioned the lieutenant at the southeast tower and gave him my spy glass. He said the same when he looked through. His warriors told me he did not leave his tower since he returned from our war council. I asked the same of your warriors about your whereabouts."

The arch-goblin captain squared his jaw and stared hard at his chieftain. Was he about to accuse him of being a spy?

"They said the same about you my friend. You had not left your post nor said anything to your warriors?"

The captain did not have an immediate reply. Then it dawned on him. But before he could say anything Chieftain Skraw headed to the southwest tower, with his five-arch-goblin entourage of bodyguards in tow.

The arch-goblins at the tower nodded in respect. A few choices but quieted questions were levied upon the arch-goblins in the tower.

"Where is your lieutenant and what has he told you about the assault?" When the chieftain was certain his lieutenant from the southwest tower had not revealed anything about the war council meeting he made his way to their lieutenant. Chieftain Skraw was directed to a room in the tower's middle floor. He tried to barge in but the door was locked. So he banged his fist on the door.

The occupant behind responded in the arch-goblin tongue, "What is so important? Are we being attacked again?" The door opened and there stood the lieutenant. In barged the chieftain and his entourage. The lieutenant was surrounded instantly. "What is the meaning of this?" he asked.

"You are the traitor?" said the chieftain. "Put him in irons!"

The arch-goblins were on the lieutenant in a swarm. An arch-goblin each grabbed an arm while one punched him with brass knuckles to the stomach. The arch-goblin lieutenant fell instantly to his knees.

The arch-goblin trying to put on the shackles was the first to notice something amiss. Save for the arch-goblin lieutenant's index finger on his right hand which held a simple silver ring, the arch-goblin's hands were suddenly bulbous, and his wrists were too large to place the shackles around. The lieutenant suddenly exploded with an uncanny strength. The two holding his arms down went flying backwards and the one trying to cuff him jumped back startled. The lieutenant's fists were now the size of large mace and he began flailing them around pushing back everyone before they could draw a weapon, save for Chieftain Skraw who drew his curved sword.

The chieftain took a stab at the lieutenant who was quicker and pulled a stunned arch-goblin in front of him. The chieftain partly impaled his own bodyguard but quickly withdrew it. However, that same bodyguard was thrown at the chieftain sending him backwards.

Another bodyguard who was standing behind the one who tried to shackle the lieutenant managed to get his sword free and stab through some of the armour of the lieutenant. That stab was comparable to a large cut and was met with a hit to the head by the enlarged fist of the lieutenant, rendering him unconscious.

Skraw by now had rolled his bleeding bodyguard off him but his sword was kicked free from his hand. A large fist came down on the arch-goblin's face. Warm blood poured from the chieftain's nose. The lieutenant was suddenly resting atop his chest.

The lieutenant turned his silver ring and vanished suddenly along with Chieftain Skraw!

* * * * *

It wasn't so much the surprise that two arch-goblins appeared in Major Goldwater's tent that alarmed the wizards Yasmina and Archibald; it was the nonchalant manner in which Major Goldwater acted. It was almost as if he had expected this to happen.

"Ah, I see you been discovered then my friend," said the major pouring a drink and handing it over to the arch-goblin with the large fists. The major had his sword out, pointed at the neck of the bleeding arch-goblin beneath him. Mimdrid's bulbous, mace-sized fists became normal again as he stood up and changed into the semblance of Mr. Night. "And who do we have here?" asked the major.

"May I present, Chieftain Skraw, the new leader of Ironhold," said Mr. Night as if he was never an arch-goblin. "Somehow, he found me out and I best not to go back there, not for some time."

"Oh, so you're the new chieftain I am up against," said the major. "Tell me chieftain, uh, Skraw was it? How did you discover our spy?" he asked smiling. "Did you discover any others perhaps?" he asked smiling knowing there were no other spies. "Best you take off that armour and help yourself to some of my attire behind the curtain in the corner before I call the guards in," he said to Mimdrid. "Does he speak common at least?" asked the major once Mr. Night came out from behind the curtain.

"He does and I need one of your priests. I am cut on my back by one of his soldiers," said Mr. Night.

"I have not seen an arch-goblin up close before," said Archibald.

"Hideous, aren't they?" asked Yasmina.

"Quite, my lady, quite," agreed the major.

"So you have another mage?" asked Yasmina referring to Mr. Night.

"No my dear, it, is a shape-changer," said Archibald. Everyone was surprised by Archibald's knowledge. "It was the large hands and almost instantaneous change that gave it away.

"Speak no more," said the major. "Guards!"

* * * * *

With Ironhold losing two chieftains in just a few days, the city was beginning to erupt into chaos. Shouts and war cries could even be heard at the Vorclaw front lines. It was the captain on the gates that took charge and eventually got soldiers ready on the walls. However, to his surprise no attack came, save for a small party about halfway between Ironhold and the front lines of the Vorclawean forces. A rider came beckoning to the Ironhold gates asking for a meeting. asking for only three to attend at the halfway point.

The Vorclaweans set up a canopy and lit torches all around it to pierce the night. The captain was greeted by five humans, two of whom were holding Chieftain Skraw.

"I am Major Goldwater of the Vorclawean Army and my associates are the wizards Yasmina and Archibald," announced the major. "You know your chieftain I presume?"

The arch-goblin captain stared at his gagged chieftain but merely growled in response.

"You do speak common?"

"Yes human, what is it you wish to discuss?"

"A trade of prisoners and peace," replied the major.

"What trade?" asked the arch-goblin not understanding.

"I will return your chieftain and twenty other prisoners of arch-goblin and lizard-goblin. And in return you return our captured citizens," said the major.

"And if we refuse?" asked the captain, arms folded over in defiance.

"Then these wizards will begin an assault upon Ironhold, the likes of which you have never seen. I don't know why you attacked our city," lied Major Goldwater. "But our citizens are paramount. I hope you place the same value on your own chieftain at least. If you don't agree, our spies, these two wizards and all the other wizards who have come from afar to aid my soldiers, will destroy you all this night."

The captain didn't budge and merely flexed his muscles looking at his chieftain. Worried that the arch-goblin might draw his weapons, the major played his next hand.

"Your chieftain has asked for this, not I. Ask him yourself. Guards remove the gag," said the major.

"Do as he asks captain," said Chieftain Skraw in the arch-goblin tongue. His breath was labored from what the captain presumed was a beating. "I have been behind their lines and seen their might. Release their peoples and we get back more warriors. Then we can lock ourselves in the mountain until they leave. Just agree to their terms. We have enough poison running through our city without dealing with this coming onslaught."

After several moments of silence, Major Goldwater ordered the gag back on and the two soldiers took the chieftain back to the Vorclawean camp. The arch-goblin captain appeared more relaxed now.

"Are we in agreement then?" asked Major Goldwater.

"One for one swap then," said the captain.

"No. You will return everyone you have for our twenty arch-goblins, fifty-two lizard-goblins and one chieftain," said the major.

"I only have one hundred of your people," lied the captain.

"Liar. We have many spies. You have two hundred and twelve prisoners. I want them all or you all die tonight.

"And what of peace?" asked the arch-goblin captain. "Do you just go away after exchange is complete?"

"Yes," said Major Goldwater. "Tomorrow I will have a treaty drafted ceasing hostilities," he said then turned and walked away. The two wizards followed him out from under the canopy. "The exchange begins at first light," shouted Major Goldwater.

* * * * *

The officers escorting the arch-goblin chieftain released him back into Major Goldwater's tent and ungagged him. The two officers were Major Goldwater's personal guards that he chose. They were also members of the Black-maskas, the secret order that General Blackpool created among high ranking officers and wealthy members who saw things his way. Once Major Goldwater returned with the two wizards, he asked the arch-goblin chieftain, "Do you really think he will return the prisoners?"

Mimdrid then changed forms from the arch-goblin chieftain and into Mr. Night. "After tapping into his surface thoughts, I do believe he will comply. But only time will tell."

In then walked General Blackpool. "I have already written the treaty," he said.

"That was fast!" exclaimed Yasmina.

"Thanks to your *charismatic* spells my dear I was able to work well with this Chieftain Skraw although I do not believe his queen will be very happy."

"So, it is up to me now to convince him that he took part in the meeting. I think I have just the spell for that to work. And it should last for a couple of days," said Archibald.

Chapter 18
Archangel

The adventurers made it to the other side of the central lake by way of a narrow path around the west. They encountered several patches of swamp along the way. They all presumed the swamp developed due to the lake's banks overflowing at several places. Far to the east, only Leif's keen eyes could see the cause. As Leif explained it, a great aqueduct lay ruined along the mountainside beneath a waterfall. The rest of the party came to see the truth of Leif's words once they had again travelled on the overgrown central road in the forest. The ruins of the aqueduct was all along the eastern mountain walls.

"I am surprised we haven't seen any elves as of yet?" said Dru. "I half expected a welcoming party or some escort this side of the lake."

"Why would they?" asked Damon. "Our elf and lizard-goblin already gave them what they wanted."

Leif did not retaliate. He was devastated that he lost the Jade Tower and got captured by a nest of lizard-goblins.

Sker was no better. Prior to losing the Jade Tower, when Leif arrived, he thought the elf was ensuring his safety but later discovered Leif was more interested in the Jade Tower, so the lizard-goblin believed.

Lorez was nervous. He was an arch-goblin after all. Elves and arch-goblins don't often mix well and often kill one another. Therefore, the local elves may not see him in the light that Leif does. He was on edge.

Bjorn, on the other hand, was becoming increasingly irritated. He had risked his own life to save his adopted brother Leif. They only needed to accomplish the mission of trapping Rom-Seti which they apparently had, with great help, only to carelessly lose device. The priest would have come close to death had it not been for the grace of Matronae and the forest-dames. He was also becoming bothered by Damon's continuous taunting of his brother Leif.

"I hope they don't decide to kill us now that they have what they want," said Damon.

Bjorn slowed his pace to let Damon get alongside of him. Bjorn towered over the assassin by at least a foot. "Damon, let it go," began Bjorn. "I am not happy either but taunting him will be of no value," he said. "And it is irritating me," said Bjorn with a stern look at the smaller man.

Damon kept on walking as if Bjorn's words didn't matter. However, it must have worked for there was quiet among them all for the next hour. Eventually the trees gave way to an amazing but depressing sight. What lay before them was an unkempt and overgrown field, taken over by brush, grasses and weeds. Beyond that was an enormous walled city, ruined. It had five tiers up a mountainside whose apex went to the top of a mountain.

Everyone could see multicoloured onion-shaped domes on buildings behind the walls. Several towers of rich green, red and blue still stood. Many of the buildings visible from afar displayed pastel colours of pink, green, red, blue and orange. However, many of the colours were faded and filthy.

"Now we know why the elves never came out to greet us," said Damon.

"It's because there aren't any," said Bjorn, finishing Damon's thoughts.

Everyone looked stunned, especially Leif. "This place," started Leif but didn't finish.

"You all right, Leif?" asked Dru but Leif didn't answer.

Lorez was already scanning the overgrown fields. "We should approach cautiously," said Lorez. "Tall grasses are perfect for elves or other creatures waiting to ambush."

Everyone drew their weapons and shields. Damon took the lead with Dru, looking for tracks or signs of lurking creatures.

Bjorn noticed Leif still staring up at the city that was now looming overhead. "Hey, snap out of it," said Bjorn, smacking Leif on the back of the head. "Focus on your surroundings."

They made it to the remains of the front gate. Huge walls were to either side, but the gate was obliterated. To the side of it rested a huge golden-stone head, well most of one.

"Does the giant head look familiar?" asked Lorez.

"Its colour is unique. Is it made of amber?" asked Bjorn.

"I believe so," said Dru. "It must've been a sight to see. But the image on the stone face is similar to images from the necropolis. It also bears the hooded cobra helm carved into amber."

"So this city was invaded and wrecked by the revenant we captured?" asked Damon.

"There is a hand!" said Sker referring to a large stone hand off to their left. It was of the same stone and make.

"A stone golem made of amber?" said Damon. "To break the gates."

Suddenly Leif stormed through the gateway. Dru made a move to stop him but it was too late. Once through he stopped and looked up.

"Leif," said Bjorn but half whispering, worried someone else might be alerted to their presence. "Get back here!"

Leif turned and said softly, "Its ruined, all of it. Come and see."

Bjorn approached first, followed by the rest. "What is the matter with you brother?"

"I don't know?" replied Leif. "I feel like I seen this place before. In a dream maybe."

"No elf-ez?" asked Sker when he came to Leif's side.

"There is at least one," said Leif who pointed up to the sky. Circling up above was that mysterious griffin rider.

Everyone looked around cautiously, half expecting an army of undead to come forth from the ruins.

"Despite the rubble and plant growth, I was able to find a roadway that leads up to the next tier," announced Damon.

Damon led them up a cobblestone road. They came to another destroyed gate at the top of the road and now they all could look down upon the first tier. It was completely in ruins and tree growth verified it had been this way for at least a decade, maybe more.

It was more of the same in the second tier but in the third tier however the devastation lessened. Many of the buildings in the third tier retained their shape and coloring, albeit faded and filthy in places.

"Would an undead army such as Rom-Seti's be capable destroying this city?" asked Dru.

No one offered an answer.

"Best we keep quiet," said Lorez. "We don't know if anyone lurks in these buildings."

At the fourth tier, they saw something they never expected. All along the main road lay skeletons. Covered in shabby and rusted armour, all appeared to be holding some form of weapon, swords mostly.

"Dead elves," said Lorez.

"Notice the difference in armour in some," said Dru. "Some have very fine, smooth appearances while others seem a bit macabre to be worn by elves."

"That's because they're not elves!" came a call from above. There stood Teodor on the road above looking down. "Well, sort of. Some of them were dark-elves," he said. "But come up and quickly, all will be explained."

Everyone looked dumbfounded at each other but they all pressed on and upward.

At the top, the fifth and final tier, the gate was also smashed in. The grounds were well kept though. A robust vegetable garden lay before them. However, separate from that also laid a large rusting body of a rusting armed statue, possible a golem. Again, that too was similar in shape to the stone golem head they saw at the city's entrance. Teodor, the griffin rider, whose griffin was nowhere in sight, was there holding a basket of freshly picked fruits and vegetables.

"Welcome, to the Archangel. Or what's left of it," he said. "Come up to the palace, my master awaits," said the elf.

Everyone's eyes were in awe of the ruined but functional place. It was once white with golden trim but now weathered. Parts to the left and up on a balcony appeared burnt out. The structure itself looked sound. The stonework was smooth and seamless. No straight edges seemed visible. Everything, the stone, the woodwork and the roof all seemed to flow into each part as if it was joined together. There was a pool just before the steps with water and fish in it, though the fountain of the pool barely worked. There was a great cascade of steps that got narrower at the top but wide enough to allow five people to stand shoulder to shoulder.

Leif was certain he had dreamt of a place like this. Only in his dream it was more lively and cheerful.

Teodor led them down a dark corridor that had some magical floating lights to guide the way. Around a bend to their right they came to a dining room. A feast was on the table.

"I took the liberty of preparing a meal for you all," said Teodor. "Sit, please! There is fish, grapes, berries, tomatoes, potatoes and assorted greens. I even killed a few rabbits. Grab your plate and fill it, I am certain you must be hungry from your journey."

"About that," began Leif, "You could have warned us about the lizard-goblin tribe before we arrived. Or warned them of our arrival since you knew them and they knew you," he said.

"An oversight on my part, my apologies," replied Teodor to Leif.

Lorez was the first to grab at the roasted rabbit.

"Arch-goblin," began Teodor, "It may be custom in your culture to put your filthy fingers over all the food but in this place, we use utensils to put food on to our plates."

Lorez dropped the half rabbit he had broken apart with his hands and split the halves between his plate and the serving platter. He then stabbed at the other half he had just put down and picked it up with his fork.

"Well, he is better than a dwarf at least," said Teodor. He then poured out some wine. "I made it myself," he said as he took a sip from his own glass.

Everyone else began to fill their plates. Everyone except Leif who stared at Teodor.

"What have you done with the Jade Tower?" asked Leif.

"It is here," replied Teodor.

"When can we have it back?"

"Whenever my master decides," replied Teodor.

"I would like to speak with your master, now," said Leif.

Bjorn interjected, "Leif, relax. Take your mind off your troubles and eat."

Leif stared at Teodor but still made his way for the food as his brother suggested. Leif wasn't sure of what to make of this elf or any of this place.

Once everyone's plates were full and were seated, Teodor helped himself to a plate and joined them. "You all undoubtedly have many questions," he said. "Let me begin by telling you the sad tale of Archangel."

"Will our host not be joining us?" asked Damon.

"No, he doesn't enjoy this kind of setting and asked me to feed you and to help pass the time tell you the tale of this place."

"I am curious to hear what happened here," said Dru.

"Archangel was once a jewel tucked away from the prying eyes of the known world," began Teodor. "Or so we thought. Rom-Seti's necropolis appeared from out of nowhere. Many other creatures unbeknown to this region also appeared. You met one on the way here, that hairy fellow you left with the forest-dames," he said. "The appearance of Rom-Seti's city was akin to a fairy tale or better still a nightmare," continued Teodor. "As we investigated, we made ourselves known to Rom-Seti. Subsequently, he invaded. He aligned with the dark-elves, orcs, arch-goblins and lizard-goblins to ravage our once beautiful city and our lands. He killed our king and the invaders killed thousands of elves, to include the few non-elves welcomed in Archangel," he said.

The old elf paused, staring at the table. It was clear to all he was reliving events of the story he was sharing.

"However, not all of us perished," he continued. "We sent our queen, her daughter and all the city's children off in our fantastic flying ships. They escaped the carnage as we fought on. Their destination was for the east to find some form of reservation for themselves. All that remains are the caretakers, who are myself and Arch Mage Pallentine, your host."

"Flying ships?" asked Damon.

Teodor merely nodded yes in response.

"So, there are only two elves here that survived?" asked Dru.

Teodor didn't answer but appeared to be pondering a response that should have been a yes or no. Finally, he said," I will let the archmage answer that when you meet him after dinner."

"Whatever happened to the elves that made for the east? Did anyone ever return?" asked Leif.

"None, ever returned," replied Teodor.

"How did it end?" asked Bjorn. "Meaning, I saw a lot of remains outside, we all saw. Were the invaders beaten back or did they leave after wrecking your beautiful city?"

"They were beaten back by Archmage Pallentine," responded Teodor. "Rom-Seti and his minions were forced to retreat but not before both sides lost dearly. War has a funny was of decimating both sides, regardless of outcome or winner."

"Was it your archmage that created Jade Tower?" asked Leif.

"Actually no, he did not," responded Teodor. "His apprentice did."

"So, there are three elves?" asked Dru.

"Who pray tell is that?" asked Leif.

"Must-ah be the Mistress of Sanctuary!" announced Sker.

"Smart for a lizard-goblin," said Teodor. "But no," he finished deflating the lizard-goblin's already fragile ego.

"I thought you already met her?" asked Teodor referring to the maker of the Jade Tower.

"Is it the arch-goblin queen, Queen Ooktha?" asked Lorez chomping on an entire apple.

"By the gods, please speak when your mouth is not filled with food," responded Teodor. "And no, I never met that creature," he said. "Do you seriously believe the archmage would have anything to do with your kind, arch-goblin?" asked Teodor, showing his disdain for arch-goblins.

"He meant no offence in playing your ridiculous games," announced Leif. "So do not give it back to any of us. We're here because you forced our hand and were in no mood for your history lesson or your games."

Teodor eyed Leif but eventually nodded in response and everyone continued to eat, silently. Damon cracked a smile and a halfhearted wink at Leif showing some small form of respect for Leif to put this mysterious Teodor in his place.

After the table was cleared of food Teodor beckoned them to follow. They went up what was once a grand staircase that had seen some repair work done to it, undoubtedly by Teodor. Down the corridor from the top of the staircase they came upon what was once a gold and glass room. Much of the gold inlay remained but only wooden panels stood in place of what would have held large glass mirror. Only the mirrors at the end of the room were still visible and where a golden throne shone dimly in the magical fires of yellow that floated around the room to give it light.

Leif again had an uneasy feeling about this place. It all seemed familiar but somehow it was a twisted nightmare.

"Let me warn you," began Teodor as they walked up to the throne, "his appearance is not that pleasing so he wears a mask. Please try not to offend him with any comments about it."

Teodor stopped them at the bottom of the steps up to the throne. He walked up and tapped on the glass behind the throne. He spoke something in elvish and backed away. He then turned to the adventurers and said, "He will be along."

The glass suddenly bowed but did not break. It was like water rippling. The whole party jumped back suddenly startled. First, a bony hand came through, withered and old looking. It was followed by a tattered black sleeve that may have had some purple to it. Next the whole form suddenly broke the plain of the watery surface. Robes of black and purple covered a skinny elven form. The creature wore a wooden mask, painted and carved into a stern but handsome male elf. It was trimmed in gold and completely covered the face of the creature before them, save for the eyes. The mirror made a reverberating hum as the figure came through the portal. He held a staff in his left hand and the Jade Tower in his right. Green dots peered through the eye sockets of the mask.

Sker turned and ran outside. Lorez was backing up the same way. Everyone was uneasy at the sudden appearance and sight.

"Be at ease my friends," came a raspy but surprisingly strong sounding voice. "I am Archmage Pallentine and Lord Protector of the City of Archangel," he continued as he sat down on the throne. "I have asked for this," he said holding up the small Jade Tower with bony fingers. Flesh was on his hands but dark and shrivelled the bone. "A creation by my apprentice designed long ago but it wasn't until now that heroes such as yourselves could be trusted enough to use it. I wanted to know of its precious cargo, to know for myself if you indeed captured the one who lay waste to my once beautiful homeland."

"Now that you have examined it, I presume you can tell that his soul is indeed captured?" asked Leif. The old wizard answered with a nod. "Then you no longer have to fear that creature and therefore I would like it returned."

"Returned..." said Pallentine.

"Yes," replied Leif unflinching. "We intend to take it to the mountains of Vorclaw. It is paramount to achieving peace in the region."

"I fail to see why I should return such a wondrous item that I commissioned. And how do I know you will not release the mad revenant inside?"

"I have no doubt of your commissioning since the command word is the same as your great city," said Leif. "But honestly, I don't know how to release him, save from breaking it with a rock or hammer."

"Ha!" shouted Pallentine with an eerie laugh. "The Mistress of Sanctuary never gave you the release command. And smashing it against a rock will not open it either. At least not one without great magical might anyway." He turned to look at Teodor. "That one, always doing things her own way. Seems she doesn't want him released from his prison," he said with a touch of humor.

"I cannot say I blame the Mistress of Sanctuary," said Teodor.

"What of you then and the one who you are delivering this to? What of that elf abomination?" he asked referring to Queen Ooktha.

Leif couldn't help but feel a little humiliated at the reference to his vampire lover.

"How do I know she won't release him, perhaps on your homes in Vorclaw?

"You know a lot about us, revenant," dared Bjorn, standing next to Leif.

"Ah, the priest of Matronae who was saved by my forest-dames," he said.

"Yes, and I suffered dearly under the hand of the one whose soul you now possess. But if we can deliver it to stop another war from erupting, like the one that ruined this fine city, then surely releasing it to us is in everyone's best interests."

Teodor interjected but only spoke in the elvish tongue, *"I thought you said the war in their homeland was already underway?"* But the archmage didn't respond. *"Also, the large elf demanding the item is the one the Mistress believes to be the lost Delvemoora prince."* Again, the archmage didn't respond. *"He said he has no memory of his homeland, found and raised by humans far away in the land where they wish to return."*

Pallentine turned to look at Teodor and then to Leif. He stood up and slowly descended to stand before Leif and Bjorn.

The two towered over the archmage and they could both see around the eye sockets of the mask. Wrinkled flesh, exposed bone and two green pinpricks for eyes were beneath for sure. The creature before them was either a revenant of something of the sort. They felt the cold emanating from

Pallentine's body strengthening Bjorn's concerns. Pallentine looked over at Leif's face and turned to walk, slowly to the throne but didn't sit.

"Tonight, you will rest comfortably here as our guests. I will give you an answer on the Jade Tower in the morning. He then backed up slowly, disappearing into the mirror from whence he came.

Teodor walked down the steps and said, "I think you impressed him. Come follow me, I will show you where you can all rest for the night."

Chapter 19
The Exchange

The line of prisoners, all two hundred and twelve, came out of the gates or Ironhold at first light. They were under escort and roped one after the other so they could not run immediately away. Arch-goblins and small lizard-goblins held crossbows, spears and swords ready in case the trade did not go as planned.

"You will go last, chieftain," said General Blackpool. "Major, release his warriors."

One by one the beaten arch-goblins and lizard-goblins walked out from behind the Vorclawean Army's makeshift barricades. Their wrists were bound with ropes and tied to their feet making walking difficult and slow. They were given simple instructions: 'ignore the citizens of Vorclaw passing you as you return to Ironhold.'

"A lot more lizard-goblins were rounded up and arrived in the night. So there now we are sending twenty arch-goblins and twenty-five lizard-goblins, more than was promised," said General Blackpool to Chieftain Skraw. "I presume that is acceptable?"

But the chieftain didn't answer. His mind was a haze of beatings and misplaced memories. He remembered some treaty to cease all fighting and to return inside the mountain. He had thought that part before being captured. However, he didn't recall the part of meeting to discuss these terms nor the prisoner-exchange meeting.

"Make certain your queen receives that treaty as my council will receive my copy," said the general. Once the last Vorclaw citizen was received behind the barricades the general cut the bonds of the chieftain. "Off you go then." He shoved the chieftain from out behind the barricades.

"Best hurry!" shouted the general. "I still intend to destroy the outer fortress of Ironhold. So best get through the mountain quickly."

"Artillery!" shouted Major Goldwater. "Loose!"

Chieftain Skraw was barely one quarter the distance when a barrage of flaming pitch was released from the five Vorclaw siege weapons. They had more distance and could hold more than what the arch-goblins trebuchets had from within their stronghold. The five shots either hit the walls of Ironhold or landed within. Chieftain Skraw sprinted to his stronghold. However, his warriors exploded out the gates instead in a rage fuelled by the anger at the sudden betrayal.

Everything was a haze for the new chieftain. Led by his own captain, Chieftain Skraw tried to stop them from approaching by holding out his arms and ordering them to return. The enraged arch-goblin horde roared past their new chieftain, savoring the kill to come.

Once within range, Major Goldwater ordered the release of his archers who were waiting just in case such an event happened. Two volleys of arrows and another from the siege weapons upon the stronghold hit the approaching horde before they made it to the barricaded perimeter. When the arch-goblins decided to retreat, not one Vorclaw soldier was harmed and another forty arch-goblins were dead. An additional twenty lizard-goblins lost their lives in the attack. More went scattering into the forest.

By now the wounded and limping Ironhold denizens were back to their stronghold which was ablaze in the courtyard. Chieftain Skraw ordered everyone under mountain and to seal the great doors. He realized that his captain was not among them. He ordered the stronghold doors shut and as they closed he saw his captain lying dead with arrows in him.

"They are charging on the walls," announced his lieutenant from the tower. "Everyone, get your bows and let's finish them!"

The chieftain's head was a whirl. He knew that was the logical idea but still he had it in his mind that he should take his people into the mountain and bar the gate, for the sake of his clan. In his indecisiveness, the arch-goblins mounted the walls instead.

"No!" he shouted, get under into the mountain. He then realized the sheer number of soldiers he saw and the powerful wizards.

And an explosion at the gates blew open the doors locking mechanisms. An additional volley flaming pitch from their nasty siege weapons set the courtyard and buildings ablaze. He counted six explosions this time though. It struck him as odd but halted anyone further from exiting the great doors from the mountain. Then he heard a shout that made him realise why he heard a sixth explosion, "Wizards!"

* * * * *

Yasmina and Archibald were at the exploded gate with six soldiers with full body shields. As if practiced, the two wizards entered the courtyard, turned and readied spells for the walls. The soldiers huddled around the two wizards as they readied their barrage. Arrows pinged off the large shields whose sole job was to protect the wizards.

Fist-sized rocks burst forth from their outstretched hands. The rocks spread outwards and up to the catwalks of the defensive walls. Whistling noises trailed as the rocks approached the walls until they exploded, taking with them arch-goblin, lizard-goblin and wall. Most of it went over the wall to land in a heap at the front of the stronghold.

Yasmina and Archibald then pulled forth wands. *Lightning strikes* emanated from those wands singeing, maiming or killing anything approaching.

With the gates blown open and the wall occupants dead or tending to fires, the Vorclawean Army didn't take long to get into the compound and laying waste to whatever creature they could find.

"Well done boys," said Archibald to those guarding him and Yasmina.

"Are we to have some fun now?" she asked.

"If you must," replied Archibald. "I prefer to watch the rest unfold. You three, escort my lady and see to it nothing befalls her. You other three remain with me."

Yasmina screamed with joy at the chance to use her power. She slowly conjured a *fireball*. Taking her time allowed her to accumulate the energy and mental acuity to devastating effects. She launched it on what was once Mimdrid's watch tower, exploding it asunder. Parts and pieces flew in all directions. Her escorts shielded her from the debris.

"Not so fast," said Yasmina as she saw a small herd of lizard-goblins running for the mountain gates as they slowly closed. Her *wand of lightning strikes* sent five lizard-goblins into fits. They were shaking and burning from the electrical blast. An arrow bounced off one of her shield soldiers. She saw the archer, a female arch-goblin from up on the wall. Another wave of the *lightning wand* sent that arch-goblin female running into a small building for protection but not before feeling the effects of electrical sting.

The Vorclawean soldiers laid waste to whatever they could find. They forcefully entered buildings, knocking over crude tables and killing anything that wasn't from Vorclaw. No building was spared. It was either wrecked or set ablaze or both.

Yasmina saw resistance up ahead. The great doors inside the mountain were closing but a barrier was formed so the remaining arch-goblins and lizard-goblins could get inside before the doors shut. Vorclawean archers exchanged arrows with arch-goblin crossbow bolts there. She made her way closer to the makeshift defensive position. The doors would be closed she realized in a matter of seconds. She broke into a trot with her guardians trying to keep her safe around her. Crossbow bolts now were coming her way but her *magical shields* protected her from normal missiles such as those. She levelled her *lightning wand* and released a stream into the barricade. She delighted at the sensation and the havoc it caused. Again, more bolts launched from her wand and her eyes lit up as fire took hold of both the barricade and the arch-goblins.

Neither more arch-goblins nor lizard-goblins would make it into the mountain. The doors were shut. It was now every arch-goblin or lizard-goblin for themselves as the army from Vorclaw poured into the stronghold.

Yasmina and her three shield-bearing soldiers walked up to the burning barricade. She cast a *wind of frost* so that it would extinguish the flames but also freeze anything left alive. She put her two hands together at their base.

She spoke some arcane words and from her came a powerful blast of cold air. She could then walk up to the great iron doors unabated. She stood about twenty feet from the doors and readied another spell.

Ash she began to harness the magical energies needed, a familiar voice stopped her.

"I know you are not about to blast open those doors, Yasmina?" asked Archibald.

She halted her spell but frustratingly so. She loved the destructive power she was capable of.

"You've had your fun. Remember, we are not going to open that door," said Archibald. "We are meant to seal it."

* * * * *

Leif was first awake. They all had their own beds but not privacy. Bjorn's snoring didn't help either as they all slept in a large room together.

Leif dared to wonder in the place he felt he had seen in a dream. Most of it was swept clean but was burned, boarded or damaged. He found his way to the front doors from where he originally entered the palace. There he found Teodor sitting on a small stone wall overlooking the city. Leif asked to join the elf as the sun rose from over the mountains to their right.

"The view of the mountains and the sunrise never gets old to me," said Teodor.

"Even the city still retains a certain beauty," complimented Leif.

"If only you'd seen it fifteen or so years ago, before the invasion," he said. "I have a question. How long ago were you found by your adopted parents in Vorclaw?" he asked.

"You were listening to me chat with the Mistress of Sanctuary were you not?" responded Leif.

Teodor merely shrugged.

"I was found about ten years ago in the mountains of Vorclaw. My father said I was wearing bloody clothes and this," said Leif showing off his light golden necklace. "It has a power to heal and hurt the undead when I deem it so or it's touched maliciously," said Leif. "That's not what's unique about it. It has no lock. It's as if it was woven around me and I have no memory of it."

Teodor looked at his necklace but said nothing. After several more moments of the sun rising over the mountains, he continued the conversation. "Tell me, Leif, is it?" making certain he got the large elf's name correct. "Have you ever heard the name Delvemoora?"

Leif sat back and paused before answering. He looked up at the sky wondering. "It sounds like an elven name, but I cannot say I have heard that name spoken allowed before."

"It is the name of the last rulers of Archangel."

"Did any of them survive?"

"The king, Ivanovh, was killed by Rom-Seti. The queen and her daughter escaped. One son is dead, buried in the mountains by the Mistress of Sanctuary, the other was captured or killed, never seen or heard from again. Of course, I divulge this for a reason, Leif."

"And that is?"

"You bear a resemblance to the Delvemoora family."

Leif suddenly laughed. Then he stopped himself, seeing Teodor was not joining him. "My apologies if I offended you," began Leif. "However, you said Archangel was destroyed fifteen years ago. I was found ten years ago. That is a lot of missing years."

"Perhaps," replied Teodor. "But possible."

"But just a coincidence," said Leif. "No, I am here to protect Vorclaw, nothing more."

"As you wish," replied Teodor staring at the valley below.

Leif took his leave of the other elf.

"One last question Leif," begged Teodor. Leif turned to hear but Teodor didn't. "Have you ever heard the name Alexie before?"

Leif didn't respond. He merely turned and walked away to wake his friends.

Teodor whispered aloud to Pallentine who was listening via his crystal ball, "Coincidence or not, he might be the lost prince after all."

* * * * *

Again, they all met for another healthy breakfast with Teodor in the morning. Leif did not speak of his discussions with Teodor to any of them. He wanted to get the Jade Tower and return to his family to save what he believed to be a war brewing.

After breakfast, the adventurers again came before the revenant Pallentine. The elven revenant was already seated in his throne when they arrived. His mask and robes were the same from the day before.

"I have decided to return the Jade Tower," he began.

"Thank you, archmage," said Leif with a sigh of relief.

"That's because none of you know the command word to release him or the other spirits you trapped with Rom-Seti."

"And thank you for your hospitality," said Bjorn.

"But only on one condition," Pallentine interrupted suddenly. Everyone was quiet, waiting for the response. "That you, elf," he said pointing at Leif, "after you delivered the tower to the arch-goblin queen, you must return it to me within a year."

"The mission we are on is, in part, to get Leif back from the arch-goblins," Bjorn protested "I will not see my brother sold into indentured servitude once more. Why him?"

"Because," said Pallentine, "he is not wise to the ways of his people. Teodor and myself could teach him much."

140

"Hurry up and agree so we can be gone from here," said Damon.

"Vorclaw is very far from here. I am not certain I could traverse the distance in a year let alone find my way back here," said Leif.

"You were transported to Sanctuary were you not?" replied Pallentine. "Your sources can do so again, I am certain."

"Do it elf," said Damon. "You will no longer have to lie about defeating a mantikhoras. Instead you will get new stories to share," he said.

"And you will teleport us all to Vorclaw?" replied Leif.

"Hardly," Pallentine replied dryly. "I will transport you to the Sanctuary, nothing more. It is up to yourselves to get home."

"But our mage is dead," said Damon, now agitated.

"I have means to return us all if you get us to Sanctuary," interrupted Dru. Everyone's head turned. "I will explain when we get to Sanctuary," he said but it did not dissuade Damon from looking at him in agitation.

"And when I come back, how long must I remain in your service?" asked Leif breaking the tension.

"Let's just say," intervened Teodor, "that will be left up to you to decide upon your return."

"We have much to show a lost elf," added the revenant. "We have much in common."

Leif looked to Bjorn for guidance.

"It is up to you brother," said Bjorn.

"I do not feel lost and I do not believe I am who you think I am. But if it will get my friends home and help me prevent further deaths in Vorclaw then I accept your conditions," replied Leif.

"You are very noble, Leif Foehammer," said Pallentine.

"An elven trait surely," said Teodor. "But undoubtedly a credit to your human upbringing to be sure," he finished with a deep bow.

"You don't have to do this Leif," said Lorez. "We can walk back, ride a boat or find another mage to transport us."

"I want to see my parents, my friend," responded Leif. "Let's all go home."

Teodor climbed down the steps from the throne and offered both the Jade Tower.

"Why can't he just transport us all to Vorclaw?" asked Leif of Teodor.

"Because, he has never been there and there is a risk involved when transporting to a place one has never been. Some of you may not arrive as you should," said Teodor.

Sker gulped at the thought of what that might mean.

Pallentine then opened a magical doorway, *mage's gate,* that put them just outside Sanctuary, as promised.

"I put a *binding* spell on the Jade Tower that will prevent Rom-Seti from calling out to undead minions to rescue him." The revenant then had another thought. "I am curious as to what she intends to do with the device. Does she perhaps intend to release him? But then why would she want to do that?"

Leif didn't have the answer to that. No one did. The adventurers turned to the portal. No one wanted to be the first to go through.

"It is quite safe," said Teodor sensing apprehension. So he tossed a small rock through. It landed in the grass on the other side, safely.

Sker went to Leif's side unsure of the door. "Hop on Sker, we go together."

Leif and Sker went through and when nothing happened, everyone followed. Then the *mage's gate* closed behind them all. They were all standing once again before the Sanctuary.

"That ended well," said Lorez.

"Not so arch-goblin, we lost our wizard mind you," said Bjorn.

"How do you intend to get us home?" asked Damon of Dru who still seemed agitated that he had a plan to return them.

"I have a ring to teleport me back home," said Dru.

"You what?" said Damon.

"You could have sent word home and asked for a rescue all along?" asked Bjorn.

"I could have left yes but would I have been able to return to you all? I have no idea. At least now my uncle Anthon knows where this place is and he can do the same as those creepy elves just did for us. No offence, Leif."

"Welcome," came a girl's voice. "It is good to see you all again. Will you be staying for lunch?" asked a girl with light gray skin, red eyes and black hair, who stood next to a large brown bear. She wore green and brown leather armour with a bow over her shoulder and short sword at her hip.

"My lady Denisia," said Leif. "We would be honored."

"I will be back to you all as soon as I locate my uncle," said Dru. He turned his ring clockwise once, said his last name, turned it clockwise again and he was gone.

* * * * *

"I am surprised you gave back the Jade Tower, you hate Rom-Seti, as do I," said Teodor to the revenant as soon as the *mage's gate* closed.

"Yes, but allowing this mission to continue will bring back that boy-elf to us. Keeping the Jade Tower would only drive him away."

"As you wish," replied Teodor.

"Besides, we now have more important work to do at Rom-Seti's lair!"

Chapter 20
Sealing Deals

"Place all the wooden items you can find into the towers of the stronghold," ordered Major Goldwater to his officers. "Include our siege weapons we recently made. Shove as much wood as you can into the tower walls. I want to burn them out. Make the stonework cracked and brittle."

While one of the captains protested that the wood alone would not be enough to bring down the stronghold walls of Ironhold, Major Goldwater had wizards at his disposal.

"The wizards have used a spell, a powerful spell, to transform some of the *stone to dirt*. By doing so at key points, the structure has become much less stable," he explained looking at Archibald. "That, together with the burning, should crack or even topple the more solid defence points."

"I have seen it work in Uden," announced Archibald referring to his time working with the Uden Army.

"In the meantime, I want the rest of our soldiers finishing their work on the iron doors that lead into the mountain," said the major.

At Archibald's direction, the soldiers were covering the doors in layers of dirt that was pulled from trenches dug from around the outer tower walls of Ironhold to further weaken the foundations. That dirt was then transported to the iron doors that led into the mountain. It took his entire force nearly two days but the door, now covered by a ramp of dirt and rock, was ready to be sealed by magic. The dirt was kept wet by collecting water from the wells inside the stronghold. The door was completely covered by mud and dirt at least two feet deep at the top and ten feet at the bottom. Archibald intended to use the same spell that transformed some of the keystones to dirt on the iron doors but in reverse.

Yasmina didn't enjoy this spell. It wasn't aggressive enough and she would rather have smashed down the iron doors instead of sealing them in a ramp of stone. Her counterpart, Archibald, loved the idea. He said they may never get out that way since the doors must swing out to open.

It took several minutes to prepare the components and the soldiers gathered to watch the two wizards work in tandem. Holding hands, they read simultaneously from their magically floating books while holding spell components; they grabbed some dirt prepositioned on a table and a placed it in a bowl of clear water. Then they said the verbal parts of the spell. The mud and dirt covering the iron doors began to harden as water vapour began to rise from the obstacle as it became stone. The soldiers cheered.

"Well done, fine job all of you!" shouted Major Goldwater. "Now let us burn this place so they know never to return to our lands!" he shouted.

Yasmina happily went to the one tower and sent flames forth from her hands igniting one tower while the soldiers burned the other. Doors, tables and wood were spread throughout to burn any wooden beam, roof or other part of the stronghold. Eventually the soldiers evacuated the entire stronghold and watched as Ironhold burned from every visible arrow slit, opening and rooftop. After about an hour, Yasmina sent a hail of fire at the base of her tower. It didn't topple. She then discharged the remains of her *lightning wand* at the same location. A slight rumble echoed and part of the external tower walls began to come down. Cut rocks and fire exploded outwards. And the soldiers cheered again!

*   *   *   *   *

Dru emerged from the underground dwellings of the Academy of Arms; it was where the ring had deposited him. Unfortunately, he returned to a horror of a sight. He wasn't certain how to feel but he did not feel well. Guilt came to mind for sure. Like his father, he too was mad at the ruling council but for different reasons. Dru disliked how they deployed the military constantly around the country for extended lengths of time where they themselves often never spent time in the military. Some soldiers were gone for years at a time. Some soldiers came back to dead loved ones, lovers who had moved on or resentful children. He was one of those resentful children.

Dru was present when his mother was killed in the crossfire of a wizard's duel, dying in his arms while his father was away with the military. It fuelled his anger for resentment to the Wizard's College, the ruling council and even his father. So he turned a blind eye to his father's plans to create the Black-masks. He turned a blind eye to his father's plans to unseat the power of the council; he never really bothered to ask how but presumed it was by way of the Black-masks. He also turned a blind eye to his father's connections to the Shadow Company, thanks to his uncle Anthon.

However, he had no idea that his father would ruin Sedgedunum, the capital of Vorclaw to exact his revenge. What may have once been a bonding moment between him and his father was now a nightmare that he never realized he was to have been a part of until it was all too late. He felt guilty by association; guilty by knowing that something drastic could happen. But how could it come to this? And how many had died?

He went to his father's office which was under guard at the Academy of Arms. Although his father was the general of the armies of Vorclaw, he kept his office at the academy. It also gave him direct access to the underground ruins Vorclaw was built upon. Dru got a brief from the guard on what had befallen the city. It practically confirmed that his father might be the mastermind behind the attack on the city, although he was not certain anyone would believe him now that his devious father made himself into the hero. Thanks to the guard's information, Dru made his way to the temporary headquarters established by his father, at the northern city gate. He had to hear it from his father's own mouth.

* * * * *

"Thank you, Mr. Night, on the update regarding the successful campaign led by Major Goldwater," said General Baltus Blackpool.

Present at the meeting was the new head of the Wizard's College, Horatio Mercutio, the general's brother Anthon Blackpool, Admiral Drake Kahee and Lord Handle Nightingale.

"Thanks to the White Eagles out of Fort Adamant, yourself of course, and the two wizards you provided. We can now work towards the restoration of Sedgedunum and the creation of a new ruling council. That is why you are also here Lord Nightingale," said Baltus.

"And what of the bishops and other lords you have under arrest?" demanded Handel. It was unusual for Lord Handel Nightingale to be defiant, especially since he helped promote the general to the council position of General of the Armies of Vorclaw.

"They will all go back to their places of worship or estates they have gained for their time after I decided I am done with them. I asked their respective clergy to provide replacements if they wished and I even added recommendations. Ones that have served in the army of course, that way, I hope they will serve for the good of Vorclaw, and not themselves," said the general now standing over Lord Nightingale. "But I understand your rash words, it's not nice to sit in a jail cell not knowing what your crimes are or how you might be punished," he said staring at him.

"But luckily for you, your presence on the council is the youngest, second only to my own and knowing your aunt for all my life, gives me some insight about the integrity of your family," he said.

"Hear-hear!" said Admiral Kahee who also knew both the Blackpool's and the Nightingales growing up. The admiral really wanted something to do other than think about his dead son he recently buried at sea.

"Therefore, you will remain on the council with me, the admiral, the new headmaster of the wizard's academy Horatio, who you already know. Your family will oversee the restoration of Sedgedunum."

"You risk civil war," said Handel as if his new appointment mattered not. "Once Lord Igor Frothbeard from Irons-by-the-Sea gets word of this."

"Lord Igor Frothbeard, the dwarven arms dealer from Irons-by-the-Sea is dead," explained the admiral. "The mayor of the city tried to take him into custody and he fought back resulting in his own death, I am afraid."

"The Mayor of the City of Irons-by-the-Sea is a female elf by the name of Dominika Gildedwing. I am told the two were good friends but her loyalty is to Vorclaw while his, I am told, to his bank account," explained the general.

"I sent a ship for her and she will arrive within a fortnight to give us the details," said the admiral.

"And what of the rest of the council?" asked Handel.

"We will get to that once the remaining are rounded up. But Sedgedunum must be healed first."

"You general have got the country in your pocket, don't you?" said Handel defiantly staring at the man from his chair.

"Handel," interjected Horatio, "Be reasonable. This is a time of war and war brings about change."

"Says the man who now sits on the throne of wizards," replied Handel. Horatio rolled his eyes in response.

After some silence Handel stood up and said, "May I leave, general? I want to report to my aunt and start supervising the covering of the scars of Sedgedunum," he said. The general nodded and Lord Handle Nightingale took his leave of the council.

* * * * *

Lord Handel Nightingale, who was usually well dressed, was not in his best outfit. Therefore, Dru Blackpool didn't even notice him when he passed him on the cobblestone road.

"Dru?" inquired Lord Handel.

"My lord?" said a surprised Dru Blackpool. "It has been sometime. How are you? What has transpired here?" he asked.

"You don't know? Where have you been? The city came under attack a few weeks ago by the arch-goblins. Led by some vampire and wizards, we're told. It is now believed they had a score to settle with the Wizards College since an iron-golem was used to wreck the college and knock down the tower. While that was taking place, the arch-goblins wrecked and plundered much of the northern city," said the lord. "Where have you been?"

"Where is my father?"

"He is in there," said Handel, pointing to a large room in the Academy of Arms. "He has taken over the council and declared military law," continued Lord Handel, still upset by it all. "Your father has used this as an excuse to seize control of the council and arrested many of them."

"Arrested!"

"I too was arrested and spent over a week in jail, just released yesterday. Your father blames the council for much of the folly of this city."

"What happened to the people, to the arch-goblins, where are they all now?" asked Dru.

"Your father's army liberated the city by abandoning Fort Adamant. That is now under arch-goblin control as well but he doesn't seem to care about that. He sent a major to lay siege to Ironhold, the arch-goblin stronghold at the back of the forest. It was from there it seems the attack was launched. Seems they have levelled that stronghold and rescued over two hundred citizens.

The good news about his father liberating citizens and destroying the arch-goblin stronghold made Dru think that his father might not be the villain he believed. But then again, Dru above all knew his father had a gift at manipulation and knew, deep down, his father was involved deeper than Lord Handel believed.

"But he has taken over the council and is replacing it with former military members or people directly loyal to him," said the lord who was now whispering. "And I worry he risks civil war in the future. Several council members are already dead from this. I am only free because my family's business is needed to help repair the city. Speak to your father Dru, for our country's sake."

"I know my father can be stubborn and may have an axe to grind against the council but rest assured I will speak to him and do my best to prevent anything like that from happening," said Dru.

"Best of luck to you Dru Blackpool," said Lord Nightingale but Dru could not tell if he was genuine or being sarcastic.

* * * * *

"Father," said Dru interrupting the meeting between Horatio Mercutio, the general's brother Anthon Blackpool, Mr. Night and Admiral Drake Kahee.

"Son! Finally, how?" began Baltus but was cut short by Admiral Kahee.

"What happened to my son on that mission?" asked the admiral.

"I would prefer to speak to you, my father and my uncle in private," replied Dru.

Baltus excused Horatio and Mr. Night from the room. Horatio obliged not knowing the admiral's son had died and respected his wishes. Mr. Night who was the shape-changer Mimdrid, was more than a little curious but an eye from Baltus signaled that he best depart.

Dru went to his father's liquor cabinet and poured himself a brandy and drank it down exceedingly fast.

"By the gods what has happened here?" Dru asked.

"One thing at a time, son. First, explain to the admiral how his son died?" Dru looked confused. "How did you know?"

"Your family is not the only ones with means," explained the admiral. "My son, my other son Ruko, retrieved his remains. What I want to know is how he died? His spirit told us it was a flesh-golem, is that correct?"

"His spirit?" Dru poured another. "Yes, that is correct, he was knocked off a cliff by the beast." Dru realized the admiral was still in grief over the death. "He was very brave, and likely saved us all. He battled the revenant with success but with much of his spells spent and other creatures closing in during our escape, he fell victim to an unfortunate moment in time," explained Dru.

The admiral came to face Dru. He put both hands on Dru's shoulders and whispered, "Thank you." He then walked out of the room.

"What took you so long to return?" asked Anthon. Dru hardly noticed the question. The last time Dru saw any kind of father's love for his son was when he saw Magnus Foehammer's interaction with Bjorn and Leif.

"Why did you not teleport or use the scroll tube to write?" asked Baltus.

"It is good to see you too, father, and you uncle. I am fine thanks," replied Dru who poured another drink but Baltus took away the glass.

"Seriously, father," replied Dru. "Do you really believe I would leave Bjorn and Leif on their own? And the one scroll tube you gave us uncle, you gave to your apprentice. It went over the falls with him."

Baltus handed his son back his drink.

"Tell us what happened and where is everyone presently. Then we will tell you what transpired while you were gone."

"I will but you're not going to believe what we experienced!"

* * * * *

Separate from the long house in the Sanctuary, Leif, Denisia and the Mistress of Sanctuary sat comfortably around a small table in her dwelling that was cut into the stone of the mountain.

"Thank you for having us again," said Leif to the Mistress of Sanctuary and she nodded in response. "Did the orcs or lycaons come seek you?"

She looked at him curiously not understanding.

Leif then addressed Denisia. "Did you inform your mother of the orcs and lycaons?"

"I did but no one came to us thereafter regarding the incident," she responded.

Leif then pulled forth the totem given to him by Rreebish. "This totem represents a friendship I made along the path back to you," he said looking to both the ladies. "It was given to me by the leader of the lycaons, a creature who calls himself Rreebish. I told him he could come and see you to verify the story of the orcs being attacked in the mountains by his lycaons. Your knowledge of the truth of that day lady may prevent an outright war between the orcs and the lycaons here in the region," he said looking at Denisia.

"My knowledge?"

"Seems his lycaons told him a different version of the events that day," said Leif.

"If he arrives, I will tell him what I saw," replied Denisia.

The Mistress of Sanctuary changed the subject. "Did you complete your mission and get what you were after?"

Leif then pulled forth the Jade Tower. "He is in there. But it came at a price. We lost our wizard and by all accounts, a friend to some of my friends. My brother Bjorn nearly died were it not for his faith and some forest-dames who shared his deity. And I was captured by both lycaons and lizard-goblins. Somehow, I made it through," he said with a half-hearted smile.

"Interesting," she replied.

"As you wish mistress, however I think the whole experience was terrible," he said. Leif thought that comment was odd, expecting more sympathy than anything.

"No, that's not what's interesting," she replied, eyeing the Jade Tower and smiling.

"Ah, what then?" asked Leif confused.

"Interesting that you referred to your human brother's deity as his and not yours," she said.

Leif was caught by surprise and almost embarrassed. He had attended the worship of Matronae, the deity of his human family. But now he pondered as if he really followed her or not. He did admit to himself that he did not feel a connection to Matronae but had never spoken it aloud.

"And the horrid creature is within?" asked the Mistress of Sanctuary. Leif nodded in response. "And what did you make of Archmage Pallentine then?" she asked.

"A curious creature," pondered Leif. "Oddly, he asked me to return to him in the next year. I think he and Teodor seem to think I am related to the former ruling family or something."

The mistress looked up and smiled. She implanted that seed in Teodor's head but said nothing.

"You will come back to see us again?" asked Denisia. "Once your work in Vorclaw is complete?"

"I would very much like too, yes," responded Leif.

"Please put that thing away and never show or speak of it again to me," she said. She abruptly got up and said to wait for her return.

"I am glad you returned," said Denisia quietly. "I feared you would not, I mean, that you might be killed on your journey," she said somewhat flustered. "You are very brave you know," she said.

Leif smiled. "It was the right thing to do, to go on this mission," said Leif. "I hope to end hostilities between the arch-goblins and my country when I return with this device. Seems this creature we captured has attacked their queen and proof of the capture of this evil I hope will end other forms of evil," he explained.

The mistress of Sanctuary returned holding something. "Have you seen this before?" she asked holding out an elven dagger. It was small but elegant.

Leif took the blade in hand. Somehow it seemed familiar. He did not answer though. This whole journey had him confused.

"It is yours," she said. Leif suddenly felt faint but held his composure; he did feel as if he had held this blade before.

"Consider it a gift for taking that abomination away from the mountains," she finished.

Leif closed his eyes and almost laughed aloud. How could this have ever been his dagger? Teodor's discussions and his tired head were playing tricks on his emotions, he reasoned.

He nodded in appreciation but she was staring at him as if waiting for a reaction of some kind.

Leif then stood up and said, "Thank you my lady I will cherish it and use it wisely. Ladies, if I may, I would now like to join my comrades in the long house for a rest."

Part III: Spoils of War

Chapter 21
The Spy Among Us

"Ironhold has shut its doors, my queen," announced Chieftain Blist. "They have retreated behind their iron doors."

Queen Ooktha's response was to drink blood from a chalice and roll her eyes as if she cared. Instead she marveled over the finest of stolen gems and necklaces from Sedgedunum. She had them laid out for viewing over her large wooden dining table where both she and Chieftain Blist often ate and discussed issues of concern. She was a mage herself and made certain these contained no magic properties before sampling.

"I like this ruby necklace," she said. "I can only imagine the actual cost of it on the markets of Uden or Dubravna," she said aloud. She then moved on to the bracelets.

"There is more to my report," announced the chieftain.

Queen Ooktha sipped some more blood as if it were wine from her chalice and motioned for him to continue as she looked over her new-found treasures.

"I have also received word Ironhold wrote a treaty with General Blackpool ceasing hostilities for the exchange of prisoners," said the chieftain. "The new chieftain of Ironhold took it upon himself to sign without your consent."

Queen Ooktha stopped marveling over the diamond bracelets and turned to view Chieftain Blist holding a rolled-up parchment. He handed it to her. It was the treaty. After reading it she dropped it to the ground and said, "Skraw is a bigger fool than Gutter was." After several moments, another question came to her. "If he has closed himself into the mountain, what is to stop the Vorclawean Army from ransacking the stronghold?"

"Nothing, my queen. In fact, it is already under the enemy's control. They have been tearing it down for the last two days. Chieftain Skraw has come to tell us so personally," he said with a toothy grin of anger.

She too looked at the chieftain in anger. "Bring him to my throne room."

The chieftain bowed and left. Once the doors were closed, she threw her chalice of blood into the fire pit and let out a nightmarish wail of anger.

* * * * *

"Don't kill me my queen!" begged Chieftain Skraw, grovelling at her booted feet. "I was bewitched by powerful magics!" he explained, panting. "I was captured and teleported by a creature that changes shape."

153

"What else?" she demanded baring her fangs.

"The shape changer and human general said they had more spies but would remove them if I signed the treaty."

"Fool! And you believed him," shouted Chieftain Blist kicking Skraw in the ribs. Ooktha merely smiled.

"No, but I was bewitched by wizards," replied Skraw once he regained his breath.

Queen Ooktha then bent low to the ground, just above the face of the prone Chieftain Skraw. She lifted his face gently with two fingers by the chin. "Tell me more about this shape changer," she inquired seductively. She used her vampirism power of persuasion upon the arch-goblin.

"My queen, I sought out a growing dissension among the ranks of Ironhold. Someone poisoned your sweet name there and tried to start a rebellion. I did a test among my officers and found one to be untrustworthy. When I confronted him, he attacked me and my warriors. He possessed the strength of an ogre. Then he used some ring to teleport he and I to the Vorclaw siege camp. I then witnessed him change instantly from an arch-goblin to a human. I was then spelled into a haze. When I came to, I was being exchanged for the human captives and holding the treaty to end hostilities."

"What was the dissension?" asked chieftain Blist. But Skraw refused to answer. He was now visibly shaking.

"Tell me my sweet chieftain," said Queen Ooktha. "It is all right to speak it so we can stop it."

Reluctantly, Skraw opened his mouth. "Several arch-goblins heard that you had no arch-goblin blood ties. That you are a full elf-witch come to poison the arch-goblins," he said.

Queen Ooktha stood up suddenly holding Skraw by the neck, the arch-goblin gasping for air. She then squeezed his neck with both hands crushing into his spine, shaking him and screaming. She threw him across the room, dead. Chieftain Blist backed away but lowered to one knee showing his obedience.

"Tell me Blist, am I not your kin?" she asked testing him.

"You are my king and queen, my lady," he said knowing the kin part was a lie. He used that ruse long ago to gain the upper hand over the other arch-goblin cities and by having the vampire on an arch-goblin throne gave him free reign to rule as well.

"Then how did this lie happen?" she asked angrily. Chieftain Blist was smart enough not to answer.

It was then she realized what Skraw was seeing. A creature who possessed great strength and could change shape. They had a shape-changer posing as an arch-goblin!

* * * * *

"I believe they have a shape-changer," said Queen Ooktha conferring with her mentor, Revenant Niss through her magical mirrors.

"It would make sense," responded the revenant. "It explains how the general knew how to find you and get letters to you undetected. The creature must've passed through one of your strongholds and came into his employment."

"How does anyone find or fight such a creature?" asked Revenant Niss, providing no real insight nor really caring.

"Have you heard from your contact in the mountains near Rom-Seti's necropolis?" asked Queen Ooktha.

"Not since the last time we spoke. If you recall he sent his minion to search for the artefact and your lover. I am meeting with him tomorrow," she said.

Queen Ooktha was only half listening now. The mention of Leif as her lover pained her. She battled his adopted parents on the streets of Sedgedunum. Once Leif finds out, how could he ever return with the same affections?

"I said the Jade Tower must be found before he returns to you," Revenant Niss repeated seeing Queen Ooktha's mind was suddenly elsewhere.

"Yes, my mentor, of course."

"If Rom-Seti is indeed in there, the Jade Tower becomes a powerful artefact to whoever controls it. But more importantly, Rom-Seti now knows that we all were in league together in this. You, me, and my own mentor," said Revenant Niss. "If Rom-Seti was to be released before being destroyed and he notified the Union of Undead, there would be war among us all."

"Then how do we kill him once and for all?"

"Once we know he is captured, I will then go to his pyramid to find his *soul-sepulchre* and destroy it. Then we will release him on our terms and we will attack him together. He is already weakened from the fight you sent him. He will be no match for us girls and my mentor!" said Revenant Niss.

"Your mentor, he would join us in battle?" asked Queen Ooktha. "I thought he sees the Union of Undead as vile and me an abomination."

"He's a xenophobic arse but he will join because he hates Rom-Seti more than anything," replied Revenant Niss.

Queen Ooktha nodded and smiled. "In the meantime, what do you recommend I do about my arch-goblins in Ironhold and this shape-changer?"

"Shape-changers, my dear value their life well above all others. Now that *it* is found out, it will not return, not for some time. As for Ironhold, it will take time but keep them sealed in; you have your other two cities to repopulate Ironhold with a new brood. In other words, let them stay sealed in until they become a healthy force again, maybe a decade from now. That is not so long even when you were a living elf."

"Very well. Thank you, my teacher," said Ooktha and Revenant Niss nodded in reply. "I look forward to hearing then from you regarding Leif's whereabouts and if he succeeded," she said.

"Until tomorrow then," responded Revenant Niss.

Dunkin Saltclaw was able to inquire with the locals as to the home of Magnus and Disa Foehammer. However, no one was home. A neighbour explained that he may best starting with the infirmary, hearing that they were both were hurt during the invasion, Disa Foehammer especially. The man made his way down the muddy Main Street of Sedgefen, destined for the farm that housed the infirmary. This small village outside Sedgedunum became the makeshift infirmary centre for the wounded of the capital city. Dunkin no longer wore armour; all was confiscated upon his incarceration at Fort Adamant for striking Mr. Night. He was armed only with a knife and wooden spear he found.

The shouts and screams still echoed in the infirmary, even though the arch-goblin horde had been driven off over a week ago. Pain, sickness and the dying however, had yet to be played out in Sedgefen. After hearing from a villager about what transpired in Sedgedunum, the now retired master sergeant was sickened that he could not be part of the city's defence. He cursed his arrogance that put him in jail in the first place but at the same time he knew something was amiss about Mr. Night and he confirmed some of that to be true.

During the evacuation of Fort Adamant, Dunkin was a straggler on his way out of the fort. At night he witnessed a large red-haired arch-goblin running along Panther Paw Pass. That arch-goblin transformed into a man he knew as Mr. Night. Dunkin wasn't certain but assumed Mr. Night was not human and must be some form of spy, possibly for the arch-goblins.

The man made his way into several tents seeing firsthand the ravages of war and the casualties it left behind. Bludgeoned, cut, amputated and burned victims moaned in pain. It was a sickening sight. Faiths of all kinds went around the tents trying to mitigate the suffering as best they could. Dunkin asked the clergy but could not locate Magnus or Disa Foehammer. Dunkin made it to another tent where the dead were sent and waited to be disposed of. Incense burned to smooth the smell of decay. Several weeping people were in there, grieving the loss of their loved ones.

It was here he found a large man sitting next to a woman's body covered by a white sheet embroidered with the markings of Matronae. Dunkin felt for the man. He obviously lost someone very dear to him, a wife probably. The man looked frail and malnourished, as if he had not eaten in days. He thought to ask the man some questions but didn't dare intrude on his bereavement.

Dunkin exited the tent of the dead and looked around for a tavern or an inn. He was given some money by Captain Ty and had several coins saved with the bank at Sedgedunum, if it still existed. But after several days on the open road he needed a place to rest. He inquired about such places but after another hour of searching, every place was full because of the evacuees from Sedgedunum. With no other place to go he went to the Foehammer residents once again. He pulled his hood over his head tightly as the rain started to fall.

He shivered outside for what seemed like an hour. The sun was starting to set and the chill from the rain was beginning to dig into his bones. He was now feeling lost and hopeless.

It was then he spotted a tall man coming down the muddy road in the rain. He too had his cloak pulled tight to keep out the chill. He suddenly stopped and stared at Dunkin, not certain what to make of him. The rain was really coming down hard as the tall man walked up to him directly and hugged him! It was then Dunkin realized this frail and tall man who was grieving hours before was indeed Magnus Foehammer.

"Sergeant Major, I bring good news for you during these troubled times," said Dunkin.

Magnus's wet face smiled back. "Come, let's start a fire and talk," said Magnus.

* * * * *

Magnus drank from a bottle of alcohol he had in his modest home in Sedge Fen. "It took her two days to die," said Magnus in tears.

"Sergeant Major, I am sorry for your loss," responded Dunkin.

"My wife saved me earlier from the same female vampire. It seemed it did not like that and hunted her down. Somehow the vampire…" Magnus couldn't even finish the sentence.

Dunkin thought he sounded confused but Magnus tried to explain further.

"I was attacked by a vampire alongside some ruffians. However, the leader of those ruffians seemed to know who I was and who the vampire was but how?"

Once Magnus's last name was spoken aloud, the vampire ceased her attack on him.

"Then Disa appeared with reinforcements and attacked the vampire. Then there was no trace of the ruffian leader or his men."

"A vampire?" said Dunkin surprised and not knowing what to say about that. "Is there anything I can do for you? Perhaps things that you need to do while you attend to laying your wife to rest?"

Magnus didn't respond but just drank some more from the bottle.

Dunkin then grabbed two cups from the shelf and took the bottle from his old mentor. "I have news that may brighten your day," he said pouring drinks for them both. "Leif is alive!" he said.

Magnus began to cry some more but he grabbed Dunkin by the shoulders as he almost collapsed.

"Tell me, how is this true?"

"I was told by your son Bjorn who arranged my release. He bade me to come to you and explain what I knew of your son and what Bjorn knew."

"Your release?"

"I was jailed for striking a man who was supposed to be our liaison to dealing with the arch-goblins in the Fort Adamant region. His information got the entire Gold Company from the White Eagles killed as well as Major Titus, the White Eagles Battalion commander and even the commander of Vorclaw's Army, Lord Brisbane," he said. "I thought I was the only survivor. I was left unconscious, attacked from behind. But Lieutenant Foehammer was taken prisoner. Yet somehow he gained favor among them and lives."

"What! How do you know this?"

"Bjorn told me. He said they were on a mission to free him," said Dunkin. "Though, he would say no more, it was secret. But Captain Ty of Blue Company was there with Bjorn when he told me. Captain Ty too seemed as surprised as I."

"Why did Bjorn not say anything to me of this?" he said to himself knowing Dunkin could not give an answer.

"He said something about bartering for his life," said Dunkin. "Likely Bjorn did not want you to worry."

Magnus sat down, totally drained. Not knowing the whereabouts of his sons and losing his wife suddenly, he thought he might descend into madness and knew not where to turn.

"I do not know the answers to a lot of the questions that must be going through your head," said Dunkin. "But I must also tell you what I saw during the battle I shared with your son," said Dunkin. Magnus looked up. "You have trained him up well He had trained him up well. He became a great young leader. He controlled the scene as well as any commander, directing archers and laying out arch-goblins with both his sword and shield. He killed several for sure."

It was a lot to take in for Magnus. He laughed loudly at the thought Leif was alive and had performed well at the ambush. It then dawned on him suddenly. Only one person could garner information about Leif and sanction such a mission, General Blackpool.

"I have to go," he said suddenly. "I have to find General Blackpool. The orders, the mission, all would have come from him."

"Wait! There is more," said Dunkin.

"More?"

"Yes, have you ever heard of a man known as Mr. Night?"

Chapter 22
Promises and Deceit

"It's carved in the shape of a lycaon," said Denisia, the daughter to the Mistress of Sanctuary. "What does the rune-work down the back mean?" Leif and Denisia sat near one of the many shrines that lay around Sanctuary. It was Leif who joined Denisia. She often chose different shrines to sit at and today she chose Airia, the goddess of air and mother to elven kind.

"I believe it means one who is a friend to the lycaons," replied Leif.

"I am told below the mountains there is a plain that is used by the lycaons," she said. "This could become useful if you make your way back to us on foot," she responded handing the totem back to him.

"You really wish me to return?" replied Leif with a smile at the half human and half dark elf female.

"I do and my mother believes you will come back as well."

"Oh. Why is that?" he asked.

"She believes you are some kind of chosen one," she said openly. "What that means and for who or what, she would not say."

Leif merely laughed but was uneasy at the comment. Teodor and Pallentine secured his return on his honor. Seems he wasn't the only one interested in him. "And what do you think, young lady?" asked Leif to see if there was more information about what the interest was in him and his unknown past.

"I just think you're a crazy elf," she said. "One who is a bit too cavalier with his own life," she said staring at Leif.

"Well, I can understand why you would say that. But I came prepared. My armour and weapons were enhanced but more importantly, it was for the greater good," Leif said to her staring back. "I believe it is for the greater good," he said turning his gaze outward, wondering how he was to get the Jade Tower to Queen Ooktha, but he hadn't a clue, not yet. "You know, there are a lot of sights to see up in these mountains."

"Are you returning?" she asked.

"My return might have something to do with the promise I made to your mother's friends," said Leif. "I will return to Archangel and therefore I intend to come this way as well," he said smiling.

Denisia then leaned into Leif's arm and hugged it. "I am glad," she said. "You seem like a good person, even if you are foolish with your life," she said.

"Tell me more about your adventure in the mountains? Tell me about the forest-dames. Were they pretty?"

* * * * *

Lorez watched on from a distance along with Sker from just outside the longhouse entrance. The two had not spoken much. Lizard-goblins were beneath arch-goblins after all. Therefore, Sker never engaged with Lorez unless the arch-goblin started it. Lorez watched from the corner of his eye how the young half elf adored Leif. Furthermore, Lorez knew full well Leif would be returning to a war-torn nation regardless of this journey's outcome. He knew of the planned assault on Sedgedunum and the betrayal his own chieftain concocted with Dru's father to obliterate Ironhold's forces. Even if Leif returned with the Jade Tower, there would be no peace waiting for them on their return.

Lorez had to make a choice, let the lie play out and deal with it on their return or make the lie known now before Dru opened a doorway back to Vorclaw.

"What do you think Sker?" began Lorez in arch-goblin, knowing Sker spoke it. "Is he to receive a hero's welcome?"

"Hero to Queen Ooktha yes but his heart will be torn apart when he returns, from what whispers Sker has heard."

"Do tell, "said Lorez.

"I know of a deal made by Chieftain Merka of Blood-helm and the human wizard Anthon, uncle to Leif's friend Dru."

"How do you know this?" asked Lorez curiously as if reading his mind.

"Iza one of a few lizard-goblins who can speak many languages. Not much good at fighting so I listen. So too does Master Leif. He is very observant. But Iza also steward to Master Leif and to Chieftain Merka."

"Does the elf know?"

"Iza do not believe Master Leif knows of the deal between chieftain and wizard," responded Sker. "But Master Leif is suspicious of this endeavour to be sure and of your chieftain."

Sker was of course speaking of the rumors he heard during his time at Blood-helm regarding negotiations between Anthon Blackpool, Mr. Knight and Chieftain Merka for the handover of Fort Adamant—all sanctioned by General Blackpool—in exchange for remaining out of the war.

"Why even do this, all of this, this journey? Why not run away?"

"He has to try for peace and would willingly stay with Queen Ooktha to keep peace in the region," explained Sker.

Lorez wondered how Leif would take to the news that no war was going to happen between Blood-helm and Fort Adamant but one between Sedgedunum and Ironhold was inevitable. No, the war Leif was led to believe this mission would stop was never going to happen because of the secret pact made by Chieftain Merka without Queen Ooktha's knowledge!

"Peace in the Fort Adamant region is not the problem," responded Lorez. He knew Sedgedunum would have been attacked by now but wasn't certain if Sker also knew that much. "There can be no peace for Leif in the end," said Lorez.

Sker did not answer but looked somewhat confused, signaling that Sker did not know as much as Lorez regarding the attack on Sedgedunum, the attack concocted by General Blackpool and his brother Anthon. For what purpose the attack served the Blackpool's, Lorez could only guess.

"If we tell him what we know, it will devastate him," said Lorez aloud.

"Iza say nothing because I know how much he cares for his human friend, Dru. But I wonder how much does Dru know about the deception playing out in Leif's homeland," said Sker.

"You have a very inquisitive mind little lizard-goblin," said Lorez now wondering that Sker may know even more than anyone! "Keep an eye out for Leif and let me know if his life is in danger."

It was the only compliment Sker ever heard from an arch-goblin, from anyone other than Leif. Sker looked up to half smile at the arch-goblin but saw that Lorez was now listening intently at Bjorn and Damon's conversation within the longhouse.

* * * * *

Bjorn was making the hot meal for everyone, uncertain how long Dru would take to locate his uncle Anthon and open the magical door to get them home. Damon and Dru sat quietly in the longhouse in front of a fire and the pot of stew Bjorn was preparing. No one else was there.

"How much do you honestly know about what we are returning to?" asked Damon of Bjorn.

Bjorn looked at the man but then looked back to his stew, not answering.

"Do you not know the truth of it all?" inquired Damon.

Bjorn still refused to look at the man.

"Ah so you do know what we are returning to at Vorclaw?" pressed Damon.

"What I know is none of your concern, assassin," replied Bjorn.

Damon rolled his eyes and chuckled. "Of course, you knew all along that this was in part, a ploy to get the general's beloved son and the Foehammer boy away from the general's plot. As if it somehow it absolved you all of the sin. Vorclaw has hypocrisy in the clergy as well as in the military I see. At least I know what I stand for."

"Ha and what is that?" asked Bjorn. "I am told you could not even follow orders which is why you were dishonorably discharged from the armies of Uden," said Bjorn scornfully.

Damon had a look of distaste now and Bjorn knew he had hit a nerve.

"You know, I was very sceptical of the general's decision to employ you as a mentor to Dru," pressed Bjorn. "But I figured it is best not to judge a person before getting to know a person," he added.

"And?" asked Damon who stood up instantly.

It surprised Bjorn how fast the much shorter and older man was on his feet.

"Thankfully for you, I report only to the general," said Bjorn, not backing down. "I will make certain your contributions of harassment towards my brother, mistreatment of his lizard-goblin friend and lack of support when surrounded by lycaons is well noted," said Bjorn now standing looking at the man.

"I led us in there and out, not you, nor your brother."

"Good," said Bjorn. "Then I will leave it to you tell Ruko Kahee how his brother Erik died," said Bjorn to smite Damon.

"After this mission is over, you would do well to stay clear of me," said Damon after a few moments of silence.

"Then you would do well to take your own advice!" announced Bjorn.

"And if you keep pushing me, I might let out that you knew all too well the general's plans to wreck Sedgedunum and take the country for himself. With the Shadow Company's financial backing of course," said Damon.

That surprised Bjorn. He had no idea Sedgedunum was to be wrecked! Bjorn was privy to the general's coup and thought it best for the good of the nation; Bjorn was a Black-mask after all. Damon must be speaking about the coup, not an attack on the city.

"You Shadow Company are a wicked brood, aren't you? You lot are nothing more than a bunch of thieves and cut throats, only caring about filling your pockets. But then again that's probably why you found a home with them," replied Bjorn.

"And yet you allow it to happen, hypocrite."

"For the betterment of the nation in the long run; you are nothing more than a necessary evil. But I don't expect you to understand anything about devotion to one's own country," replied Bjorn. "And I know how to follow orders so I don't need a lecture from the likes of you."

Lorez and Sker then entered the room. Seeing the two humans facing each other, it was obvious they were in the middle of a disagreement. Sker just stood there pretending not to notice and looked down while Lorez stared at them intently. Then, as if he suddenly realized he didn't care about either of the two humans, Lorez went to a spot in the long house and laid down on a bed roll. Sker didn't stray far from Lorez. He was unsure of Bjorn but definitely afraid of Damon.

The presence of the arch-goblin and lizard-goblin seemed to cease the argument between the two humans, for now.

As Lorez lay down on his bed roll he asked, "Why are you two at odds?"

Neither answered and a long silence followed.

"So, you two are at odds. Is it because you are wondering what we are returning to?" the arch-goblin said with a laugh.

"What do you mean?" asked Bjorn.

"I know Dru's father, the general has swindled a deal with my chieftain to keep my clan out of the coming war," explained Lorez. "Surely you two knew that?"

Damon cracked a smile at Bjorn, turned and walked over to a dark spot in the longhouse he claimed with his bedroll. Bjorn instead turned back on his stew.

Bjorn was brewing inside from the second notion of a war. Was Damon correct about General Blackpool planning to wreck Sedgedunum and take the country for himself?

"You know Bjorn, that Leif will be at odds when he returns to your capital city," said Lorez aloud.

"What are you talking about?" asked Bjorn.

Lorez saw Damon roll his eyes and lay down.

"That human there knows," said Lorez pointing at Damon, pressing the issue hoping someone would inform Leif about the plot between General Blackpool and Queen Ooktha. He was also told by leader Chieftain Merka that Damon was aware of the plot too.

Damon did not return a concerned look back to Lorez, so the arch-goblin decided to reveal even more to Bjorn.

"Don't presume that war was something all the arch-goblins wanted," continued Lorez. "My chieftain, my clan, wanted no part of the war with Sedgedunum. The other two arch-goblin cities did however. Which is why my chieftain agreed to a deal to secretly stay out of the war in exchange for Fort Adamant. But make no mistake, the creation of Fort Adamant so near to my home was a preemptive act by your very people that helped call for it," said Lorez.

"Curious?" piped up Damon who was not aware of Lorez's knowledge. "If you were so knowledgeable about the facts about the war with Sedgedunum and your clan was not participating in the war, then why would you come with us? I do know you were ordered yes, but you could have abandoned us at any time, you still can. Why do you reveal the plot to us and remain?"

Lorez sat up and looked to the doorway for anyone coming. Then he laid back down staring up at the ceiling as if contemplating the questions for several moments before answering.

"Let me understand you arch-goblin," interrupted Bjorn confused by the revelation that Sedgedunum was or had been attacked and everyone knew about it, save for himself. "Are you saying you are fine with your own tribe betraying your queen and she plans to attack with Sedgedunum?" asked Bjorn.

"Of course! I do not want an arch-goblin queen that is part-elf but all vampire," Lorez said, although he did not know that she was fully elf. "Chieftain Blist concocted the lie about her heritage to bring the other chieftains to him. Lorez speculated that if it were true, she would have been killed at birth."

"If you had told us this in the beginning, we could have skipped this horrid mission altogether!" said Bjorn.

Privately, Damon agreed with Bjorn's assessment.

"You know why this mission exists?" asked Lorez. "Leif believes it will grant him his freedom from captivity and in return we eliminate Queen Ooktha' s enemy, Rom-Seti," explained Lorez.

"But now you are telling me that is untrue and why did we go forward with this mission?" demanded Bjorn.

"At the time, I didn't understand Leif, but now I consider the elf, a friend," continued Lorez who laughed aloud at his own statement. "When have our two races ever got along?" Lorez asked jokingly. "When I look at this lizard-goblin, who follows the elf, Leif treats him as a friend does, regardless of his race or people's history. He does the same to me. I could have let him die in the coliseum but the elf for one, wouldn't die. Even the mantikhoras couldn't kill him," he said looking at Damon who doubted the story. "Even Queen Ooktha tried to kill him at one time. Whoever raised him must have never seen him as elf or even human, they see him as Leif and made him resilient. And after years of warring, his view is different and I think so is mine now. So, I did not want to tell him. This journey has changed me and Sker and it is because of Leif Foehammer."

"He ah-saved me," added Sker. "Saved hundreds of arch-goblins and orcs from fighting."

"That's right!" added Lorez.

"That doesn't explain why we still went on this mission," said Damon.

"We went in case Queen Ooktha survived the assassination," said Lorez.

"What assassination?" asked Damon.

"The wizard Anthon intends to kill her after the attack on Sedgedunum is underway."

There was a long pause in the longhouse before anyone spoke again.

Both Dru and Damon were surprised by all this information the arch-goblin was revealing about Leif and himself.

"So why don't I leave?" began Lorez again. "If Queen Ooktha survives I need to be able to explain that we accomplished the mission. But also, perhaps I truly worry about what you two or Dru or the general or the wizard Anthon might say or do to the elf."

Bjorn stood up coming to realise the truth of it all. Both Damon and Lorez said an attack on Sedgedunum was inevitable. There never was going to be a peace.

"Wait!" said Bjorn to everyone. "If peace was never on the table and your other two clans were going to attack Sedgedunum anyway, why did the general send us?"

"Because he needed the attack to happen to make his coup happen," said Damon. "This mission was also Queen Ooktha' s price to begin the attack."

Leif walked into the longhouse then with Denisia. The two were talking about their recent adventure and was at the point about leaving the forest-dames grove.

"Leif, we must talk," said Bjorn.

Leif just stared back. Sker looked away and Lorez stood up as well.

"Oh, this should be good," said Damon who also stood up.

"The mission it seems never needed to happen. Lorez here wasn't really a spy to ensure the mission was attempted, or accomplished or whatever. He too hates his queen."

"I would not have begun the discussion like that," said Lorez.

"What are you two talking about?" asked Leif as he walked further into the longhouse.

"Your arch-goblin spy here, as it turns out, was never really a spy and seems to like you more than his own vampire queen! We could have simply waited here until..." Bjorn said but stopped suddenly.

"Until what?" asked Leif.

"Until the general's deal with Lorez's chieftain was done," said Damon "And the battle between Ironhold and Sedgedunum commenced."

There was a long silence but once Damon's words set, they were like a knife to the gut for Leif and Bjorn.

"The whole premise for this mission was to prevent war!" argued Leif. Confused, he tried to speak but some gibberish came out. He then made his way slowly to a bench opposite Lorez and hung his head low while seated.

Lorez made a move towards him and so did Sker but Leif shouted, "Stay back! All of you, stay back!" It was uncanny as the elf was usually calm, even in danger. "Then why are we here if a war was going to happen anyway?" asked Leif softly.

"Because" began Damon but was cut short by Bjorn.

"Brother, the war with the arch-goblins," began Bjorn but was cut short by Lorez.

"Was inevitable," finished Lorez. "Ironhold and Skulls-thorpe wanted it with Sedgedunum. The general made a secret deal with my chieftain in Blood-helm to stay out of the assault on your capitol and in return, the general would hand over the unfinished Fort Adamant to my chieftain."

It was only half true. Lorez omitted the part about General Blackpool asking for the assault on Sedgedunum so he could depose the current ruling council. Lorez knew of this from his dealings with his chieftain, Mr. Night and the Wizard Anthon but was reluctant to further wound Leif and didn't know the details.

"Why Sedgedunum?" asked Leif.

"Why not?" replied Lorez.

"No, there is a reason why."

"Arch-goblins are bred to war, are we not?" said and Sedgedunum was an unsuspecting target."

"No that's not true," said Leif. "You just said the war was known, even to you brother," said Leif pointing at Bjorn. "Surely Sedgedunum was warned by the general and prepared the city," reasoned Leif.

"Perhaps?" said Lorez.

"And Queen Ooktha, she knew and kept this from me?" asked Leif to the point of breaking.

"Because she helped plan this war with your general," said Lorez.

"What did you say?" asked Leif in shock. Again, Leif felt like he had been punched in the gut.

"They planned this war together," said Lorez.

"Impossible," said Leif in disbelief. "Why would she?

"She too needed a war to justify her rule among the arch-goblin chieftains. Otherwise, why follow her?" said Lorez.

Who else knew?" asked Leif.

"Leif, I knew some of it," started Bjorn. "I knew of the general's desire to rid the ruling council, but I knew nothing of the attack," said Bjorn. "Damon knew of the general's part because he is an agent of the Shadow Company, the financial backers of the general's schemes it seems."

"What schemes?" asked Leif.

"The Black-masks," said Bjorn.

Leif drew his *dao* sword, eyeing them all "This is all a lie! I was sent to help bring peace to our lands. You tell me the truth! And you Lorez, why would you then betray her?"

"Because, if we are lucky, she is likely dead by now," responded Lorez.

Leif raised his sword and prepared to strike Lorez. The arch-goblin backed away suddenly.

"No, Leif!" shouted Denisia. "You will not harm him here in Sanctuary!" A great brown bear suddenly appeared in the doorway behind Denisia. It was Grommel, her companion and part of the muscle that kept Sanctuary safe.

"Leif!" shouted Bjorn, "It is true and not his fault or your fault or my fault or even Damon's fault. All was going to happen it seems. Even the loss of Fort Adamant, the assault of Sedgedunum and the death of their queen. But we are guilty of keeping you in the dark."

"I didn't tell you because I know what a saint you are," said Lorez.

"That I cannot argue with," said Bjorn. "At times, I feel like you should be the clergy, not I or mother. I didn't want to tell you everything I was aware of because I knew it would devastate you and at the time, I didn't know about Lorez who actually cares for you too. He is the reason we are telling you the truth of the matter. He is probably the most genuine one of us, apart from Sker. So if you strike anyone," said Bjorn throwing his mace to the floor, "it should be me! In keeping the truth from you, I have betrayed you, I see that now. I just wanted you back!"

Leif threw down his *dao* sword and walked out of the longhouse. He went to the shrine to Matronae and knelt down. "What a fool I am," he said.

* * * * *

It was nightfall when Denisia finally decided to make her way up to Leif, Grommel alongside her.

"I am sorry dear Leif for what they just put you through," she said standing over him. Leif had no response. "Clearly though, from what I heard, both the large human and arch-goblin both care for you enough to shield you from both the truth and all the wickedness."

"You should go back to your mother, young lady," said Leif. "The night will be cold."

"I have Grommel to keep me warm," she replied as the large bear plopped down next to Leif, sniffing him. "I think he likes you."

That did bring a smile to Leif's face. "At least someone does."

"You don't know how lucky you are Mr. Leif."

"Lucky, huh?"

"You have friends down there willing to hide a horrible truth from you. They even risked their lives for you to go on this mission. Your brother Bjorn almost died and was willing to do so to free you from this queen."

"I don't wish to offend you but you don't understand. They did it because they were following orders."

"You don't believe that?" she responded but Leif didn't answer the question

"I thought Queen Ooktha was a good person trapped in a terrible circumstance, making the best of the hand life had dealt her."

"And what do you believe now?"

"Now I don't know what to believe and I don't want to speak about this any longer," replied Leif. Grommel then lay down next to Leif. Leif then leaned back on the great bear and Denisia sat next to him.

Leif let out a sigh and put his hands in his face. Denisia just stared at the elf, concerned but also smitten.

Chapter 23
Revenants Will Be Revenants

Revenant Niss was very upset. Her mentor and silent partner in many of her endeavours was silent indeed. She had planned to meet him once the sun was over the mountains of Archangel. She arrived precisely then but he was nowhere to be found. It was very uncanny for any revenant to leave one's own refuge. She called out his name in the rundown palace but no answer returned. Nothing seemed different, nothing out of place, save Pallentine was gone as was his steward, Teodor.

She walked up to the throne where Revenant Pallentine often sat and thought about doing just that but she could sense it had magic upon it and was not willing to risk being harmed by attempting to sit and wait. Therefore, she waved her bony fingers and an invisible seat materialized from behind her. She waited for Revenant Pallentine's return.

* * * * *

Revenant Pallentine *teleported* with Teodor to stand before the rampart that led to the opening of Rom-Seti's red-stone pyramid.

"It was clear they had to fight their way out," said Teodor. There were remnants of destroyed skeleton warriors on or near the rampart. Teodor drew his sword when he saw a zombie coming down the rampart from the top.

"Stay yourself, my friend," said Revenant Pallentine. Pallentine could control the undead and command them to do his bidding. If two powerful undead beings tried to control the same creature, confusion often set into the lesser undead minion. Pallentine commanded the zombie mentally to stop and then throw himself over the side of the rampart. The zombie did as Pallentine instructed.

"Oh, what a marvelous day my friend," said Revenant Pallentine to Teodor.

Although Teodor was glad that Rom-Seti was gone, he was concerned Leif, or his Vampire Queen might release their enemy and return. "Let us be done with this place my mage. If you recall though, our intrusion here many years ago is what started the great war in the first place."

The two were once in her Rom-Seti's pyramid long ago, escorting their once beloved king. Many years ago, King Ivanovh Delvemoora, ruler of Archangel, wanted to explore this ancient splendor as soon as he heard of its existence. That incursion is what started Rom-Seti on his path to destroy Archangel and the king's death.

"Not this time," said Pallentine. "This time Rom-Seti pays for his crimes against our people. Today we pillage his treasures."

The two elves, revenant and elf, had longed for the day they could exact their revenge. Now, thanks to Revenant Niss and Queen Ooktha hatching a plan against Rom-Seti, he could take what he wanted. Revenant Pallentine had the power to control all the undead here and no one could stop him.

The pair made their way up the pathway that the Vorclawean party used. They were both stunned at the vast library.

"We never saw this place when we were last here!" exclaimed Pallentine.

"That's because we only made it into the lower levels below the pyramid and that was as far as we got with King Ivanovh," replied Teodor.

"Do you think there is more down where we were at?"

"That was about sixteen years ago. I like to believe he was smart enough to consolidate given what we took from him," replied Teodor.

Revenant Pallentine nodded and remembered the papyrus scroll-set that King Ivanovh had taken from Rom-Seti. In those scrolls contained the guidance, magical incantations and spells to create wondrous flying machines. The elves of Archangel built several of them shortly afterwards and in fact used them to evacuate the children from their city to escape Rom-Seti's assault.

Another undead came into the library from an opening up high. It was the opening that led to Rom-Seti's throne room. This one was armored, and more than a mindless warrior. It had a connection to Rom-Seti and Pallentine found it not so easy to control.

"That one seems to be giving you some trouble," said Teodor again drawing his sword.

"This one is an angry soul indeed," said Revenant Pallentine. "And he doesn't like you it seems."

"Of course not," said Teodor. "Send him after me once I am out of the library so I can deal with him. Don't want to make a mess in the library."

Revenant Pallentine held the creature in place until Teodor was through the doorway from which they came. The revenant kept back a distance in case the armored undead warrior changed its mind and attacked him. However, Pallentine also knew most evil undead creatures hated the living more than anything. The creature pursued Teodor though, and its head was cut from its body as soon as it entered the foyer outside. Teodor put his sword through the skull just to be certain.

The pair reunited again and made their way up the stairs to the catwalk that led to the throne room. There they discovered a charred room. Melted and shattered mirrors hung on the walls or what remained of them. The framework of the doorway, to the side of a damaged throne, shone that something big came through it.

"It is how she described his throne room. The mirrors are how they communicated," said Teodor.

Pallentine then launched some *mage's darts* and destroyed any remaining mirrors. Sparks flew from the impacts.

The noise alerted other creatures in the pyramid. From the damaged opening behind the charred throne came another set of beasts.

"I haven't seen creatures such as these since the last time we were in this place," said Teodor. These creatures were wrapped in strips of cloth. Two mummies made for the intruders.

"I am your new master now," said Pallentine in their own tongue, a spell he cast upon himself so any undead would understand him. "I command you to stop." The mummies did as commanded by the powerful undead revenant. "To gain my favor, one of you must destroy the other," said Pallentine.

The mummies wasted no time clobbering each other. The larger finally defeated the smaller and once done, Pallentine cast *flames* from his hands, burning the victor to a husk.

"I think I enjoyed that as much as you did," said Teodor.

The pair walked over the now destroyed mummies and in through the damaged portal. Behind there they found a grand gallery. Two rows of decorated columns, six on each side dominated the chamber. Each column was decorated in rich colours showcasing blues, greens, reds and yellows. No one column was alike. A brazier burned before each lighting up scenes of harvesting, fishing, warriors, laborers and alien-gods carved into the stone. Lines of hieroglyphs ran the lengths of the shaft telling a story in some language of which the elves knew not. Every inch of the walls boasted decorum in the same fashion. There were opened sarcophagi nestled along the walls in between each column. The lids were all slid down towards the feet leaving an opening at the top where the head should be. It was large enough to fit a person through the opening. All seemed decorated in gold with more hieroglyphs and the face of someone on the top.

"This place is beautiful," said Teodor.

"This place is an abomination and should not be on our world," replied Revenant Pallentine.

Like many elves, the Revenant Pallentine was xenophobic even in undeath. Teodor come to accept Pallentine's ways but was able to see beauty for what it was. And in Teodor's mind, this grand gallery was just that.

Pallentine continued on his way to the end of the room. The walkway between the columns were four times as wide he was tall. To became clear the room's purpose was not only built to impress but the columns themselves were what held up the top of the pyramid.

Teodor pulled out a wand and said an elven incantation. The wand glowed blue and so too did anything magical near the elf. Revenant Pallentine stopped as different objects around the room glowed blue, signaling their magical property. Every brazier and every sarcophagus glowed blue as Teodor neared

170

it. At the end of the room was another sarcophagus that also glowed blue. It too was open like the others.

"It must be his," said Teodor. "There was magic glowing all about the floor."

"Trapped no doubt," responded Revenant Pallentine. "Remain here," he said and floated above the floor. The revenant scrutinized the lid to the sarcophagus Then, when he was satisfied, he used a spell of *telekinesis*. The lid was heavy, heavier than he imagined. It took all Revenant Pallentine's magical might just to move it. Both he and Teodor got back once the lid was ready to drop on to the floor. Sparks, explosions, fire, acid and spikes shot up from the ground.

When the spectacle finished, Pallentine again floated above the sarcophagus. It was empty. He even performed a *discover enchantment* spell but found nothing inside it. "A pity, I was hoping it would be in here."

"Did you really think it would be that easy?" asked Teodor.

A hiss suddenly emanated from upon high, followed by an eerie screech.

"A spectre," said Pallentine aloud. "She is none too pleased."

"Why would she be?" said Teodor drawing his magical blade and a wand.

"We're invading her home." Teodor moved around looking up, around and behind.

"Something odd about her," said Pallentine.

Behind them appeared a ghostly female apparition. She was young in appearance but also showed she was from whence Rom-Seti came. Her hair was cropped to her shoulders and she wore similar motif as some of the statues seen around the necropolis. She took one look at Teodor and screamed; all spectres hated living things. Revenant Pallentine floated in front of Teodor hiding him from her gaze.

"Calm yourself my child," said Pallentine. "Your master is gone and I have no desire to do harm to you but cannot let anyone harm my friend. I sense your pain is not for endearment to the former master of this pyramid," said Pallentine.

The spectre nodded in response but was unwilling or unable to speak.

"I sense you hated he who ruled here, is it Rom-Seti?" Again, the creature nodded in response to Revenant Pallentine. "I will free you of your curse spectre but I need your help first. Can you lead me to where your oppressor hides his *soul-sepulchre*?"

The female spectre floated by Revenant Pallentine who was careful to keep Teodor from her direct gaze. She was on a small quest for her freedom but the sight of the living could enrage her. "Stay behind me, Teodor," said Pallentine. "Keep yourself from her sight."

The female spectre hovered over the lid of the sarcophagus, putting her hand over the painted and carved face upon the lid.

"Ah yes," said Pallentine. He raised the lid off the ground and flipped it over. It smacked to the ground, echoing the empty chamber. The lid was made of stone but there was a compartment inside that flew open near the centre. It was nothing more than a piece of the same stone, carved so well into the back of the lid it appeared seamless. What fell out of the compartment was what intrigued Revenant Pallentine.

The spectre pointed at a small yellow-stone alligator that fell free. It was amber, set with two small ruby-red eyes. It was carved in great detail with a rough-ridged back, just like an alligator. The item itself was no bigger than the width of Revenant Pallentine's bony hand. Using his *telekinesis* once again, he floated the item up to his grasp. He sensed its power. This indeed was the *soul-sepulchre* of Rom-Seti.

The female apparition floated at the feet of Revenant Pallentine, hands held in praise as if asking for her death. In her own language, Pallentine told her to lower her head and not look up. The spectre did as she was asked. She remained in a kneeling position with her head down.

"Come Teodor," said Pallentine. "Let us end this spectre's torment. Stab her with your enchanted blade so we might begin to cleanse this place."

Suddenly she felt the sting of an enchanted device strike her but did not realise the pain it would cause. She forgot what pain was. Again, a stab went into her back. She wanted to flee but she no longer wanted to remain the spectre of this pyramid. She then felt scared, another feeling she hadn't experienced in many decades; her ghostly form began to dissipate as her vision became a blinding light. She could see a woman in that light. It could only be one person, her mother. She heard this newcomer's voice again speaking in her language.

Pallentine was aware of what she was experiencing as his mind could share in hers. "Go to her my child," he said.

She did as Revenant Pallentine commanded. She was no longer scared nor in pain any longer; she was happy again to be in the waiting spirit of her own mother.

* * * * *

"We will use the rest of the remaining undead skeletons to collect books, scrolls and other materials," explained Revenant Pallentine. "I will have them bring everything to the library."

As magical alarms sounded by the removal of scrolls and books from their shelves, it forced undead creatures to react to the alert. But Pallentine could control the undead and return them to do his own bidding.

When everything was in place, he opened a portal to a designated spot he had picked out in his own ruined city of Archangel. It was a place large enough to house this massive collection. It took hours to move everything. Teodor was already on the other side back in Archangel waiting to instruct the creatures where items should go and be placed. By late into the evening, the entire library of the Red-Pyramid was emptied. Teodor watched the last of the skeletons returning through the portal from whence they came. Pallentine set fire to the remains of the Red-Pyramid along with all the undead within and closed the portal.

It was nightfall and the two walked their way back up the winding road from the third tier of Archangel. There housed a building, an old meeting hall of sorts; it was a facility large enough to hold Rom-Seti's library,

"And what of the *soul-sepulchre*? You intend to destroy it?" asked Teodor.

"I need Niss to collect her Jade Tower from her vampire disciple to complete my revenge," said Revenant Pallentine. "Then I will destroy it with him in it!"

"You know this could have been solved today had you not given it back," said Teodor.

"I know, I know, but then our young prince would not return to us so easily," said Pallentine referring to Leif. "Once he finds out what a monster she really is, he will come home," he said. "But for now, I must send my regrets to Revenant Niss. We were to meet today to discuss the whereabouts of her soul sucker.

"And what of it?" came a shout from upon high. Revenant Niss floated down to meet them in the road. "I have been waiting hours for our meeting."

"And so, you deserve an apology," said Pallentine. "I was working on another project that needed my attention. I lost track of time," said Pallentine.

Teodor wondered if the subtle movement of female revenant's dead skin was a sign she was pleased or displeased with the answer. "I take my leave of you both," said Teodor with a nod.

"And has he found them?"

"Yes, he brought them here."

"Good so you have my Jade Tower?"

"No, I let him, uh them, leave with it."

"Why?" begged Revenant Niss. "I want that beast dead as much as you. How could you?"

"The elf stated he needed to sue for peace in his land," said Pallentine.

"Then you are a bigger fool than he is," she responded. "There is no peace in Vorclaw. His lover and his master conspire together to bring about the downfall of the land for their own dark purposes. Where are they now?"

Revenant Pallentine did not respond. He just started walking back towards the palace.

"I asked you, where are they now?"

Revenant Pallentine then turned to face her. "You are the reason why I despise the known world and why the elves of this world have retreated because of deceit, lies and half-truths."

"Me, how dare you after all I have done!" shouted Revenant Niss.

"Had I known that your precious vampire lied to the elf, I would never let him leave with the soul sucker. This is your fault for keeping me in the dark, again. You always played these games with me, even in life!" shouted Revenant Pallentine.

"I created the Jade Tower for us so we might finally have revenge on the filthy monster, Rom-Seti. You should have known better than to let it slip away!" she yelled.

Revenant Pallentine could not deny they both hated Rom-Seti and for the same reasons; he knew she built it for both their sakes.

"And do not sound so surprised. You have always known what I am about my old master, creating wondrous magical artefacts is what I do best. I care not for Ooktha' s war, only for the opportunity to use what I create. This was to be my greatest achievement to date and you let it slip away!" she said in a rage.

"Where are they now?" asked Revenant Niss for a third time.

"I presume they are home in Vorclaw," he said. "If you are lucky then your pupil already has the Jade Tower and you have nothing to worry about," and walked away.

Chapter 24
The Return to Sedgedunum

Leif eventually returned to the longhouse but many hours into the night. He didn't feel it was appropriate to share a night under the stars with a young girl he didn't really know. Leif also suspected she was smitten and could not promise her anything, especially at her tender age. He told her, "Goodnight and thank you," before he returned.

The next morning Dru was standing in the doorway to the longhouse along with Anthon Blackpool. "Time to go," said Anthon, who turned and walked out. Everyone jumped up and gathered their belongings.

"Where is it that we are going?" asked Lorez.

"My uncle will open two gates, one leads outside of Fort Adamant. That is for you Lorez and for Sker," explained Dru. "The rest of us are ordered back to Sedgedunum," said Dru.

"Iza wants to stay with Master Leif," said Sker.

"It is too dangerous my friend. Isn't it Dru?" asked Leif. "Is Sedgedunum under siege?"

Dru looked to Bjorn for an answer.

"We told him about the coming war," said Damon.

Dru simply turned and went outside. Leif was the first to emerge, leaving behind the sword he was given by Queen Ooktha. Lorez picked it up and followed him out.

"I want to know wizard!" shouted Leif, "Is she dead yet?"

Anthon who was talking with the Mistress of Sanctuary and Denisia, turned to Leif. "Is who dead?"

"You know who?" said Leif. "Your name was used casually while I was in Blood-helm. At first, I didn't realise who it was but I finally put it together. You were there pulling the strings, were you not? You and your brother," said Leif angrily.

"Lieutenant, as far as I know you were a prisoner of war and your commanding officer wanted you retrieved for some reason. Was I part of it? Yes. He even put his own son and your brother at risk to retrieve you. So don't turn your anger on me if your lover is dead or not. Or if she used you as a pawn to get what she wanted," said Anthon.

Those words stung Leif, even somewhat embarrassed him. The Mistress of Sanctuary was wide eyed as Denisia turned and walked away.

"Many pardons for the young lieutenant's interruption," said Anthon to the Mistress of Sanctuary.

"I think it is best you take them all without delay. Seems they have inadvertently disturbed the peace in the region and now I am told lycaons and orcs are at odds, once again."

"We were trying to save the orc from the lycaon," announced Leif to the Mistress, advancing on her.

"Leif, that's enough," said Bjorn.

Dru then came up to Leif putting himself before them to slow him down. "We're done here Leif. Let's be gone from this place and let my father explain everything," said Dru.

That did seem to calm the large elf.

"You two," said Anthon pointing to Sker and Lorez. "Your master awaits." He then created a doorway that took them back to the exact spot in the mountains in Vorclaw from whence their journey began.

Lorez and Sker went to say their farewells but Leif ignored the arch-goblin.

Sker jumped up and climbed up on elf. Leif's demeanour then melted somewhat. He hugged the little lizard-goblin. "You have been my only friend throughout this entire journey," he whispered. "I shan't forget you?"

"Nor I, Master Leif."

"Keep him safe," said Leif to Lorez. The arch-goblin nodded in response and waved a hand to Leif but he did not return the gesture.

Both the arch-goblin and lizard-goblin walked through the gateway and were gone from all their lives.

* * * * *

General Blackpool's office door slammed open and a young lieutenant, the steward outside the general's office, fell over backwards through the door.

"What is the meaning of this?" asked the general.

Baltus was about to draw his own weapon but saw Magnus Foehammer come through the door with another man who looked relatively familiar but couldn't quite place the name. Neither was armed and so Baltus relaxed.

The lieutenant however, once he got back to his feet, drew his rapier.

"That will be all lieutenant," said the general. The lieutenant didn't move and eyed the two men "Stay your sword young man!" said the general. "And leave us!" It got the lieutenant's attention and he complied.

"What brings you to my door old friend?" asked Baltus.

"My wife is dead," he said bluntly.

Baltus closed his eyes. "Oh Magnus. I am some sorry," he said. Baltus refused to open his eyes and look at the man, knowing full well he was ultimately responsible. The death toll was coming in and he knew it would. The general once had such hatred for the city and the leaders of the country;

he thought he could stomach it. But now with Disa dead, the guilt became all too real.

"Where is my son?" asked Magnus now standing before the general's desk.

The general slowly opened his eyes. He was indeed teary eyed. "I am sorry for your loss my friend," he whispered.

"I want to know where both Bjorn and Leif are," he said. "I know they are alive and I want to know what is going on," said Magnus. "All of this?"

"All of what? The war?" asked Baltus. "We have been invaded and repelled the invaders."

"No, you are not getting off that easy. You had a part in this, all of this," said Magnus.

Baltus was taken aback.

"Who is Mr. Night, really?" asked Dunkin Saltclaw, standing just behind Magnus. "How did you know to evacuate Fort Adamant and get them here so quickly?" he asked.

"Ah, now it makes sense, I know who you are, you're the soldier who hit him in the face after the battle at the mine," said Baltus. "Magnus, what stories has this man been telling you? You know you're lucky you were never court-martialed."

Dunkin was about to respond but Magnus cut him short. "Who is Mr. Night and what is his affiliation to the army," demanded Magnus.

"That is none of your concern," responded Baltus dryly.

"It is where my son is concerned. If what I heard is true, that man put my son and the White Eagles in danger," said Magnus. "And it cost me my son."

"Don't you think I know that!" spouted the general. "Leif is a good man, a good person, a good soldier, a good elf," said Baltus looking down at his desk, feeling the weight of guilt. "I would never want harm to come to him. I was told his company wasn't even supposed to be on that mission, but Major Titus decided," said General Blackpool, but paused. He may have revealed too much. It was his own order relayed to Major Goldwater for Major Titus to send another company other than Leif's into the mountains for the ambush. It was Major Titus, the White Eagle Battalion commander, who ignored his order and sent Leif's Gold Company on the mission instead. Furthermore, these two army veterans were arousing suspicions about Mr. Night, who was indeed a shape-changer working for the general. That might be the more pressing issue to quell.

If on cue, Anthon came out from the hidden door to the far side of the room behind the fireplace. It was the hidden door that led down into the ancient ruins the Academy of Arms was built upon. However, few knew of its existence; only elite Black-masks were privy to its location and entrances. Both Magnus and Dunkin looked to their left in surprise to see the wizard.

Dunkin quickly developed a suspicion that perhaps this wizard might be the one involved in the arch-goblin ambush of Gold Company. Only a mage could have concocted the spelled-explosion needed at the mine.

Magnus however knew much about Anthon Blackpool from the tales confided in him by the general himself. He knew Anthon left suddenly from the Wizard's College, rumored to have been expelled. Rumoured also to have joined some dark order but not certain which. The two men even met long ago when Magnus served as the Sergeant Major for Baltus in the White Eagles which was when Baltus confided in him about his brother as being a disgrace.

"Now it makes sense," said Magnus. "The resurgences of your brother, the downfall of the Sedgedunum Wizard's College. You are behind this," said Magnus pointing not to Baltus but to Anthon.

Anthon put up his hands to show he was innocent and said, "I am behind nothing Magnus. I was requested to come to my brother's side after the college fell," he lied.

Baltus wanted to quickly defuse this situation. Magnus was close to the truth, some of it anyway and decided to take him into the ruins, hoping to take his mind off this line of questioning.

"Are they here?" asked Baltus of Anthon.

The wizard nodded, yes in response.

"Good then let me show Magnus why my brother is here and put your mind at ease. Come I have something to show you," he said and led them all down the secret passage.

"I came across this underground ruin many years ago Magnus," began Baltus. "It was built by elves long ago and I am sure the city is built on other ruins."

The passage was narrow but well-lit with ever-burn torches. Finally, they came to a locked wooden door. It was different from the brickwork used in the construction. It was very new with modern locks. "I use this for special meetings and mission of great importance. By coming down here you are now bound to keep this place secret or forfeit your life. Do you both understand." The two men merely nodded.

Anthon pushed open the door that emptied into a large underground chamber. It was the ruined remains of an elven court but beneath Vorclaw's Academy of Arms. There were elves depicted in the statues and glyphs decorating this underground chamber. Sitting on the stone bleachers was a rag tag group of soldiers.

"My sons!" shouted Magnus.

Leif and Bjorn made their way to the large man and the three hugged, meeting in the middle of the chamber. Magnus was not as big as Bjorn but was able to but his big arms around them both. "You brought him back to us Bjorn," said Magnus staring at Leif.

"Yes father, we all did," said Bjorn. "Dru too helped."

"Only a little, sir," said Dru trying to lighten the mood.

"Are you ok, boy?" said Magnus holding Leif's by the face. "I thought you were lost to us!" Tears welled in his eyes.

"I am ok, father," responded Leif.

"Thank you, all of you," said Magnus.

"Good to see you made it, sirs," said Dunkin.

"By the gods, it is good to see you," said Leif who ran over to hug Dunkin Saltclaw.

"Good to see you," said Bjorn to the man.

"And to you, sir," responded Dunkin. "And thank you, for all your help in procuring my release."

Damon Crag made no comment or overtures to Magnus nor Dunkin. He simply made his way past them and over to the Blackpool brothers.

Dru walked over to Magnus and put his hand on the man's shoulder. "I don't think I ever seen you cry before old man," said Dru with a smile. He patted the big man on the shoulder but Magnus engulfed Dru.

"Thank you," said Magnus hugging Dru. "I am in your debt young man," he said.

"And mother?" asked Leif. "How fares she?"

Dunkin put his hand on Leif's shoulder to ready him for the answer. The corner of Magnus's smile turned upside down. He couldn't say it. He looked at Bjorn for support.

"Father," said Bjorn. "What's the matter? How is mother?"

"She is no longer with us my friends," said Baltus suddenly. "The war has taken many things including our beloved Disa," finished Baltus solemnly. He too broke down when he spoke her name aloud.

Magnus merely shook his head confirming what Baltus said.

"No!" shouted Bjorn. "How?"

Magnus merely hugged his large son.

"Father?" said Leif. "Tell me it's not so."

Magnus outstretched his arm to have him come join him and his brother Bjorn. Bjorn's face was awash with tears. He leaned his head on his father's shoulder trying to stay awake.

"You told me none of this," protested Dru to his father.

"I just found out," replied the general.

Dru looked at the Foehammers. For once they looked as broken a family unit as he and his father. Dru too loved Disa. She helped raise him when his own mother was killed in a wizard's duel, many years ago. That same act is what started his father on this quest to take the city, the country and wreak havoc. Only now it had cost him his second mother. "How?" whispered Dru.

"It was the leader of the arch-goblins, the vampire queen," announced Baltus.

Leif froze.

Bjorn looked up at and turned to the general.

Dru's eyes looked to his father and then to Leif.

"What did you say?" asked Bjorn.

Leif stood there, eyes closed. He couldn't move.

"During the siege of the city, Disa saved your father's life when the vampiress attacked him. She retaliated the next night by attacking the

179

infirmary Disa helped create. In her attack, she set it all ablaze with her magic and struck your mother herself."

"Father," began Bjorn. "Is this true?" The man grabbed Bjorn and cried, shaking his head confirming it was.

Leif collapsed to his knees. The elf started shaking.

"My boy are you ok?" asked Magnus, sniffling and crying.

"Tell me Leif she is not the same!" shouted Bjorn. Bjorn knew Leif was her lover. Leif also explained to Bjorn that he believed their mission and the relationship Leif had with the Queen Ooktha could prevent war. Bjorn never thought it would, he only went on the mission to get Leif back from her.

"What's all this?" asked Magnus.

Leif was breaking down. His body was shaking as if crying although no sound came forth.

"Tell me Leif it's not the same vampire!" shouted Bjorn.

"Bjorn," began Dru. "Perhaps now it is not,"

"Stay out of this, Dru! Tell me what you know Leif?"

Leif began to cry. He then looked up at the ceiling in a panic. His eyes were darting all around, his head was shaking from sadness, regret and embarrassment. "No!" he cried out at the top of his voice.

"This is your fault, Leif," shouted Bjorn.

"What is this about?" asked Magnus of Bjorn. "Have you gone mad?"

"I should have left you there to rot with her," said Bjorn. "We would have all been better off."

Leif sobbed into his hands.

Dru made a move to comfort Leif but was held back by the firm grip on Damon Crag. The assassin didn't appear to be enjoying this but seemed weary of Dru intervening.

"It was his lover!" shouted Bjorn. "That's how he survived, father!" announced Bjorn. "You slept with a vampire to save your own skin and now she has killed our mother!" Bjorn walked up and punched Leif in the face, knocking him to the floor. Leif's vision blurred. He slowly lost consciousness.

Magnus was frozen. He couldn't move. His heart pounded and he fell to the ground in shock.

Bjorn grabbed his large mace and went to crush Leif's head. It was Dunkin Saltclaw who tackled the large priest, sending him, Bjorn, to the ground.

"That's enough I say!" shouted Dunkin. "You all have been through a lot, more than anyone should in such a short time. Captain Foehammer, you will not lay your hands on my lieutenant again or you will answer to my own fist."

"Agreed, that is enough," said the general.

"This is also your fault, general!" shouted Bjorn. "We were told all about your involvement in this war and how you conspired with the same vampire to wage war so you could enact your own coup!"

"Dru, help Magnus up," he said as the large man appeared to be struggling to get off the ground.

"Magnus?" inquired Dru of the man who now appeared to be more than struggling. "Magnus!" shouted Dru. His body was shaking; he was having some kind of fit. It was the shock of it all. "Bjorn! To your father!"

Chapter 25
Chieftain Merka

"The elf was ordered not to return but was not going to once he learned his mission would have no effect on the war," said Lorez to Chieftain Merka.

The chieftain sat on his throne of fine animal furs. He still had a patch over his eye. It was a remnant of his battle in the mountains, the ambush that led to Leif's capture.

"Was the mission successful? Did they vanquish the revenant or capture him in that green trinket she gave me?" Merka asked referring to the Jade Tower.

"Yes, my chieftain. Or at least they all led me to believe they did. But his runty lizard-goblin was there and witnessed it all. I am told he was the one that held on to the trinket during the capture."

"Where is the green trinket, the Jade Tower now?"

"With the elf, my lord," said Lorez.

"A pity. A powerful weapon like that could ensure our safety from her," explained Merka.

The two talked openly against Queen Ooktha. It was daylight after all and the windows were open, protecting them with precious sunlight. Neither liked her but both feared her.

"So, she not dead yet?" asked Lorez inquiring about Queen Ooktha.

"She is not but our deal to remain in the mountains in exchange for the evacuated Fort Adamant and a chest of coins had been secured. Revealing she intended to kill the wizard once he finished his work on the Wizards College turned into profitable information. Unfortunately, she never met him in battle. Therefore, she remains their queen."

"What is our next move my chieftain?" asked Lorez.

"I must report to her and explain what you have told me," said Merka. "You my friend will oversee the reconstruction of our new wall using the stones from Fort Adamant. I want a wall built at the narrowest point between the mountains; the place they call Panther Paw Pass. I do not want anyone from Vorclaw coming through that wall. It is to repel their army if need be. This land, all of it is now ours!"

* * * * *

"Sker, you are now my ward," said Lorez who had the lizard-goblin accompany him on his trek to Fort Adamant, or what remained of it. "You have proven your worth and I want you as my eyes and ears," said the arch-goblin.

"Yes, my lord," replied Sker. "My lord, do you think Master Leif will return?"

Lorez pondered that for a few moments before answering. Leif was returning to a different reality. He was surrounded by people that loved him but also deceived him. "When his eyes see the damage done by the arch-goblins of Ironhold and Queen Ooktha, I doubt he will return, except for one thing, revenge," said Lorez.

The lizard-goblin let out a weird sound not too dissimilar to a baby alligator's first calls, only that sound meant Sker was saddened by the revelation. Sker grew quite fond of Leif even though Sker thought Leif might be using him, Leif made it clear that thought was untrue when he entrusted the lizard-goblin at their farewell. Sker tapped his pocket making certain he still had the parting gift.

"If he does return, I want him to see you immediately," said Lorez. "You are the only one he truly trusts and he truly cared for you although I admit I know not why lizard-goblin. Yet you have grown on me too and certainly proven your worth over many other lizard-goblins I have seen," said Lorez.

That was the best compliment Sker ever received for an arch-goblin, let alone his own kind. The only other person to praise him was Leif. Sker was beaming a small toothy grin.

* * * * *

Chieftain Merka sailed aboard the Bloodknuckle that very afternoon and arrived in Skulls-thorpe that night. He wasted no time in going right to the citadel to see Queen Ooktha. He brought with him a small chest, no bigger than a jewelry box containing small pieces of gold, copper and silver. He had hoped it would suffice as tribute.

"I provide to you my queen, a mix of treasure!" lied the skinny arch-goblin chieftain while down on one knee. "It was what was left behind in the fort which is now being dismantled," he said. "The coins within were actually a small part of those he received from General Blackpool for betraying Queen Ooktha.

Chieftain Blist was there, he was always present when any of the other two chieftains arrived. He took the small box of coins and poured them on the floor. "That's all?" asked Chieftain Blist.

"Perhaps we could find more as we continue our search," responded Chieftain Merka, grovelling a bit. "But I am not here to boast of my victory of which you already know. I am here to inform you that Lorez and the elf have completed their mission."

Queen Ooktha stood up suddenly from her throne and Chieftain Blist backed away from the kneeling Chieftain Merka.

"Tell me what you know?" she said

"The mission was a success I am told. But the elf, Leif, has decided to return to his family," said Merka.

"He what?" said Queen Ooktha.

"His brother it seems, revealed the true plot between Vorclaw and yourself," explained Merka.

"And the device he was given, the Jade Tower?" she inquired.

"He kept the thing," replied Merka. "But have assurances from both Lorez and a lizard-goblin witness, the mission was a success."

"A lizard-goblin witness," bellowed Chieftain Blist. "Those little things will tell you whatever you want to hear. Why does Lorez not come to explain this then?"

"I have him overseeing the wall being built between the mountains. The wall is already defensible and when Lorez finishes, the pass to our lands will be unpassable for any army."

Queen Ooktha paused a moment and let the statements presented to her sink in. Then it came to her suddenly.

"Rise my chieftain," said Queen Ooktha who was now descending the steps from her throne. "You have done well. No casualties in your conquest albeit easy when the garrison was emptied. You have secured a truce with your rivals, the orcs and now you block out Vorclaw so your clan can mine and grow in those lands unabated," she said standing before the tall, slender arch-goblin. "You have proven yourself a capable leader," she said affectionately.

"I thank you my queen," he replied and nodded.

"Which is why I want you to go and take charge of Ironhold," she said, walking around him.

Merka stood there in shock. He didn't know how to answer. He clearly did not want to go. He had carved out his niche and was in fact hoping to enjoy the fruits of his labor.

"I sense your tension, Merka. Are you not pleased with the reward I have for you?"

"I am just uncertain why I am to go to Ironhold. I was told its stronghold was overrun, its doors shut and it has a new chieftain," he said apprehensively.

"Well, all of that is true. But, the new chieftain turned out to be, um, not up to the challenge," she said. "Which is why I want you to take control of Ironhold. Take twenty of your best warriors from Blood-helm with you. Chieftain Blist will give twenty of his. Take an additional one hundred lizard-goblins between your two cities. Tell Lorez he is now Chieftain of Blood-helm until I say otherwise," she said judging Merka's reactions.

It was clear he was ruffled by the revelation she had just imposed upon him.

"I want you to re-establish that stronghold over the next year. And if you are successful, you can stay or return to Blood-helm. But if you are not successful well, let us hope it doesn't come to that my friend," she said with an innocent smile. "Go celebrate tonight in Chieftain Blist's fair city," she said. "And make me proud, once more."

When he turned to protest, she was already gone. Only Chieftain Blist was standing there smiling a yellow toothy grin.

* * * * *

"Don't blame me Merka, I knew nothing about it all," said Blist in one of the few cleanly eating establishments in the underground city of Skulls-thorpe. Or at least it was clean because Chieftain Blist frequented it. No lizard-goblins, orcs or other creatures were allowed.

"What do you know, about Ironhold?" asked Merka drinking a think dark beer.

"Ironhold was thoroughly defeated and its slaves exchanged for the new chieftain's life who went and got himself captured. Somehow," said Blist eating a barely cooked side of some large animal leg, "You will find a decimated people."

"Is it true what they say, the doors are shut and sealed from the outside?" asked Merka. Blist nodded. "And of the wizard Anthon, he has betrayed us completely?"

"He has," began Blist with his mouth full. "He only used us for iron ore to build his iron-golem and then his brother turned on us. That is why your army was unaffected."

"If only I'd attacked sooner," said Merka. "You might still be there and Gutter or whatever the new chieftain's name was, might still be alive." Merka of course knew Blackpool would be gone. He was in on that, hoping he would be rid of Queen Ooktha and have his own separate kingdom. What did he get for betraying Queen Ooktha when he revealed her plans to betray General Blackpool, the annihilated stronghold of Ironhold!

"Perhaps but who cares now?" said Blist leaning forward. "You have a job to do and that's to recapture that stronghold in a year's time."

"Nothing more?" asked Merka.

"Of course, the iron and ore must flow but not as much as before," said Blist still eating and drinking. "Oh, and I almost forgot, our queen's name was tainted among the inhabitants. You need to bring them back into the fold. The human general placed a spy or spies there and one Queen Ooktha believes to be a shape-changer. They are the ones we believe who tarnished her name."

That was news to Merka; it seemed the shape-changer was known to them now. Merka only knew the shape-changer as the red-haired arch-goblin; was there possibly another or was this the same one?

"What clues do you have to make you think it was a shape-changer?"

"Your predecessor saw him change. Seems it captured him. It was also feeding information to the enemy outside the walls of Ironhold. At the time, no one knew what it was until it was too late," explained Chieftain Blist.

"Spies, iron ore and a breakout, anything else?"

He loved war and battle like all arch-goblins are taught. However, Merka was not the strongest fighter. He was tall and lanky and only had one eye thanks to his battle with Master Sergeant Saltclaw. He was just an average military commander on the field—he barely survived the ambush in the mountains. Where the arch-goblin did excel was his ability to plot and scheme.

That night Chieftain Merka, while lying awake aboard the Bloodknuckle; he felt defeated at the news that he was to restore Ironhold in the next year. Suddenly, he realized he now had influence over two of the three arch-goblin cities!

Lorez was loyal to him, always has been. The only reason he didn't let Lorez lead the ambush in the mountains where Leif was captured was because it was his task given by Queen Ooktha to him to accomplish. With Lorez loyal to him, sharing in his own disdain for Queen Ooktha, surely there was opportunity to be gained in this revelation.

Chapter 26
Unhinged Undead

Queen Ooktha went to her private quarters where there she made her way to her small throne room that contained the mirrors she used to commune with the Union of Undead. She sent out a telepathic call to the mirror of her mentor, Revenant Niss and waited for three long and agonizing hours before Revenant Niss appeared.

"I am told interesting news my dear," began Revenant Niss calmly. She had recovered from her outburst on Revenant Pallentine. Although Revenant Niss was reclusive and preferred making magical items, she tended to become unhinged when one of her creations did not work or, in this case, went missing. "Your elf champion was successful. Rom-Seti is captured and your elf is on his way back to you, with my Jade Tower. I tried to have the Jade Tower taken by my ally, but it seems your young champion is so convinced that his return will prevent war in your region that he demanded it. Silly I know but unfortunately, with my displeasure, my friends returned it to him. When he arrives, I must have it."

"My mentor, I have called because I have heard similar news. He and his companions did return and successfully captured Rom-Seti," said Queen Ooktha. "However, Leif will not be returning to me. He has been informed of the war by his family and friends; he chose to return to his home. I will not likely get the Jade Tower, my mentor."

There was a quiet pause between the two undead females. The dead skin of Revenant Niss twisted slightly. Queen Ooktha could tell it was anger as the revenant began to shake with rage.

"Listen to me child and listen well," said Revenant Niss in a manner and voice that unnerved Queen Ooktha. "You came to me with the notion of eliminating Rom-Seti. I spent years researching, crafting and spell casting an item powerful enough to trap that monster. I didn't create that wondrous artefact so your elven lover can casually sell it into obscurity or place on a mantel in his home waiting for a would-be thief to steal it. And what if it is damaged or destroyed, releasing him? That scourge would be back upon our world and no doubt who he would seek his revenge upon."

"But how can I?" said Queen Ooktha beginning to argue but was cut short.

"Silence, woman!" said Revenant Niss. "You have many means at your disposal other allies, do you not?" she asked.

Queen Ooktha presumed the revenant was referring to the few other creatures in the area that she had dealings or encounters with. In particular Skagsnest, the underground trading town that lies between Blood-helm and Skulls-thorpe, held many kinds of creature there. Surely, she could find someone to go to the surface and retrieve the Jade Tower.

"Have them find your elf and find my soul sucker; it is my creation. Go to war again if you have too!" shouted Revenant Niss. "I only loaned it to you for your own personal satisfaction and it has accomplished that which you sought. You assured me he would return did you not?" she asked. Revenant Niss didn't wait for an answer. "Now I want it back. I give you a fortnight to recover it or face my wrath! And if Rom-Seti is released and manages to contact the Union of Undead, we will both suffer!"

* * * * *

Revenant Niss sat back in her stone chair. It was larger than her by far. It was a creation she made for herself. She called it her Seat of Power. She often sat there for days on end, contemplating as revenants do. Covered in runes in symbols, the Seat of Power was the one place where she felt safest and at ease. From this chair alone, she could unleash a barrage of attacks upon anyone daring enough to enter her home.

She lived in a tower that had three levels from the outside but held many more than that on the inside. The same could be said for the circumference of the tower; from the outside the tower looked narrow but her magical creation allowed for a more spacious interior than what the outside circumference suggested. She kept her location near to Pallentine but, she kept her present location secret to all save her old mentor Revenant Pallentine.

Revenant Niss grew worrisome at the recent events. By now she had hoped to vanquish Rom-Seti at the side of her mentor and her mentee, Queen Ooktha. Instead, her magical creation was missing and within it, Rom-Seti. The meeting of the Union of Undead was soon upon her and her involvement in Rom-Seti's demise might be uncovered. She wondered how she might defend against allegations or attacks from the union as she had little faith that Queen Ooktha would retrieve the Jade Tower before the next meeting.

Revenant Niss was also extremely upset by her own mentor. Not only did he let the Jade Tower slip away, she had also learned he had also pilfered Rom-Seti's pyramid. She too went after finding out Rom-Seti's fate. There, she hoped to capitalize on the secrets of her enemy. Oh what she might learn from another culture from another world. However, she returned empty handed and now had to grovel before her mentor for access. ?

* * * * *

"I sense your disapproval of Revenant Niss once again," said Teodor to Revenant Pallentine. He was sitting at the table eating some freshly pulled tomatoes, cucumbers and broccoli.

"Revenant Niss seems always to have some alternate agenda playing out in the background," replied the revenant. "It is so upsetting that we let that young elf go on a fool's errand," said Revenant Pallentine watching his friend drink some water. The revenant forgot what it was like to eat and drink. He was pleased for Teodor's company and insight but sometimes during meals, it pained the revenant for giving up so much, like food, just to save his home.

He also thought Teodor was brave for dining with him. That or he had a strong stomach. Pallentine knew his skin had deteriorated and was now hideous to the living eye. But the two had known each other for nearly one hundred years and true friends they were.

"Wait till she finds out that we've already taken all of Rom-Seti's scrolls and books. Even his *soul-sepulchre*," said Teodor.

"Yes, she will be upset," said Pallentine amused at the notion.

"But perhaps you might better control her now if you wish. She will want access to Rom-Seti's scrolls after all," said Teodor smiling. Teodor cared not for Revenant Niss, not even when he knew her as a living human wizard. But he held no malice towards her but knowing she was once a human and now a revenant, he wanted to know if any of her dealings might one day come back to haunt them at Archangel.

"Interesting thought," said Revenant Pallentine. "I could impose stipulations upon her for access. But she must never know where we are keeping the entire collection. Instead I will provide her access to what I deem worthy. Well done, my old friend!"

* * * * *

Queen Ooktha travelled on her own barge, the Blood Bearer against the stream. The current was slow and almost unnoticeable but provided a challenge nonetheless for the slaves rowing her. Queen Ooktha insisted on dwarves, humans and orc oarsmen. She looked down at the oarsmen rowing in the bowels of the ship. These were races that she disliked, even before she became a vampiress. It was clear they feared her as they all put down their heads when they noticed her looming above. Queen Ooktha saw their sweaty necks and considered biting into one of the oarsmen but the lights of green and gold that signaled the isolated island city of Skagsnest changed her mind.

It was a large island where many kinds of boats were moored. It was a market town where the races of the underground traded goods and found services. In the centre was a great natural pillar that reached from the ceiling of the overhead cave to the bottom of the lake in which it sat. A small waterfall ran down one side of the pillar feeding the lake. Inside that pillar housed the keeper of Skagsnest, old Skags herself.

As the Blood Bearer docked, Chieftain Blist was first to come off with his entourage of elite arch-goblin warriors. They were all well armored and armed to the teeth, twenty in all. Queen Ooktha soon followed. She was dressed in a scarlet red gown that exposed her white skin shoulders, chest and navel. Her eyes were painted over in black-like a mask. Arch-goblins all cleared her path and surrounded her ensuring no one or thing came in contact with her. Orcs, ogres and goblins scampered out of the way. A pair of dwarves popped back into the seedy tavern from which they came. A dark-elf male, a rare sight, presented them a path and stood back allowing passage.

Much of Skagsnest was an island surrounding the great pillar; it was old ships, tied together with buildings and pathways placed atop them. The whole lake-town shifted at times on the water. There was dry land, rock nearer the great pillar. The entourage, led by Chieftain Blist, made its way over the boats and around the pillar to the front door of old Skags. The metal portcullis was up but a large stone door to the rear barred any further entry. The chieftain walked in and beat on the door with the pommel of his dagger. A panel in the door slid open. Chieftain Blist took a step back, startled by a large eye peering back at him. It was surrounded by what appeared to be a scaly fishlike head. In a watery voice, it said in the common tongue, "What is it that you want arch-goblin?"

"Queen Ooktha, ruler of the arch-goblins, demands an audience with old Skags," he replied.

The large fisheye moved around, peering through the panel. Its unnerving pupil grew and shrunk. Then the portal shut, and watery voices could be heard behind the door. It only took half a minute when the bolts on the door unlocked, and the door opened.

In the doorway stood a two-legged creature, it had sea green scaly skin with the head of an angry fish. It wore a sleeveless robe of yellow, tied with a blueish rope around the waist. The creature was called a lemurian. It held a staff with a red octopus like creature who had eight arms but two were red-clawed and two were five fingered arms of sea green atop it. Chieftain Blist knew it to be the likeness of their deity, Mermanta who was goddess to many water-breathing Merfolk.

"Come!" it said holding out its arm. "Most of your soldiers may wait in the foyer but she will gladly see her highness and six of her bodyguards."

Queen Ooktha looked the lemurian over with a bit of disgust but motioned for it to lead the way for her. Chieftain Blist and the six bodyguards followed. The spiral stairs shimmered like the inside of a seashell. Soft pinks, aqua-marine greens and pale blues decorated both the wide stairs and banister. The walls were painted in another soft blue, a staunch difference over the outsides of the great tower they now climbed.

They came to the first landing where they saw a shrine to the water god of Mermanta. The statue of the red octopus-like creature with her eight arms, two red-clawed, two five fingered webbed hands of sea green and the remaining were octopus tentacles, boasted a beautiful pearl necklace around its bulbous head. There were two more lemurian laying and bowing before the statue, whispering prayers. The light in this room was magical and given off only by the red claws of the effigy.

The leading lemurian led them up to another floor. It was set with pillows all over the floor. There was no carpet, just a stone floor. It too was lit by magical stones placed in the walls. No fire, just illuminating stones. The room was domed painted with pictures of lemurian battles with human seaside towns where captives were being dragged into the sea. Across from Queen Ooktha and the arch-goblins was a dark blue curtain. Before it was a plain stone chair made from the same material of the pillar, they were now in.

"Sit!" said the lemurian in a watery voice.

"I will stand as will my warriors," replied Queen Ooktha.

The lemurian did not answer nor show any sign of distaste or concern. They were almost an expressionless race. It walked away and went behind the curtain. After several moments' refreshments were brought out by slaves. Three beardless female dwarves brought out clean water, beer and mead for the arch-goblins. Two beardless male dwarves brought mushrooms, flesh large subterranean lizard chunks and other seafood delicacies for them. Lastly a dainty human female with barely any clothes on, bore a large goblet and decanter of blood for Queen Ooktha.

"I am told to tell you it is fresh from our supply of human slaves," she said in tears. The young girl was so frightened and knew what Queen Ooktha was.

"Thank you my dear," said Queen Ooktha. She took a sip and it was fresh and warm. "Delicious," she said and motioned for the girl to refill her glass. She complied but continued to cry. "Aww, don't cry my little one. I will not hurt you," she said. She then motioned for one of the beardless dwarven females to take the decanter and goblet. She picked up the young girl like she was a dolly and looked her over. "Go tell your master that I thank her for her hospitality and I am anxious indeed to discuss business post haste."

The slave girl ran back as fast as she could behind the curtain. Moments later the dwarves followed as well. Then out came the same lemurian that led them up there. Additional lemurian soldiers came out armed with tridents and spears. Lastly, out came a lemurian hunched over and supported by a staff like the lemurian they had met at the gate but much more decorative. This one was seemingly older, grayer and had longer whiskers than any of the others.

"May I present Lady Skags of Skagsnest," said the lemurian in a gurgle-sounding speech.

"How is it that you have come to me, queen of the arch-goblins?" she said in a watery voice. The voice was distinctly different from that of the other lemurian who spoke to them. This creature's voice was more feminine but more in an old hag kind of way.

"Lady Skags, Skagsnest is known for its trade, its ability to procure a variety of goods and has a reputation for finding rare items or even specific people," said Queen Ooktha.

"You came all this way to ask me to find something one of your arch-goblins took?"

"No, not in the least. I wouldn't waste my time nor yours if it were that simple," replied Queen Ooktha.

"I need something from the City of Sedgedunum, something and possibly someone, both precious to me. And I don't have the resources to find them both, quietly."

"Ah! You lost something in the city you sacked," replied Skags. "Yes, we know much of your endeavours on the surface. I had hoped your attack would produce an increase in export in goods to there but instead another power has moved into Vorclaw. Are you aware of that?"

Queen Ooktha looked as if she didn't care but in reality, she did not know what Skags was referencing.

"You, my queen," started Skags pointing a bony green and gray finger. "You brought the Shadow Company to our doorsteps and you don't even know it."

"So, what of it?"

"They bring complications my dear, complications that impact our ability to supply goods," explained Skags cryptically.

Queen Ooktha was beginning to understand. Skagsnest was indeed a trade port for the subterranean races but also had merchants connected to the surface. Those merchants would soon fall under the eyes of the Shadow Company. It also helped explained the source of funding for the Blackpool's.

"Luckily for you I have one who might find your precious something and someone," said Skags. "He is there now. But his sum will be considerable, as will mine for the chaos you have just created for me."

Chapter 27
Breaking of Foehammers

Leif woke up from the hit Bjorn laid on him. He was still in the underground ruins, the meeting place of the Black-masks. He sat up but everyone was gone save for Damon Crag of all people. The assassin sat on the one of the marble benches. A silver serving platter with a sandwich, fruit and two goblets was next to him.

"You took a nasty hit, elf," said Damon. "You been out for hours."

Leif had a swollen eye from Bjorn's fist, realizing now the source of his groggy head. He nodded in agreement but only just. Even that hurt.

"Where is my father? Where is everyone? And why in all the hells are you here?"

Damon responded by pouring some wine into one of the goblets. "Drink, it will help and here is food for you sent by the general," he said.

Leif sat up and made it to the bench next to Damon. He took a drink and ate the sandwich. He hadn't realized how hungry and drained he was until he ate some proper food. "What is that rumbling noise?"

"It's raining up there. What we just heard was thunder," said Damon.

"Oh good," said Leif. "I thought it was all in my head," he said not trying to make a joke but it came out that way. Damon even smiled a bit, a rare sight.

"You know, the more I learn about you elf, the less I dislike you," said Damon.

"I don't know why you disliked me in the first place?" responded Leif.

"Never been a fan of elves, arrogant, cocky, sure of themselves. Much like the aristocracy of the land I come from. I hated them all too."

"You seem to have a lot of hate in you," said Leif.

"Aye, that I do," responded Damon looking blankly across the way. "I used to be you once. I too was someone who would sacrifice himself for the good of others. I think it is a rare thing indeed to meet someone who genuinely gives a shite about the welfare of his people like you."

Leif looked at the man, but he didn't return Leif's look. Leif assumed Damon was once a goodly fellow as he said. But something turned him, made him angry and mistrusting.

"Why did you stay behind with this fool of an elf?" asked Leif who was staring now into his near empty goblet. The thought of his mother was now coming back to him.

Damon stood up suddenly. "Come, we have to take you to your father, he was not well," he said.

The two made their way out of another passage that somehow Damon was aware of. They emerged in a storage room, the basement of the compound. Damon took Leif to the infirmary, where his father was lying on a bed. He was pale white. His mouth was open like he had been gasping for air. Bjorn was kneeling over him, praying to Matronae no doubt. Dru was kneeling opposite Bjorn, holding Magnus's hand.

Dunkin Saltclaw was also there and made way for Damon and Leif. "Your father may not have long for this world, lieutenant," said Dunkin. Leif's mouth opened in horror, his eyes wide and watered. "He has been asking for you. Come!" said Dunkin.

Bjorn eyed Leif with hatred, a look Bjorn had never known before from his adopted brother. Leif kneeled on the other side of the bed next to Dru.

"What happened to him?" asked Leif.

"He collapsed from the shock of your lover killing our mother," bit Bjorn.

Leif's eyes watered once again. Dru directed a stern look towards the big man, showing how out of line that comment was. Bjorn stood up and walked to the other side of the room.

"Why can't you heal him? Why can't we get a healer here?" asked Leif.

"What do you think I been praying for?" shouted Bjorn.

Dru put his hand on Leif's shoulder to comfort the large elf but also left the bedside to give Leif his time with his father.

The man's breath was labored and to Leif he looked pale. "Father," said Leif. Magnus did not answer so Leif grabbed his hand. It was cool, almost void of blood. Magnus reacted and squeezed Leif's hand.

"My boy," started Magnus. "I am sorry for what happened to you at the ambush. Master Sergeant Saltclaw said you fought bravely and so very well," he said barely managing a smile.

"Be still father, you must rest and get better," said Leif.

"There is nothing more the healers can do for me, my son," whispered Magnus. "My heart is broken but not by you my son, but by the death of your mother. I will see her soon." he said. "Forgive!" shouted Magnus as another wave of pain came over his chest. "Your brother," began Magnus whispering again, "he has not walked in your boots; he does not understand your plight."

That was the man's last words.

"Bjorn," shouted Leif.

Everyone rushed to the bedside as Magnus had departed his corporal form to join his wife, Disa.

"Orderly!" shouted Dru. "Send for my father at once!"

Bjorn jumped down to the bedside of his father. The large man began chanting prayers to Matronae, begging for her healing grace to save his father. Bjorn's watery eyes showed he knew that sometimes things aren't repairable; broken hearts were often one of them.

Dru knew Magnus as a second father. Dru could often be seen in the Foehammer household on any given day or time. Dru's eyes watered.

Dunkin Saltclaw lowered his head in reverence. "The gods have received a great man and warrior this night. May Matronae guide him into her arms and reunite him with his beloved," said the Dunkin.

Damon said nothing, did nothing.

Leif stood up, his face a tirade of emotions. He made his way to the door.

Dunkin called to him as did Dru. Damon let him pass. Leif did not respond to any of them. He made his way out of the infirmary and out to the wet parade grounds. He ran out into the middle of the rainy field and fell upon his knees crying.

* * * * *

General Baltus Blackpool and the wizard Anthon Blackpool stood staring at Leif from the general's balcony. Neither man said a word but the general reasoned that Leif felt a great shame from sleeping with the creature that killed his mother and his father was now dead.

The answer came at the knock of his door, being informed that his son's presence was requested at Sergeant Major Magnus Foehammer's bedside.

Anthon was with him. "Shall we go and pay our respects to your friend's brother?" asked Anthon.

"You know it is my fault he is dead," said Baltus turning to face his brother.

Anthon hadn't seen his brother cry since his own wife Merriam died. And that was barely a tear. Baltus pulled out a decanter containing a dark substance. He also set up a chess board on a small table with two small chairs for players. Baltus walked over to the chess table and sat down, leaving Leif to his own grief.

"We used to drink this, Magnus and me. It's called *Hair of the Dwarf*. We would play chess and talk about how broken this country's leadership was and so too was the military. Or at least I used to and he would hear me vent," said Baltus to his brother.

"Was he any good at chess?" asked Anthon.

"He was good. He taught me a lot about the soldiers under my command too. He was always thinking of their needs and not his own."

Anthon knew his brother was regretting this whole endeavour; even though the property loss and damage to the city was over thousands in gold, even though the loss of life to the city was in the hundreds. Anthon worried the loss of the Foehammer parents may drive his brother over the edge.

"We should go and see him and his sons," said Anthon. "They need you now," he said.

Baltus shook his head in agreement. He stood up, downed his drink and pushed over his king on the chess table. "I must first get my soldier out of the rain," said Baltus.

Baltus walked alone in the rainstorm to the middle of the parade ground. He stood before Leif, kneeling and bent over in deep sadness.

"Stand up lieutenant," said the general. "At attention before your commanding officer," he said in a stern voice. Leif's military experience and training created a natural reaction to do just that. He even stopped crying.

"Pull yourself together, man!" began the general. "Do you think your parents would want to see you like this? Saltclaw was right. You have endured more than anyone should and in such a short time, my son. But crying in the rain for all to see is not how officers conduct themselves in my army."

"So has he, unjustly so," said Leif referring to Dunkin Saltclaw. The general raised an eyebrow in response. "We might have won the day had the sergeant major not been dropped from behind. He almost killed their chieftain."

"Do you know why he was put in irons?" asked the general.

"Because he cares about his soldiers and Mr. Night's expertise let us down," replied Leif. "He does not deserve to be retired when he survived the ambush as well," said Leif again referring to Dunkin Saltclaw.

Baltus knew the battle was staged and the ambush was partly by his design; it was to prove he was not going to double cross Queen Ooktha and give her a victory. He made no promises to her of a victory but did give her that fight with a clear advantage to her arch-goblins. It also allowed him an opportunity to usurp the position of commander of the armies of Vorclaw by being rid of his predecessor, Lord Brisbane. And after surviving that ambush, Baltus could hardly argue with Leif's logic.

"I see where you are going with this lieutenant and it amazes me that even now, you are looking out for others. You are a credit to your father, you know that? Even on this sad day you fight for the welfare of Dunkin Saltclaw. Very well, I will consider reinstating the man at his rank. But he needs to let go his line of questioning about Mr. Night," said Baltus. "And you need to take a leave of absence and mourn your family properly—not out here on my parade field, soldier."

Leif thanked the general with a nod but Leif did not know what nonsense he was referring to about Mr. Night. However, his mind was all over the place and he needed to think about how next to address his deceased family. Baltus had the answer as if reading his mind.

"Tomorrow, we will hold a feast in honor of both your mother and father. Master Sergeant Saltclaw, if he accepts his reinstatement, will recover your mother and they will be buried together in the army cemetery. You lieutenant will remain on the installation but you will not remain a lieutenant. I am promoting you to captain. You more than earned it for what you endured. Don't ask for anything more for Saltclaw, he is lucky I am allowing him to come back to his full rank."

"Thank you, sir," replied Leif.

"Leif, I need you to put this behind you and start anew. You need to resolve things with your brother, let Dru help you," said Baltus as he saw his son Dru now coming out to join them in the rain. "Here comes Dru now," he said and Leif turned to see his lifelong friend coming over. Baltus waited for Dru to get close enough for him to hear. "Now, work with him to mend things between you and Bjorn and tell Master Sergeant Saltclaw my offer. And lastly, get rid of that disgusting arch-goblin armour. I never want to see it on you again," he said to Leif.

Dru and Leif left the general standing in the rain.

"Oh Magnus, how I failed you my friend, I am so sorry," said the general walking away.

* * * * *

The next evening, Baltus held a feast at his residence but the mood was sour. Bjorn would not speak to Leif and ended up leaving as soon as Dru tried to bring them together. Dru of course ran after him but neither returned. Leif was left with the general and Master Sergeant Saltclaw for company. The general explained that Master Sergeant Saltclaw would report to Captain Ty who was on the mend; they would be patrolling the city's northern border and look for any straggling arch-goblins or lizard-goblins. Leif however would remain at the Academy of Arms, for now.

The next day it was still raining but not nearly as hard. Magnus ensured the graves were dug side by side for Magnus and Disa Foehammer. It was a solemn ceremony and a high-ranking priest of Matronae performed the burial rites. Several soldiers raised their swords in salute. Nearly everyone was beyond crying and with the rain, no one could tell if anyone was shedding a tear anyway. Master Sergeant Saltclaw attended. He was now back in uniform. Captain Ty was present as was Damon Crag. Dru stood between Bjorn and Leif and their tension hung in the air.

As the funeral dispersed, the rain picked up. Bjorn must have seen it as a sign. He turned to Leif with anger in his eyes.

"Listen to me, Leif! You and I are not brothers, we never were. You betrayed your own soldiers when you slept with that monster to save your own hide. Now your lover has killed my mother and the shock of it all killed my father. I wish my father never found you. You are a curse, Leif. Go back to the elves from which you came or go back to your demon lover. I never want to see you again. If you ever come to Foehammer residents in Sedgefen, it will be the last thing you ever do." Bjorn stormed off in the rain, leaving Leif standing with Dru, Baltus, Damon and Dunkin.

"You get back here at once, captain," said the general.

Bjorn turned with another angry glare. "I think not, Baltus. I resign my commission and will no longer take part in your new world order for Vorclaw. I believed in you once general, but I am done with all that. You're partly to blame for my parents' deaths and this farce of a war." Bjorn turned and stormed off.

The general sighed but he too turned and left for his office.

Dru moved to console Leif but saw the elf was frozen staring at his brother's departure. Dru instead thought maybe he should console his father but when would he ever listen to Dru? So Dru stormed off after Bjorn to try and talk some sense into the big man.

Dunkin walked over to Leif. "Sir, I am moving out today with Captain Ty. I would be honored if you would request a transfer to join us."

"Quite right," said Captain Ty. "There are several arch-goblins left to be killed and lizard-goblins to round up. It would indeed take your mind off matters."

"Dunkin, keep my father's memory alive as long as you can," said Leif not turning to look at either man. "You honor me once again with your wisdom," he said and he walked off.

Dunkin turned to Damon Crag, a man he knew little about and just recently met. "What happened to him, to them, these many months?"

"Oh, they came to realise how twisted this world truly is," said the assassin.

Damon left Master Sergeant Saltclaw and Captain Ty standing there in the rain to ponder.

Codex

Creatures of Vana

Arch-goblin: Arch-goblins who are pale blue with ape-like canines and faces. They live as long as humans. True goblins no longer exist as far as anyone on Vana knows. Arch-goblins are a manipulation of the smaller extinct goblins by human wizards for the purposes of war.

Dark Elves: These outcast-elves live within Vana, not on the surface. This breed of elf has ashy-colored skin, red eyes and golden hair. The sunlight pains them greatly. The reason they're so different from other elfkin was when humans arrived, elves were introduced other gods and ways of thinking. Subsequently those who turned away from the elven goddess Airia, were punished for their blasphemy. Those banished from the surface often became Crom-Cruach worshipers and atheists. They live about twice as long humans. However, lore states Airia regrets her punishment.

Dwarves: About half as tall to two-thirds as tall as an average human. These pious Terra worshipers live within mountains and highland forests. Like humans, they come in a variety of skin tones, eye and hair colours. Their height is deceiving as they are stronger physically than any humanoid. They live two to three times longer than average humans.

Elves: Slender humanoid creatures just under the height of an average human. Like humans, they come in a variety of skin tones, eye and hair colors. They have a great grasp of knowledge and fighting prowess but are in retreat due violent interactions with humans, orcs and arch-goblins. They live two to three longer than average humans

Kelpiefolk: A short two-legged aquatic humanoid with webbed hands and feet. Its skin is dark green or brown and smooth, like an amphibians. These creatures have great orbs for eyes, small fins protruding from their frog-like head. The do not have great intelligence and live more like wild animals. It is not known how long they live.

Lemurian: A two-legged creature with sea green scaly skin and the head of an angry fish. They can breathe in water and on land. They worship to the water god of Mermanta. They live about twice as long average humans.

Lizard-goblin: These are small bipedal lizard-like creatures of various colors. They often act as servants and fodder for larger races. Their scales are often seen as either green, red or orange. They had no relation to arch-goblins who seem to keep them for afore mentioned purposes. They live half as long as an average human.

Lycaon: Tall humanoid creatures with jackal like heads whose tall pointy ears extended above their heads. Their skin is dark with short dark hair that covered their shoulders up to their tall ears. Their skin and fur is black while elite of the species are golden in fur and skin. They live as long humans. They are very rare and only seen in the northern mountains.

Mantikhoras: A rare creature found in the mountains. Its body is orange tiger-like but without stripes. It has the head of a man-like creature with a furry face; it has a very long whip-like tail with spikes at the end. It is rumored to be a magical creation by human-wizards long ago and is rumored to have magical capabilities.

Orcs: These creatures have a face like a pig. Their skin varies from dark green to solid black in color. The have tusks the protrude up from their mouth like a boar. Their hair over their head and body tends to be dark in color. They live about twice as long as humans.

Shape-changer: These very rare creatures have the ability to take on the shape of those they see. They tend to study first those they intend to imitate. In their basic form they look like an albino human with no hair and blue eyes. These are very rare and believed to be a manipulation of humans by wizardry.

Undead

Note: Depending on their experience, all clergy of all faiths can manipulate the undead by either destroy or control using their own divine power bestowed by the god or goddess.

Ghoul: Horrible undead humanoids who were equally evil in real life; unlike skeletons who were either animated to follow orders, ghouls hungered for flesh and bone of the living.

Mummy: Undead guardians that lay in wait in tombs. Traditionally they are wrapped in bandages to help stem their decay. The creatures animate upon disturbance or on command of a more powerful undead creature like a revenant or vampire.

Revenant: Powerful undead who refuse to truly die; they maintain their consciousness while their body decays. They also must hide away their soul in an item called a *soul-sepulchre*. The *soul-sepulchre* allows them to keep their soul from the afterlife so they can toil as undead but retain their consciousness. Once the *soul-sepulchre* is destroyed, the soul moves into the undead body and then they can then be killed. If a revenant body is destroyed but the soul remains in a *soul-sepulchre*, the revenant can move its consciousness into another dead form.

Skeleton: Mindless undead used as labor or for fighting.

Spectre: Also known as a ghost or spirit.

Vampire: Undead creature who have unique powers such as animal control and weather manipulation. However, they require near daily fresh-blood for sustainment.

Mentioned Lands

Anubia; Rom-Seti homeland from another planet.

Dwarven Mons: Home of the dwarven kings to the west of Vorclaw.

Fort Adamant: Fort built around The Tor to protect it and the region near Panther-Paw-Pass.

Mistful Forest: Forest area north and west of Sedgedunum.

Sanctuary: A small patch of land in the far north where violence is forbidden and all are allowed to worship whatever gods they see fit.

Skagsnest: A center for trade under the Spine of Vana Mountain range. It is overseen by Lemurians. It is named for the Lemerian leader, Old Skags.

Spine of Vana: Mountain range all along the north of Vorclaw.

The Land of the Great Glaciers: Lands near the top of Vana.

The Tor: Ancient tower built by elves long ago before the advent of humans to the area.

Human Countries of Vana

Dubravna
Lotus
Karthia

Uden
Vorclaw

Vorclaw's:
Seaside cities and towns
Sedgedunum
Seaforth
Irons-by-the-Sea

Mountain and hilled cities and towns
Cairnloch
Cairnhold

Wooded cities and towns
Exbury
Wrexbury
Nortbury

The arch-goblin cities in the Spine of Vana

Blood-helm
Skulls-thorpe
Iron-hold

The indigenous four elemental gods of Vana and primary worshipers

Terra (Female) **Dwarfkin**: Depicted as a short muscular woman with white haired woman whose face was light brown in color. Terra is often depicted in a black armor adorned in silver and trim to match.

Magmum (Female) **Orckin**: Depicted as a robust orcish woman with black hair and fire-red veins protruding through her black skin.

Airia (Female) Elfkin: Depicted as a winged woman with silver hair and wings whose color pulsated the colors of a rainbow.

Mermanta (Female) Merfolk: Depicted as a red octopus like creature who had eight arms but two were red-clawed and two were five fingered arms of sea green.

Non-indigenous Gods of Vana primarily worshiped by humans

Matronae: Is the mother goddesses of birth, harvest, and the seasons. The symbol of Matronae is an X that has four additional symbols within the X. The sun is represented within the top of the X. A circle represents the planet

Vana within the bottom of the X. To the left is a wavy line that represents water while a cloud formation on the left represents the wind.

Dagda: The father figure and god of strength, war, weather. The symbol of Dagda are two lightning bolts crossing one another to form an X.

Children of Matronae and Dagda

- **Ogma** (male): God of wisdom, hunting, forestry, good. The symbol of Ogma is an oak tree. He is depicted as a man of the forest with a green beard and hair.

- **Lir** (male): God of endurance, oceans, lakes and river. The symbol of Lir is three wavy lines. He is depicted as a man with blue beard and hair that flows like water.

- **Crom-Cruach** (male): God of the underworld and often prayed to for revenge. The symbol of Crom-Cruach is a cloaked and hunched over figure walking with a scythe. No face can be seen within the hood, only boney hands holding the scythe.

Organizations:

Black-Masks: Underground network of soldiers loyal to Baltus Blackpool.

Dragoons: Vorclaw's cavalry units.

Knights of Uden: A noble elite knights that do the King of Uden's bidding, good or bad. Rumored to be one hundred strong.

The Council of Twelve: The ruling council of Vorclaw.

The Shadow Company: A greedy network of merchants, wizards, and thieves; believed to be ruled by either a secret council or powerful wizard referred to as the One.

Union of Undead: A confederacy of powerful undead forces whose members are vampires and revenants of different but unknown species.

CPSIA information can be obtained
at www.ICGtesting.com
Printed in the USA
LVHW050918210723
752909LV00048B/9